SUNDOWN & SERENA

Promise Me Origin Tales

Tara Fox Hall

Published by
Melange Books, LLC
White Bear Lake, MN 55110
www.melange-books.com

Sundown & Serena ~ Copyright © 2015 by Tara Fox Hall

ISBN: 978-1-68046-150-3

Cover Art by Caroline Andrus

To my father

******

In memory of Jess, who will live on in the pages of this series

SUNDOWN

Chapter One

It felt like the day from hell. Everything had gone wrong for me. I'd gotten hit on by an overzealous, middle-aged buffoon who'd fondled me intimately on his second lap dance. That had put me off so much, I'd been a beat behind when I took my turn onstage. The men in the audience hadn't cared, but I had. I liked to think I was the most sought after girl in Hotcakes, and how could I, feeling like some amateur her first night on the pole.

"Shit." I drank my seven-and-seven down in a gulp, and decided to pay my tab. It was time to go home.

Leaving some money on the bar, I motioned to Bill, the head bouncer at Hotcakes. He came over grinning snidely, his tanned face sharp, yet still friendly. "Another, Sun?"

"No," I said tiredly, getting to my feet. "I should go home."

He leaned in close. "Even though you've got a fan still here?"

I gave him a look that said he'd better not annoy me in the mood I was in. "What are you talking about?"

"That guy in the corner," he said, with a discreet hand gesture. "He came in when you were on stage. He watched your set like he'd never seen a woman before."

"Good for him," I said dispassionately, though inside I was pleased to hear of the special attention. "It's nice I can still give a man a lift, even as bad as I was."

"You weren't bad," Bill replied seriously. "Just off by a few seconds."

"Not good enough," I replied stiffly. "I strive for perfection. I'll see you tomorrow."

As I went for my coat, a soft yet deep voice called out, "Please wait."

I turned back to see my admirer coming toward me. As men went—especially compared to the type who came in here usually—he was a solid nine. He was handsome, tall, and his body was nicely muscular without being too bulky. He looked sort of young for some reason, yet I reasoned that he had to be at least twenty-one for Bill to have let him in the door. His straight dark hair was pulled sharply back in a short ponytail, which made me think he was older than the early twenties I pegged him for. That hairstyle wasn't popular with the twenty-something crowd, and the clothes he was wearing also spoke to him being at least thirty-something.

"Can I take you for coffee?" he asked softly, his dark eyes staring at my breasts before looking up to my face.

At least he's close to my age. It was nice to have a man come on to me who wasn't old enough to be my father…wait. The stranger's eyes had seemed red for a moment. Now they were dark again. It must have been a trick of the light. The bartender had just shut off the flashing neon signs in the front windows and announced last call. Maybe it had been the glare of the strobe lights that were still going strong? *Maybe I'm drunker than I thought…Nah.*

"Or something to eat," the stranger added, when I didn't reply. "You look like you could use a good meal."

"Listen, buddy," I replied sarcastically. "This isn't <u>Pretty Woman</u>, got it? I'm not looking for a savior."

"What woman is these days?" he stated bitterly. "I was just offering company, if you wanted some."

I was surprised that someone so young could sound so bitter. Maybe he only looked young. Or maybe he'd had a childhood like mine. I reached out and ran my hands over his chest. His muscles bunched reflexively under my hands, making a shiver of desire snake its way through my body.

Maybe this is a good way to end the night. "What are you offering?" I said suggestively, giving him my best bedroom eyes.

His eyes closed, and his breathing quickened. His skin seemed to be radiating heat. I was glad of it; I'd been feeling cold in my skimpy

2

jacket. That's what I got for caring so much about looking hot.

He didn't reply. I continued to run my hands over him while he acted as though he couldn't get enough of feeling my hands on his clothed chest. That was weird. Men usually came here because they wanted to touch me or think about touching me, even though they knew no touching was allowed. And if they wanted me to touch them, I gambled that their fantasy was never my hands on their chests, with all their clothes on.

"What do you want?" he said suddenly, his tone shaky.

Definitely weird. Too weird to take a chance on tonight. "Nothing, sweetheart," I said, dropping my hands. "Nothing but sleep." He looked so crestfallen at my brush-off that I took pity on him. "Come back tomorrow if you want," I added with a lopsided smile. "I work from eight to two. You can buy me a drink."

"I'll be here," he promised, then kissed my hand gently with his hot lips.

While the romance bit didn't impress me, it came off as sincere rather than staged for effect. Whoever he was, the man wasn't just out for sex. But that didn't mean he was my Mr. Right, either.

Taking my hand back, I staggered out to the street, and down to my little apartment. I walked up the back stairs, and let myself in. I passed out from sheer exhaustion and alcohol before I hit the bed.

* * * *

I woke up on the floor at noon.

Stupid, Sun. I always told myself to go home after my set, and not hang out in bars. What had it ever gotten me? A string of lovers that was too long to remember and a lot of tears. I was tired of tears, promises that never were kept, and calls that never came.

I sat up, got to my feet, and staggered to the bathroom. I took an extended shower, washing my long blonde hair. Well, dirty blonde, actually. I knew I'd get better tips if I dyed it a lighter shade of blonde, like platinum. But I took pride in my natural color; I was the only stripper at Hotcakes who didn't dye her hair. Everyone there was ash blonde, platinum blonde, a jet-black, or a bright burgundy redhead. That fake color looked cheap to me, the way it was so obvious and overly

3

bright, just like the deep red lipstick most of them wore. I didn't wear much makeup, except eyeliner and mascara, which was pretty much mandatory. The sequin, spandex, and spangled costumes required were also fine by me; I'd always loved to play dress up as a child. But when it came to my hair, I could dye it when it started turning gray. That would be soon enough.

My eyes were pretty, at least. They were a soft blue, not washed out, yet not bright sky blue, either. The blue of the sea, a blue that sometimes looked green in the right light when I was wearing the right colors. My eyes were my best feature, and I was proud of them.

Not that I was bad-looking or anything. While a girl didn't have to be beautiful to be a stripper, both a good body was needed and the attitude to flaunt it. My body was good, taut and firm in all the right places, even though I wasn't very tall. It was genes, not exercise. My daily workout was dancing and gyrating, and the half block walk to and from work. Still, I'd never been refused by a man I'd approached, and that counted for something in my book.

I had a late lunch, and spent the rest of the day sleeping. I didn't have any pets, children, or a boyfriend to take care of. Owning my small apartment, I didn't have any snow to shovel in winter, or grass to mow in summer. And that was the way I liked it, free and footloose.

* * * *

Later that night, my admirer came back to Hotcakes. He was sitting at his same table when I arrived, and he stayed there the entire time I worked. Curious, I motioned one of the bouncers to come backstage during my break.

He came over to me with a leer on his wide mouth. "Feeling like a roll later?"

What a surprise. But Hunter was almost always on the make, like most men. "Fuck off," I said with a polite smile. "I want to know about that guy in the corner."

"Mr. Polite?" he said, losing his happy face. "Why?"

"Because he's been here all night. I want to know if he's been drinking or—"

"No," Hunter said with a snort. "He's eaten a pizza, and had several sodas. He's not bothering anyone, so we're letting him stay. But if he doesn't spend some serious cash soon, his ass is out the door."

I felt bad suddenly for the stranger, though I didn't know why. "Go ask him if he wants a lap dance with me."

Hunter gaped at me, incredulous. "You sweet on him?"

My hackles went up. "I could use the money," I snapped harshly. "My rent's due tomorrow. Just do it, jackass."

Hunter sidled up to me, and patted my ass through my skimpy costume. "I'll give you some cash if you want," he said huskily. "Just come home with me, Sun."

"I'm not a whore," I hissed. "I fuck for pleasure, not money. Get your hands off me."

"So come home with me and I won't pay you," he amended with a grin.

I wanted to slug him, but knew there was no point. Besides being the nephew of the boss, this bullshit—'I'm God's gift to women' routine— was just Hunter's way. He treated all the girls here like that, no matter what they looked like, which had earned him his nickname. He was good-looking, and there wasn't much upstairs besides his sex drive. But while no one who'd spent a night with him had any real complaints, word around Hotcakes was that Hunter was rough, that he liked oral sex a lot, and that he expected a girl to swallow whatever he told her to swallow. While I might go for the first two, I absolutely, positively, did not ever do the last.

"No, thanks," I said with a fake smile. "Now bring me some easy money."

Hunter laughed under his breath. "Sure thing. Wait here."

I went to the bar and downed a quick shot. To my surprise, Hunter was back in a few minutes, alone, a strange expression on his face.

"He didn't want to dance. He wanted to know when you got off, because he was taking you for breakfast," Hunter said slowly. "He's odd, Sun. Maybe you shouldn't go with him. He could be one of those crazy guys."

"I'm thinking about it," I said loftily. "I probably won't."

Chapter Two

Yet when my set was finished—in spite my reservations—I put on my clothes and strolled out to see my handsome stranger.

He got up the instant he saw me. "Ready?"

"Sure. Lead on."

He took me outside, and opened the door to his pickup truck so I could get in.

His gleaming, full-size Chevy had to be brand new. "Very nice."

"You like it?" he said quietly. "I bought it today."

Maybe my luck was changing. Not only had I met a well-off man, I had met one who had a sense of chivalry. I nodded and got in. My handsome stranger took me to the only place that was open this late, a local diner. They were serving early breakfast to the blue-collar class. We got a booth, and looked at menus.

"My treat," he said, and then smiled at me.

"Okay," I said happily.

We both ordered a large breakfast. After the waitress took our menus and left, the hard part came. I hated small talk. But my handsome stranger made it easy.

"Tell me your name?"

"Sundown," I answered with a smile. "But you can call me Sun. Most people do."

"Where did you get a name like that?" he said with surprise.

"It's not my stage name," I bristled hotly. "I—"

"I'm sorry," he placated. "I didn't mean to make you think I was insulting you. I just think it's both pretty and unusual."

"Thanks," I said stiffly. "What's yours?"

"Terian," he supplied hesitantly.

"You win," I replied, cracking a smile. "Yours is more unusual. Your mother gave you that name?"

"Yes," he said with a sad look. "She died a long time ago."

"I'm sorry," I said more respectfully, then added, "Mine abandoned me."

Terian blinked at me. "You're an orphan?"

I looked away, and didn't reply.

"Sorry," he said again. "I'm one. I—"

"It's okay," I said, letting out a sigh. "No, I'm not. My father is alive and well. But we don't speak. I haven't seen him in years."

Terian seemed not to know what to say, his expression uncomfortable.

"So why offer me breakfast?" I said quickly, trying to fill the silence. I hate silence. "Why take me to eat?"

"Because I wanted to spend time with you," Terian said earnestly.

"Why?" I asked suspiciously.

"Because I find you attractive, and I wanted to know if you're a good person, and this was the easiest way to find that out, by getting a chance to talk to you alone."

He was frank; I'd give him that. The way he said things was so honest, it made me want to trust him... *No. I don't trust men, not any men. Men are assholes.* "I'm not a good person," I murmured. "I'm just a person trying to live."

Our food came right then, to my relief. As we ate, we made some small talk about the weather and current events. While Terian was up on all the current badness—like the climate change that was in the news all the time these days, and the way things in the world were bleak with all the natural disasters and political unrest—his attitude was still buoyant.

"You must be an optimist," I kidded him.

"I have hope," he admitted. "I didn't for a long time. But I do now. I think that the world's going to be okay. There are good people—"

His cheerfulness suddenly soured my mood, turning it nasty. "There aren't," I said disparagingly. "Most people are useless wastes of resources—"

I abruptly stopped and cringed, hearing my father's words in my bitter declaration.

Terian just looked at me sadly. "Not all people are," he comforted. "Sometimes it only takes one to make a big difference."

It was easy to see he believed what he was saying. It was equally easy to see he was talking about a woman that he cared for as more than a benefactor. Sure, he could be referring to a man, but then that extra affection I was hearing would make him gay. If he were gay, he wouldn't be here with me having breakfast, or getting so excited when I'd touched him. Whoever she was, she wasn't my concern. When we finished here, I was going to ask him to spend the night if he wanted to. "Maybe."

When the bill came a few minutes later, Terian paid it. We walked back to his truck, and he drove me to my place. As he had all night, he opened the door for me, then helped me out. "Thank you for coming with me," he said almost formally. "I'd like to take you out again, if you had fun."

"I did," I said slowly, realizing with surprise that I wasn't just being polite, I was telling the truth.

"Tomorrow?" he said quickly. "I can be there by ten—"

"No," I said flatly. "You can't hang out at my job."

That upset him. "Are you embarrassed I waited for you?"

"No," I said, thinking him very naive that anything would embarrass me in my profession. "But my boss makes money on the girls getting guys to pay extra money for drinks, and especially lap dances. Hotcakes is not a Pizza Hut, it's a stripper bar. He'll tell you to leave if you do what you did tonight again."

Terian made a face. "What should I be doing then? Ordering more drinks?"

"For starters, come inside with me now," I said in a sultry way, heading to my back door. "But lock your truck first. This is a bad neighborhood."

Terian looked like he was going to melt with desire, but then oddly he shook his head. "I don't want to rush things. I want to get to know you, Sun."

His attempt at being some kind of boyfriend wasn't necessary, or wanted tonight. "Either come inside, or leave now and don't come back tomorrow," I said abruptly, losing my patience. "I've got to get to bed. You can come with me or not, it's your choice." I walked inside, then turned and held the door open.

Terian came after me, blushing. As soon as we were inside and I'd locked the door, I reached for him. Then I was in his arms, kissing him passionately as he trembled, letting out soft, eager cries.

Poor guy. Terian must need a woman badly, which was surprising. He was cute enough that he wouldn't ever be a pity fuck. Why had he waited so long to get some?

As I slipped my tongue into his mouth, I pushed back my hair from my sweaty face with my free hand. *God, it's hot in here.* I unbuttoned his shirt, then stripped it off with his help, then his T-shirt, running my hands over his chest as Terian trembled harder.

"That feel good, baby?" I murmured.

"Yes," he moaned softly. "I love your hands on me. I could feel them like this all night."

Does he have a fetish? What man didn't want a woman's hands playing his organ? Go figure. "Come with me."

Grabbing his hand, I pulled him to my bedroom, and sat him on the bed. "Grab us some protection," I instructed, stripping off my shirt and jeans. "It's in the drawer."

Terian hesitantly grabbed out a condom from the nightstand. Before he got it on, I pushed him back on the bed.

"God, I want you," I said in a heated rush, feeling his hard, lean body beneath mine. It had been a month or so since I'd last taken a man to bed. I'd just not felt like it, or so I told myself. "God, you're so hot—"

Terian was pulling back from me, grimacing.

What the hell? "You okay?" I asked, my hand paused over his pant's zipper.

"Don't talk about a higher being," he said quietly. "I'm sensitive to that."

Ah shit, a Christian freak. I should have known this was too good to be true. "I'm not Mary Magdalene," I said contemptuously, pulling back from him. "I didn't invite you here to—"

"Who was she?" Terian asked, dumbfounded.

Ah. He must be just one of those people who didn't believe in saying

9

God or Jesus unless they were praying or something. One of the clients I had was like that. He didn't like me referring to God in idle conversation when I gave him his monthly lap dance. That was understandable, him being a lay preacher. "Sorry," I said with a nod. "I'll try not to say it."

Terian pulled me gently down to rest on his chest. I lay against him, liking the warmth of him. "Tell me you want me again," he said with hesitancy. "Please?"

He seemed so young, I laughed lightly. "I want you, Terian. Take me."

Terian took my face in his hands gently and kissed me. Then he was sliding his hands lower to caress me gently. But he didn't move to take off my remaining clothes.

Why is he taking so long? I reached down to undo his pants myself, but he stopped me. "I want to take my time," he said quietly. "It's the first time. I want it to be special."

I was touched he wanted to play the romantic lover for our first time, and then immediately irritated that I felt like that. But I couldn't make myself say something sarcastic. "Okay," I said, caressing his skin again. "Take your time."

Terian kissed me for a long time. At first, he did it very cautiously and carefully. Soon, he was delving into my mouth with his seeking tongue, and licking me urgently, as his hands roamed my clothed body. Finally, he removed my tank top, then caressed my bare skin, kissing me all over, making soft wordless sounds of excitement. I couldn't wait anymore by then, though, so I pushed back from him, unhooked my bra in a deft practiced motion, and tossed it aside.

Terian looked at me for a moment like he was awestruck. Then he reached a hand to cup my breast. The moment his hand closed on it, he lost a little of his self-control. He shoved me back on the bed, sucking my tit hard into his mouth, his hand rubbing my other nipple. He felt so good I let out a groan, and then he was rubbing his face on my breasts, licking and squeezing them. I groaned loudly, moving urgently beneath him. But I'd always liked men who enjoyed my whole body, and gave it attention. Too many men slipped off their jeans, and before I knew it, they were snoring.

Terian was still writhing on me, panting. Suddenly, I felt his erection pressing against my hip. *Shit!* That couldn't be him. He was huge! Riveted, I slid my hand down between us and gripped the hardness. He went completely still.

It is him. Hell. I opened his jeans with ease, and slid the whole of him out. Then I pushed him back on the bed so I could get a good look. *Wow.*

"Very nice." I ran my hand over his penis, massaging the head and then the shaft. Terian was bucking all over on the bed, and then suddenly he came. He spurted out with a cry, his hot semen spattering my hand. I jerked my hand back with a cry.

Terian looked at me, his face scared. "Did I hurt you?"

Why in hell would he think that? "No," I said, disappointed. "But I was looking forward to sex, and now it'll be a while."

"I'm not done," Terian said lustily. Then he grinned. "Babe."

Blinking in disbelief, I saw he was still erect. I'd never seen a man come, and have him not go soft on me. "How'd you do that? Viagra?"

Terian grinned wider, and pushed past me to the bathroom, stripping off his jeans as he went. "I don't need drugs, Sun. I'm special," he said. "Give me a second."

When he returned, he stopped in the doorway, looking at me. I'd taken the opportunity to shed the rest of my clothes and pose on the bed sexily. As he got into bed, I handed him another condom. He slipped it on quickly, then began pressing down on me with his hips.

"Tell me if I hurt you," he whispered. "I know I'm big."

"You are," I groaned, feeling the length of him push into me inch by delicious inch. "God, it—"

Terian let out a cry, stopped his movements, and gave me a hurt look.

"I'm sorry," I assured quickly, pulling him back towards me. "I won't say anything else. Please don't stop—"

Terian nodded. With a thrust, he pushed the rest of himself in and began to piston deeply, clasping my body to his. As before, he came within a few seconds, his groan of release almost inaudible. Again, he hurried to the bathroom, cleaned up, and returned, eagerly taking up his same position within me. "You feel so good to me, Sun," he whispered. "So right...Mmm..."

I held his body close to mine, panting slightly in arousal as he moved on me. I didn't mind his already coming twice, but I would be the one coming next or I was showing him the door, no matter how good he felt.

It wasn't long for me, but then it usually wasn't. I climaxed hard, screaming out wordlessly over and over. As I began to scream, Terian increased his pace, hammering into me, his own shout loud as mine as he came.

He withdrew, lay beside me, and then looked at me impishly. "Tell me when you want me to stop, Sun. I don't want to hurt you."

I looked at him in disbelief. "You can go again now?"

He nodded.

"Keep going then," I requested with a wicked smile. "Give me everything you've got!"

Terian grinned, then pulled me beneath him.

Terian fucked me over and over that night. I loved it, loved the feel of him rubbing me, stimulating me. But three hours later, I did stop him. I was beginning to get sore, plus he'd exhausted my supply of condoms and his. I'd come six times, a new record for me. And he'd come at least twenty times. I couldn't believe it almost, but I'd lived it. For me, that meant it was real.

We slept for a while together. I woke up first and began running my hands over him. He's asked for that all night, over and over, for me to touch him with my hands.

Terian yawned, then looked over at the clock. "I have to go," he said apologetically. "I've got work."

Well, that was understandable. It was close to noon. "That's fine," I said, feeling a little hurt for some weird reason. *Let it play out. You can't stop it happening anyway.* "I should get moving myself." I went to get up.

Terian stopped me, grabbing my arm. "I'd still like to take you out tonight," he said quickly. "What time should I pick you up?"

This was a new one. "Three a.m.," I got out. "But you don't have to, if you—"

"I meant what I said," Terian insisted as he pulled on his clothes. "I want to get to know you." Then he reached over and took my hand, putting it to his lips.

I tried not to be touched by his efforts to be romantic. "You know me now," I said, shrugging. "This is all there is."

"No, it's not," he said, hugging me gently. "But I want to see all there is, if you'll let me get close to you, Sun."

Was he asking to be a boyfriend? And did I want one? I hugged him and didn't reply.

"Do you want me to pick up more protection for us?" he asked.

Ah. He wanted to see me again because he wanted more sex. I understood that. "Sure."

"We don't have to be intimate again tonight," Terian said quickly, drawing back to look at me. "But I used all of yours, so I thought it only right I offer."

Who is this guy, that he's so...well, so nice? I'd never met a handsome man that was so nice, ever. Usually, they were pricks, with egos as big as the Montana sky, like my father...*Leave it alone right now, Sun. You think about that, you'll ruin this. Don't ruin this.*

I locked my past up, threw the key into the racks of some leftover dreams, and focused on Terian. "Sure," I said, shrugging again. "It would be a good idea to get some more."

"Do you like flowers?" he asked shyly.

I gaped at him. "You want to buy me flowers?"

"Only if you like them," he added quickly. "I thought you might be allergic. I—"

He's too good to be true. And that means something bad is coming. "What is this?" I said, getting out of bed. "We had sex. That was it—"

"I want there to be more," Terian interrupted. "Don't you want more?"

I was going to say "no," then I realized I did maybe want more. He'd been a good lover, and I'd liked being with him. Maybe it was time for a change.

You're going to get hurt, if you let anyone in.

Fuck off and die, I told that familiar voice inside me. *Just once, I'm going to see where this goes, instead of driving him away.* "Maybe," I admitted. "But I'm not sure."

"Then try it out," he said, giving me a dazzling smile. "What have you got to lose?"

My heart, maybe. "All right," I said tentatively. "I'd love some flowers. Yellow roses are my favorite."

"Then I'll bring you some tonight," he said gallantly. Terian took me in his arms, kissed me once tenderly, and left. A second later, he was back, "for one last kiss" and then he left again, grinning widely.

I was smiling, too, in spite of myself. It wasn't often that men made me smile, at least, not in a good way like this. Usually I was amazed at how dumb they acted. Maybe my luck was changing.

Chapter Three

Terian showed up right on time that night, bearing a dozen yellow long-stemmed roses. Again, we went to an early breakfast at the diner and then to my place. Being with him was just as good this night as before. But there was one surprise.

"Tell me if you want me to…um…touch you in…um…if you like…if you want me to do anything other than I'm doing, Sun," he said awkwardly. "I'm not very experienced."

"It's not like you're a virgin," I teased laughingly.

Terian went crimson.

I knew what that meant, and my mouth fell open. "You're telling me that you—?"

"Yes," Terian choked out, turning redder. "Last night, okay?"

I'd never even **met** a man who was a virgin before, much less been with one. Last night I'd taken his virginity. God, he had to be in his twenties, if not thirties! What had taken him so long?

Terian was clearly uncomfortable, so I didn't ask what I was dying to know. Instead, I touched his shoulder softly. "Don't worry about it. You were great so far, and that's all I need for now, okay?"

"Okay," he said with relief, and hugged me.

* * * *

A week passed like water, then two. We ate, fucked, and spent time together. And late one night, he just stayed. I can't remember which of us suggested it. It wasn't a problem for me; it saved us having to worry about making plans for the next night.

But after a month of living together, Terian told me that he wanted me to quit stripping. I hit the roof. "I was a stripper when you met me."

"Sun, I know that. I just think that you should quit, because you

15

don't have to—"

"Why don't I have to?"

"I'll support you," he said stoically, taking me in his arms. "I'm happy living here, with you. I'd like—"

"I like to strip," I said in a low, flat tone. "I like the money, and I'm not giving it up."

"Would you feel the same way if you were my wife?"

Nervous butterflies swarmed suddenly in my stomach and chest. It was loud and clear that Terian was thinking of marriage already. It was also clear that he thought that I was going to be June Cleaver to his Ward Cleaver once he popped the question.

No. Fucking. Way. "I'm not cut out to be anybody's wife," I said with a sneer. "I don't want to quit."

"Don't you care about me?" he asked in a small tentative voice.

For some reason, that made me so fucking furious I lost it, the bitter lie forming on my lips to spill out before I could stop it. "What we have is just sex to me, like I've had with dozens of men."

Terian gave me an unbelieving hurt look. Then, without a word, he gathered up his things and left.

I cried that night like I hadn't in some years. But I told myself it was better this way, as he would have hurt me if we went on much longer. Hurting him first was the best thing to do.

* * * *

I didn't hear from Terian for some months. I did my job, slept with a few losers I regretted as soon as I'd seen them naked, and soon it was Christmas. As usual, I sent my father the requisite card, and I sent my mother flowers to her burial plot.

My tale of childhood woe I'd told to Terian had been true, from a point of view. My mother had committed suicide when she found my father cheating on her with a sixteen-year-old girl. That the girl was her foster daughter was too much for her. So she took an overdose of Valium, went to sleep, and never woke up.

I was two at the time.

My father raised me, if you counted the endless nights of me watching TV and eating dinners I microwaved myself while he fucked a stream of women in the trailer's one bedroom.

16

Sundown

When he wasn't balling some babe, he was working: driving trucks, hauling furniture, fixtures, and God knew what to who knew where.

Given that description of his character, it might seem unbelievable that so many women wanted his company, that they gave him money or would consent to watch his brat—me—while he was off driving for days on end. The easy answer was that my father was incredibly handsome. He had dark brown hair with a slight curl that he wore long, and rich blue eyes like cobalt that seemed perpetually knowing. Even though he drank beer, and ate only fast food, through some trick of genes his body was lean, and powerfully built. But the most captivating thing about him was his charm. God, he was charming. I knew that he was shallow as a rock, and just as caring, but he faked emotions so well that it was hard not to believe he meant every word he said. Hell, he was so good at it, women looked for a reason, any reason to believe what he said, and when there was no logic to follow in his given argument, they usually made something up.

I was not immune. Over and over I believed him when he said he'd changed and seen the error of his ways, and repeatedly I was hurt when he went right back to his old habits within the space of a few days. It took me the better part of fourteen years with him to wise up. When I did, I left.

That was when I started dancing. I'd watched enough of my father's stripper-friends as they practiced their routines to know how to move, and gotten tips from a few of the more friendly ones. Wanting at least a few states between us so he wouldn't accidentally find me some night, I'd moved out here to New York, trading the desert for forest, and never looked back.

* * * *

One night in March, I looked out in the crowd and saw Terian was there, watching me dance. When my set was over, my boss told me to get my ass over to him, because he'd paid for me for private dances for the next hour solid.

I pasted a smile on my face and nodded, because I knew to refuse was to get fired. Then I went over to Terian, and began to dance. I expected…well, I don't know what I expected. Maybe for him to maybe

17

have brought me some roses, or for him to offer to take me out for breakfast. Instead, he just watched me dance.

Not to make it seem he was distant or uninterested. All his focus was on me. When I sat down on his lap, his hard erection bulged through his jeans against my bare thighs. Yet he made no move to touch me. When I was done and the hour was up, he leaned in close and whispered, "Want me to meet you outside after you get off work?"

"For what?" I replied, half-interested, half-cautious.

"For breakfast and sex, baby," he said bluntly, then grinned.

His shyness was gone, his expression and tone direct and calm. "Got some more notches on your belt?" I teased, smiling to soften the cutting edge of my remark.

"A couple," he said, grinning again in a way I found very sexy and yet boyishly innocent. "But they weren't like you, Sun."

I only had to hear him say my name like that, and I knew my answer was going to be yes.

* * * *

I got off early at six thirty by trading shifts on Monday with a friend. Terian and I got a quick breakfast, but the both of us weren't thinking about food, even as we ate. We raced to my apartment in record time.

Terian and I were all over each other, which made undoing my simple door lock a formidable task. Finally, I got it open, and we fell through the doorway, landing on the floor as we grappled with each other's clothes. We somehow made it to the bedroom, but not to the bed.

I unzipped his pants, and took out his erection, stroking him with my hand. Terian let out a growl of need, and pushed me back to the floor. He slipped on a condom from the drawer above my head, and with a thrust of his hips, he was inside me. I let out a sigh of pleasure.

Terian chuckled low and kissed my throat. "Did you miss me, Sun?"

"Duh," I said sarcastically, and kissed him hard, reaching around to caress his firm, bare ass.

Terian's phone rang suddenly, then repeatedly. He made no move to answer it, his hips pumping on mine, as we groaned together. Just as we came, the phone stopped, our shared cries loud in the sudden silence. As we lay there still joined, trying to catch our breaths, it began ringing again.

Grumbling, Terian pulled out of me and rolled onto his back, reaching into his discarded pants for his phone. "Yes?"

Terian's mouth suddenly dropped open. "Theo? I only gave one person this number! Why are you calling—?"

Terian cut off abruptly, then rubbed his eyes, his muscles tensing. Fury came off him, mixed with despair. "It was you," he said quietly. "Damn you, it was you she dreamed with."

He sat up, and hurriedly pulled on his jeans, using his head and shoulder to hold the phone. "Meet me at Alan's Creek" he said quickly. "I can make it there in fifteen minutes! Shut up, and meet me there!"

Terian hung up, slid on his shirt, and then hugged me tightly. "I have to go," he said, his eyes scared. "I'll be back in two hours or so. Stay here, Sun. I'll explain when I get back."

He raced out the door, as I was still trying to figure out what the hell had just happened.

* * * *

I worried about Terian all night, but a few drinks helped me relax, at least to the point I didn't pace. About one a.m., he returned with blood on his clothes.

"What happened?" I asked warily, pointedly looking at the bloodstains.

"Don't worry, it's not mine," he said tiredly. "Can I use your shower?"

"Sure," I assented.

Terian was in there a long time, at least an hour. I wondered how he could stand it, as given the tiny hot water heater this apartment had, the water had to be ice cold. Oddly, it didn't seem to bother him.

When Terian came out toweling his hair, he was clean, his expression resigned. "I have some things to tell you, Sun, and some questions for you. But I want to answer the questions you must have for me first." He put down the towel. "About what happened, if you want to know, that is."

Fuck yes. "Whose blood was that?"

"Some bad guys were holding a friend of mine against her will. They were going to kill her. Her boyfriend was the one who called. I

19

helped him get her free." He paused. "The blood was from some guards we had to kill, Sun."

That warning light came on again in my brain. "You killed people tonight?"

"They were going to kill me and Theo."

"Why not call the police? And who is Theo? You sound like you don't like him. There is resentment in your voice."

"The police wouldn't have helped, Sun. These people…they operate outside the law. The police are in their pocket, and they're utterly ruthless. They have connections to the highest state levels, some federal officers—"

"Enough with the conspiracy theories, Terian. Why did you risk your life?"

"The woman who was being held saved my life a few months ago. She risked herself for me back then and got hurt for it." He paused. "I owed her."

There was a lot more emotion in his tone than mere obligation called for. "Who was holding her? How did they get her in the first place?"

"A guy named Devlin Dalcon grabbed her at her home when Theo wasn't there. Sarelle shot some of his men, but they overpowered her and took her to Devlin's brother, Danial—"

Sarelle was the woman's name, the one he's carrying a torch for. "Why take her there?"

"Danial and she were…married before. Devlin wanted her for himself. He wanted to run it by Danial first, I guess."

He's stumbling over words and pausing a lot. I concluded Terian was leaving out much of the truth. "Why would a crazy guy willing to do a home invasion with armed guards care about checking with his brother for "ex" permission'?"

"Danial told him to do what he wanted with her, since she'd left him."

This was beyond illogical; this was crazy. "No man has that kind of power over his wife, much less an ex."

Terian nodded in agreement. "It didn't last even a week. Danial's too much of a possessive bastard. He hit her."

Anger focused my thoughts, remembering times I'd been hit myself by people who professed to love me. "Bastard. Did you smack him around a little, I hope?"

"Yeah. They won't be bothering her again." He flashed me a proud smile.

I didn't reply. I had too much on my mind and it had nothing to do with what he'd just said. Every time Terian mentioned Sarelle, it was obvious that he still had feelings for her. While it hadn't mattered when she'd merely been a woman he liked a few months ago, it was bracingly upsetting to know he still felt the same way now. Worse, he'd run off with barely two words to me, to risk his life to rescue her.

"Do you mind if I stay here with you?" he asked awkwardly, coming closer to hug me. "I'd like to be like we were, back before I left," He took a deep breath. "I won't pressure you for anything more, Sun."

Leave off discussing Sarelle for now. Don't ruin this. "Okay," I said, squeezing him in my arms.

Chapter Four

The next six months were blissful. It was summer, the flowers were blooming, and I was in love. Terian and I went on picnics, went hiking in parks, swam in the local pool, and made love at every opportunity. Yet even as I was blissfully having it all, I began to wonder at some of my lover's odd habits.

Terian never seemed to get too hot, even on the hottest day. He didn't seem to sweat at all, except when we made love for hours, and even then, it was barely noticeable. Yet sometimes his skin seemed hotter than it should be, to the point where touching him was uncomfortable. Weirder still was that happened most often when I startled him.

He seemed to like food of all kinds, but sometimes he ate meat that was so rare it sickened me. He always said he'd cooked it, but it looked completely raw to me. I told myself that was quirky, but not abnormal. And if I felt my skin crawl sometimes when something upset him, I chalked that up to my empathizing with him. But what bothered me the most, was our sex life.

It was plain weird that he refused to have sex with me without a condom, even after I got a clean bill of health from my gyno along with some birth control pills. I used all the normal arguments guys had always used on me: it will feel better, its more natural, we're protected, but to no avail. Terian just repeated that it wasn't safe, and that he wouldn't have sex without a condom, period. So I shrugged and agreed, thinking him paranoid.

What broke us wasn't any of this, though; it was his refusal to let me see his real eyes.

Terian had worn colored contacts the whole time I'd known him. Sure, they were the kind people wore for a month at a time; that wasn't the problem. After being with him for six months, I just wanted to know what color his eyes really were. Yet Terian flatly refused to let me see him when he changed his lenses out. I tried asking nicely, then bluntly, then angrily. He just refused, quietly reiterating again that the eyes he was born with weren't very pretty, and then requested that I leave it alone.

I didn't leave it alone, of course; I just bided my time. Finally, in October, I got my chance.

Terian was opening his new contacts in the bathroom behind a locked door when his phone rang. When I heard him answer it, I knew I had just a few seconds to get in there and solve the mystery. Jimmying open the door quietly with the top of a pen, I peeked in. Terian's back was to the door, so he didn't see me. I still don't know to this day how he missed hearing me, but some of his distraction likely was because the person he was talking to was the infamous Sarelle, known as Sar to her friends.

She called every week now, though Terian didn't tell me why or what they talked about. But he'd often go for walks alone after they talked, and then return home eager for sex. I didn't need it spelled out for me that Theo wasn't in the picture with Sar anymore, and that Terian was thinking hard about leaving me to go to her. He'd slipped once and said something to the effect that I resembled her. After that, I couldn't help feeling jealous of her, even though I knew he hadn't been with her or anyone else since he'd come back to me.

Terian looked up in the mirror. I let out a gasp. I'd expected hazel eyes, grey eyes, or maybe even icy blue eyes. But his eyes were none of those. His eyes were bright, deep red.

I turned to run. Terian had hold of me before I'd gone a step, angrier than I had ever seen him. "You wanted to see! Go ahead, look!"

"What are you?" I demanded.

"I'm half demon," he grated out.

"How?"

"My human mother had sex with a demon," he said sarcastically. "You do know how sex works, right?"

"I'm sorry."

"I'm not," he said suddenly, hugging me. "I wanted to tell you, Sun.

23

I was afraid though, afraid you'd be scared of me." He swallowed hard. "I didn't want you to be scared of me."

"I'm not," I said slowly. "I'm not scared."

"Good, because I've been wanting to ask you something," he said anxiously. He went to one knee. "Would you marry me, Sundown?"

I felt like throwing up.

"I love you," Terian went on. "I should have told you sooner, but...I needed to work some things out for myself. Now that I have, I want to be with you."

"What about Sarelle?"

Terian blushed. "She told me she didn't like me as more than a friend. Nothing's changed. She...she's—"

So I get you by default. No. "I can't marry you," I said, letting out a long breath. "I don't want to get married, Terian. Not even to you, and I like you a lot—"

"You wouldn't have to give up your, um...lifestyle. Things would be like they are now."

"Then why can't they stay like this?" I asked bluntly. "I couldn't wear a ring for you, not even an engagement ring, not to work. My boss frowns on that, says it makes the customers think they can't ask us to dance, if we're married."

"Then he's an asshole!"

"Terian—"

"Look, I have a lot of money now! You don't have to sell yourself! You could do anything you wanted, go back to school, get a degree—"

I felt one of my legendary rages coming on. *Who is he to think I needed to better myself? I'm fine like I am!*

"I don't want a fucking degree! I want my own life! I want to do what I want, and that's not marrying any fucking demon!"

"Half-demon! I'm only half!"

"What's that mean anyway? You tell me you want me to marry you, but only because I accidentally find out what you are?"

"No," Terian said, hurt. He went to his drawer, and took out a box. "I got this for you a month ago. But I didn't want to rush you. I was willing to wait years if that's what it took, decades even, until you began to age, and maybe decided marriage wasn't so bad."

I got an ominous feeling and went perfectly still, as what he was saying sunk in. "Until I began to age?" I repeated in slow measured words. "'I'? Why not 'we'?"

"I don't age," Terian said sadly. "I'll look like this in another fifty years, Sun. But—"

"How old are you?" I whispered, staring at him.

"Seventy or so," he said in a low, broken tone.

I lost it right there. "Seventy!" I cackled. "And you were a virgin! How could you have waited seventy years to get laid?"

"I thought I might hurt a human woman, if I was with her," he replied, tears in his eyes. "I didn't know what I was." He swallowed hard. "I only recently learned that I wouldn't, but that I'd have to use condoms, always."

"I'm not marrying you! You love Sarelle!"

"She doesn't love me!" he roared, and I felt an unseen wave of black evil come out of him and wash over me. I let out a scream, and like magic, it dissipated as if it had never appeared. But the memory of it lingered, making my skin crawl. I backed away from Terian, my eyes wide and scared.

He started toward me. "Sun, I'm sorry."

"Get out!" I spat at him. "You're evil! I can feel it, Terian! Get out! Get out and don't come back!"

"Sun, I love you!"

"I don't love you! Get out, or I'm calling the cops!"

Terian gave me one last pained look, and then he packed his things, and left.

When he had gone, I spent the rest of that night crying, because I had lied to him. I did love him. And I'd quit my job earlier that day, because I knew he wanted me to, and I had been hoping that he was going to pop the question.

* * * *

I moped around my apartment for a while. What was the point in going anywhere? I no longer had a person who wanted to spend time with me. I told myself that he'd lied to me about what he was. He'd kept it from me, and he was an evil being, the kind every religion in the world

25

said was in league with the devil. So what if he was half-human? So what if he'd been the one man who'd never hurt me? I told myself repeatedly that it didn't matter, and didn't stop repeating the litany until I finally believed it.

I went later that day and got my job back at Hotcakes. It wasn't as if I needed the money right away. Terian had left me money in our joint account, enough to live on for a while. But it was going to run out eventually. It wasn't great to be ogled again, especially after I'd been telling myself all week I was done with that, but I'd done it before. And I took to it like I'd never left.

Days passed, then weeks, then a month. But the time that went by didn't help the loss I felt at not having Terian in my life. If anything, it made it worse. Every day I'd spent with Terian seemed to have taken on a rosy glow, like the best memories always do. I remembered all the good times we had touched, and been happy together, and how good it had been, having someone for the first time in my life who had loved me, really loved me.

Had I made the biggest mistake of my life? I was feeling more and more like I had ruined the only good thing I'd ever had. That feeling of self-destruction lingered and grew day by day, as I became more and more sure that there was no point in anything I did, and that the pain I felt was not only permanent, it was warranted.

Eventually, that self-contempt drove me to my worst dive bar. It was a rough place, one I went to only when I was feeling truly awful, and wanted to find a man to make me forget my pain. Davy's was a good place for that. There were always a lot of rough men there, no matter the night. If I was blatant about what I was looking for, I knew it wouldn't take long to find one. Maybe if I had sex with someone else, I could move on. It was a given that whoever I picked up here wouldn't be a knight in shining armor—he'd be a coarse bastard. Yet I was confident that I could handle any situation that cropped up; I always had before. *And if something happens, it's just what I deserve.*

Oddly, when I walked in that night, Davy's was practically empty. *Where is everyone? It's Saturday night.*

The jukebox was on, playing "Sympathy for the Devil" by Guns and Roses. The weird thing was it was playing quietly, the normal super loud volume turned down to barely audible. I could just hear the song over the sound of some scuffling noises coming from the back room, where the pool tables were.

I wandered into the back room, and found the source of those noises. A man was sitting on the pool table, a woman astride him, and she was riding him so hard the table legs were rocking. He had her hair gripped in his fist, pulling it back as she rode him.

God, that's bizarre! Who the fuck has sex like this out in public? I was so shocked I couldn't speak. I just stared at them with my mouth open.

"You shouldn't be here," Gary the barkeep whispered. He was cowering behind the bar, his eyes scared. "Get out of here, Sundown."

"Why?" I murmured.

"Now, Gary," a clear and beautiful voice intoned. "You'll frighten your one legitimate customer. And we wouldn't want that, now would we?"

I turned to the sound of the voice, and saw a tall dazzling blond man in back of me. He was very good-looking, his build much like Terian's; tall and broad shouldered. But his coloring was fair, very fair, his heart-shaped face almost like an angel's. His eyes were a weird light shade of brown I found unsettling. *Wait, are those red tints? Is he a fucking demon too?*

"Come and sit with me," he whispered, taking my hand, and bringing it to his lips. "My friend doesn't like to be watched."

I looked back over to see both man and woman had stopped having sex, and were staring at me with hostility. Though I had every right to be where I was, I blushed red and turned away.

The handsome blond led me into the other room to the bar, where we both sat down. He picked up a glass of white wine. "Want a drink? You look like you could use one."

Hell yes. I was no voyeur. And hearing those scuffling noises start up again was unsettling, now I knew what was causing them. "Sure."

He motioned to Gary. The bartender poured me a glass of white wine, and pushed it to me, his hand shaking hard.

"I don't want any of that shit!" I said belligerently. "Give me a drink! That's what I asked for."

27

The blond smiled faintly, and motioned for Gary to pour me a shot of whiskey. "You heard her."

Gary poured me a shot of some kind of fancy scotch, and pushed it to me. I took it and drank it down in one gulp, admiring the smoothness. I asked for another one, and he poured me more. I downed that one, too. Now I was feeling a little better, I turned to the blond man and offered him a sexy smile. "Thanks. So how's your night so far?"

The blond was studying me. "Want to come home with me?" he offered, looking pleased.

I'd heard a lot of pick-up lines in my life, but this was the first time I'd been propositioned so bluntly. *Maybe, but I'm going to make you work for it.* "No."

"To a hotel, then?" he said, unfazed.

"No," I said again. "I don't go home with men."

"Fine then," he said, nonplused. "We'll go to your place."

"Aren't you getting ahead of yourself?" I snorted.

"Don't you want me?" he said bluntly. "Didn't you come here to find someone to bed?"

Well, I had, but doing it and admitting it aloud were two different things. "I—"

"Don't lie. I can tell by your eyes you're thinking about how much fun we could have together." His voice was a dangerous purr.

This guy's not the usual hard-drinking brawler who hangs out here. Maybe Gary had been right to tell me to leave. Maybe I should go. I got up from the barstool unsteadily.

"Don't you want to have at least one orgasm, before you go home to your lonely bed?" the blond murmured softly. "Cin is coming right now."

The scuffling noises were faint, and very, very fast. There came a woman's soft cry of climax. A few seconds later, the sounds abruptly stopped. The jukebox had stopped playing, too.

Utter silence descended. The blond man moved closer to me, and I felt him kiss me lightly, very lightly up my neck. His lips were almost cold, and so were his hands. But his caresses were practiced and skilled, his deft hands and lips moving over my skin like an enveloping fog of pleasure. Before long he had me sighing as he touched me. Then he

28

began to sing to me softly.

"I can see you lying back in your satin dress, in a room where you do what you don't confess."

His captivating voice washed over me, making my knees go weak and my resistance waver hard. His choice of song wasn't surprising, but his voice was so beautiful, like an angel's.

"Come home with me, Sundown," he purred seductively. "We'll have a good time. I'm a considerate lover. I promise you, you'll love every moment of our time together."

I liked the feel of him and wanted more. *To hell with him being dangerous.* I turned to him and said, "Okay."

"I should ask you now, are you willing for other kinds of sex, besides the kind you just saw here tonight?" the blond asked quietly. "I like the full experience, so to speak."

Chapter Five

I felt a thrill, then wariness. "I don't go in for anything that hurts, or leaves scars."

"I'll do nothing that causes you pain," he said with a gentle caress. "And if you tell me to stop at any time, I will. I promise."

"Then you're on," I said with a sultry smile.

"Good," he said, a pleased note in his words. "Drink your scotch, and we'll go."

I turned to see Gary had vanished. But there was indeed a scotch there on the bar near my hand.

I drank it down in a gulp, and then he began to touch me in earnest. "Do you need some money?" he whispered in my ear, massaging one breast through my clothes, his other arm pulling my body close to his. "I'll give you some, if you're open to another man joining us."

As interesting as I found the idea of a threesome, I took offense at the offered money. "I'm not a whore," I said mildly. "I don't fuck unless I want to."

"Too bad," he said with actual reluctance. "I was hoping to pay you, so my friend and I could have you together."

"I don't do blondes," a disgusted, hissing voice said. "You know that. And I have my own woman. Leave me out of your games."

I turned. The dark man from the back room was standing there in the doorway, dressed now, his dark woman beside him. She was baring her teeth at me, and they looked kind of funny, almost too long.

"She looks like that topless dancer from over on Prospect Ave.," the woman said with a sneer to the blond man. "I should have known you were paying for it, now that you're nothing."

"Go fuck yourself, Cin," the blonde said pleasantly, "You're done here for tonight. Get your ass out that door before I kick it out myself."

Cin gave the dark man a look, like he should defend her. But he just motioned with his head that she should leave. She hissed at him with those odd teeth of hers and he just looked back at her as if he wasn't impressed.

"Fuck you!" she hissed at him. He reached out to grab hold of her, but she jerked free. "Don't come to O'Malley's again, expecting me to lie with you," she hissed once more, then left, grabbing a purse and going out the door.

I eyed the dark man. He was eyeing me in return. But his expression had no lust in it, no real emotion at all. *Weird. Doesn't he care he's just been broken up with?* Well, maybe she hadn't meant it, for all I knew this scene played out every Saturday night; I hadn't been here in more than six months.

"You should reconsider joining me, seeing as it looks like you're single again," the blond said snarkily to the dark man. "I'd love you to show her your other form, and then watch you have her."

"Other form?" I said in confusion, my words slurring. "What the hell are you talking about? I'm not into threesomes unless the other partners are male."

"I don't want any of her, or what you are planning," the dark man hissed. "Leave me out of it."

"You sure, Lash? She looks just like her."

I fainted, or passed out, because the next thing I remember, I was waking up in bed beside another woman. She was naked and also blonde, but platinum blonde. I thought I recognized her from a club across town, but I could have been wrong. With enough makeup and a wig, one woman can look like the twin of someone she normally wouldn't resemble at all.

"Who are you?" I said, pushing myself up, only to discover my clothes had been replaced by a black velvet robe. *What the hell? Why is she naked, and I'm not?* "Where are we?"

"I'm Cassy," she said quietly. "Where are we? I was in a bar with a blonde—"

"So was I."

"And here I am," the handsome man said, reappearing and strolling over to us dressed in a gray robe. "Cassy," he said enticingly. "Come

31

into the shower with me."

"But I'm clean," she protested.

"I asked you to do it," he said with a growl. "Do it now. Or else leave."

Cassy got up, and followed him into the bathroom. Water began running.

The next thing I knew, I was waking up again on the floor. I got to my feet unsteadily. The water was still running. With effort, I got to the doorway and looked in.

The man was kissing Cassy in the shower, touching her intimately, and she was moaning and writhing. The guy suddenly reared back, I saw long fangs, and a second later, he'd buried them in her throat. She cried out, then pulled him to her, caressing him with longing, her moans loud over the rush of the water.

Suddenly, the blond jerked backward, and blood fountained up. He had ripped out Cassy's throat. She struggled weakly, her mouth gasping soundlessly. He pushed his face into her neck, closing his eyes as her blood covered him, running down his face. He fastened his mouth over her throat, and began drinking.

The fangs, the cool skin, the blood... God, he's a vampire.

I slid down to the floor, and collapsed.

I awoke back in the bed. I screamed when I opened my eyes and saw the blond beside me. I tried to run, but he grabbed my arm tightly, preventing me from leaving.

"Vampire...you're a—!"

"Shh," he said calmly. "You just had a bad dream. I had to wake you. You were screaming."

I rubbed my eyes, noticing that I still had on my own clothes, not the black robe I thought I'd been wearing. *What happened?*

"You passed out in the bar briefly. But you drank six straight scotches, so that's not unexpected. You passed out again in the car on the way here. Do you remember?"

"No," I said hesitantly, wondering if he was lying about the amount I'd drunk. "And I usually do."

"Lay there and rest then," he said reassuringly. "You're safe. We'll have sex when you wake up, if you want to. If you don't, I'll have one of my men take you home."

I eyed him dubiously, but he didn't make any moves, just looked at me with a bemused expression. I stretched out, and fell asleep again. When I woke up, I felt a lot better.

I rolled over to see the handsome man beside me. He was naked now, and I drank in the sight of him. He not only looked sexy as hell, he was well-hung, a solid ten-plus on the scale of one to ten. The sight of him stiff for me excited me as though I'd been without a man for a year.

"Are you feeling better?" he purred, his odd-looking eyes almost happy.

"Yes," I said, my tone like thick syrup as I hurriedly undressed. "I want to feel you in me so bad—"

"I aim to please," he said and chuckled. He slid me over to him, helping me with my clothes and pushing them aside, so he could see all of me. He caressed me with his fingers, and I shivered beneath his hands, spreading my legs wide so he could touch me intimately. He slid his finger inside my vagina, and sighed, feeling my instant wetness for him.

"Tell me you want me to fuck you," he hissed, his eyes suddenly red-gold. "Say it!"

Vampire. He's a vampire for real! I did see him kill that girl, Cassy! Strangely, I wasn't afraid. I knew on some level I should be, but I wasn't. All I could think of was how much I wanted him. "Fuck me, please," I moaned. "Please!"

"Beg me!" he said with a sneer.

"Please!" I said, almost crying. "Please, I'll do anything."

"Anything?"

"Anything! Please, please!"

"Come here then," he purred, rolling onto his back. "And show me a little appreciation first. And then I'll fuck you, I promise."

I knew what he wanted, just from the expectant look on his face. With how large he was, it would probably be uncomfortable for me to deep throat him. But I didn't care. There was only my need for him that was insatiable. *I have to have him. I have to!*

I got up on my hands and knees, and crawled to him. I put my hands on his dick, and saw belatedly he wasn't wearing a condom. "We need protection."

33

"I don't use any, ever," he said arrogantly. "I'm sterile. Now get to it!"

"I—"

"Get to it, or leave," he said scornfully. "I have plenty of others to ask to my bed. You can go back to the bar I found you in."

I was drowning in a well of loneliness and hopelessness. I couldn't leave: I wanted to be loved! "No, please, you promised—"

His tone was tender and soft when he spoke, though his words were cruel, his expression pure relish. "Suck me now, or leave, you bitch."

I bent my head, and took him in my mouth. He immediately thrust the full length of himself into my throat. I gagged a little, but managed to take him all in.

Terian was big too, I'd had practice…

Tears began to fall down my cheeks at thoughts of Terian. Of how he would feel, to see me like this, doing this to someone else.

The blond was thrusting into me hard, and a second later he came. When I felt him begin to come, I tried to draw back, to get him out of me, but he had hold of me, and he wouldn't let go. Worse, he pulled himself out of me enough so I tasted him on my tongue, as he pumped into me over and over, growling loudly. "Take it," he spat at me, his eyes fully red now. "Swallow it, bitch!"

I was crying hard now, feeling so debased. But I did what he said, choking a little on his semen. He slipped out of me, his penis still hard. Abruptly, he pushed me onto my back, and slipped inside me with a growl. He stroked me skillfully as he thrust, his fingers rubbing my clit, and within minutes, I was coming for him hard. The orgasm was so powerful I felt as though a train had hit me. I convulsed under him, screaming out loudly.

"You want me to fuck you!" he hissed, stroking me as I cried out. "Tell me you do!"

"Yes, I do! So badly! Please fuck me!"

"Harder? Deeper?"

"Yes!" I gasped.

I felt him grab hold of my hips, and then he was plunging into me, bringing pain. There was too much of him to take. But I also couldn't seem to get enough.

"You're mine," he panted. "Not his! Say it! You're mine! Not his!"

"I'm not his! I'm yours!" I screamed. "All yours!"

"Ahhh!" he cried out, shuddering, and I felt him spurt into me again.

But he didn't stop. He didn't even pause, his thrusting still hard, deep and fast, the sex too rough. I couldn't seem to care, though. It felt incredible, what he was doing to me, better than any sex I'd ever had, ever!

I came again and again, shuddering in his arms, and he kept having me, over and over, kept telling me repeatedly to say I was his. Soon I was slick with sweat and our come, but he wouldn't stop. I didn't want him to. *Not ever! This was the most incredible sex I'd ever had.*

I began to feel weak, but I couldn't seem to care about that, either. *Nothing mattered but my next orgasm.*

He cried out again, shuddering.

Something was pricking me a little. I looked down to see where he was holding my hips. His nails had grown to talons an inch long. They were sunk into me, the deep wounds seeping blood. I was sitting in a puddle of it. There was some blood on his hips, and on mine, mixed with glistening semen.

Was this real? *This can't be real. I can't feel anything but pure pleasure.*

My vision blurred, and my head lolled. He was licking at my neck, and moaning. He came again, and then finally rolled off me. I looked over, blinking my eyes, trying to clear my head.

The bottom half of his face was shiny with blood. My blood.

"Want to know my name?" he said with a smile, his fang tips showing. "Or can you guess it?"

Horrified, I grabbed all of my willpower and resolve, and fought my desire for him. "No," I whispered, shaking. "I want you to stop. I don't want you to touch me again!"

The man's grinning face became a mask of rage, and he bolted out of bed with a growl. He picked up his phone, and began speaking into it. Two minutes later, there was a knock at the door.

The blond man got up and answered the door, letting another man in.

"You wanted me, Boss? Hey, she looks like—"

"You want a piece of her?" the handsome man offered with a grin.

"You offering, Boss?" The man's tone was rough and lustful.

"Sure, Kev. Sun said she was open to a threesome, so long as she was the only woman."

"Whatever I want?"

"I know your proclivities," the blond purred. "That's why I called you."

Kev unbuckled his jeans, and started toward me. I wanted to move but I couldn't. My muscles just wouldn't obey me.

"Use protection," the blond cautioned.

"I'm clean," the other man protested.

"You were with Klara last night. I can't be sure of that." The handsome man pointed a taloned finger. "Obey me, or leave, Kev. Now."

"Okay, Boss, but why do you care?" the man said in surprise. "She's not special."

The handsome vampire's expression darkened. "Yes, she is. I enjoyed this night with her a lot, more than anything for the last few months, and I want her to last more than tonight," he growled. "Have her, but don't hurt her. You do and I warn you, you'll have the same done to you ten times over."

Kev slipped on a condom the blond tossed him, then rolled me over to lay on my stomach. I fought to move, managing only to clench my hands. Kev began easing into me, groaning. I didn't feel pain, but I knew where he was putting himself. I twitched in revulsion and fear, scared he was going to hurt me. *Keep calm, you're fine, hold still, you know it's easier to take when you hold still.*

"She's tight," Kev groaned. "God, she must never have done this before, it feels so good."

"Take her hard," the blond growled. "Make her scream. I want to see you bring her to climax."

"She probably won't—"

"Oh, but she will," the blond replied with a nod. "Sundown's on a drug that makes her reach orgasm quickly. Just stroke her a little with your hand, and she'll come. I want her to feel nothing but pleasure."

Kev began to slide himself in and out of me, but it wasn't painful, it was gratifying. And I felt him touching me gently with his hand,

36

manipulating me. I began to groan almost at once, my enjoyment building. Kev sped up, and soon I was climaxing hard, screaming. He roared loudly, pushing himself all the way in as he came. Something seemed to give way inside me, but there was no pain.

Kev slipped out of me, then pulled on his pants. "Thanks, Boss," he said with an easy grin. "I loved pretending it was—"

"I know you did," the blond answered with a brief nod. "So did I. But I need to tend to her bleeding, or she'll have scarring, something she specifically spoke out against. So leave now. If you're good, I'll invite you back next time she comes to play."

"Thanks again, Sundown," Kev said, looking over at me with a last savoring glance. "You were fantastic." Then he left.

"He's right, my dear. You were perfect, right down to your tears," the blond said, giving me an approving smile. He kissed my hand gently, then took me in his arms, positioning me on my back. "Rest now and I'll have your wounds tended to. I promise you, there'll be no scars or pain." He took my hand in his, then rubbed it against his cheek briefly before letting it go and standing. "I'll be around to visit you again soon, Sundown. Very soon. Adieu."

He caressed my cheek once gently, and I shuddered under his touch. Then I slipped into unconsciousness.

Chapter Six

I awoke in my own bed.

God, had I dreamed all that weird stuff? I went to move, and whimpered in pain. Then I pulled back the sheets, afraid of what I'd find.

Oh God. I had no visible bruises, but my entire body ached. There was a little blood crusted on my pubic hair and on my thighs. There were wounds at my sides, bandaged, but still seeping blood. *Those are the wounds from his nails...it wasn't a dream.* It had all been real. *Everything he did to me was real!*

"Are you too hurt to move by yourself?" a hissing voice asked. "You shouldn't be feeling any pain."

I looked over with horror to see the dark man from last night. What had the blond called him? *Whip? Blade?*

The whole night came back in a rush. *That blond asshole!* "You're saying I gave consent? I didn't! Not for that! Not for any of it!"

His eyes were very flat, and unreadable. *Scary eyes, almost like an animal's.* I didn't feel particularly scared of him, though his face had a cruel cast to it.

"If you didn't want rough sex, why the hell were you at Davy's?" he said pointedly. "When you agree to a threesome with two men, oral or anal is part of the package. What did you think was going to happen?"

"He date-raped me," I whispered. "He let his man—"

"You thought you knew what you were doing last night in that bar," the dark man said scathingly. "You thought you'd find a man to bed, maybe some rough trade to make you forget whatever it was you wanted to forget. But this time, you got in over your head, girl. Because some men want more than sex for a night. Some want everything that you are."

"He's a vampire! An honest to God vampire! A monster out of a movie!"

"He is vampire," the dark man stated in a correcting tone. "So what? It changes nothing about last night, Sun."

I began to cry again.

He hugged me tighter. "Don't think about it, any of it," the dark man whispered. "Forget it like a nightmare. You'll need to stay in bed this next day or so, but you'll be okay after that. You don't have an STD, vampires never get them. Your wounds won't scar, and should be healed by tonight."

"How would you know?" I cried piteously. "He hurt me."

"Because I am the one that dressed them, and cleaned you up," the dark man said. "I used a salve that took most of the pain away, and won't leave a scar. They were bloody, but not deep, or life threatening. This is not the first time he's done this to a woman. Or the first time I've sat with one after." He studied me. "Why do you females always consent when he asks if you're up for anything?"

"How can you stay with him?" I whispered, appalled and angry. "He's evil."

"He can be," the dark man admitted. "I've seen it, what he's capable of. But monsters aren't born, they are made. He's not always like this. He's been worse these past two months, since he was hurt badly. His brother took his power, with the help of a half demon and—"

Terian. I swooned and collapsed. The dark man caught me, and eased me back to the bed, looking worried.

"Devlin," I whispered, shaking. "The blond man's name was Devlin."

"Yes?" the dark man asked curiously. "But how did you know that? He didn't tell you his name. He said you didn't want to know it, he was so pissed about that."

"Terian was my lover at the time you're talking about," I said, starting to cry again. "He told me about saving Sarelle that night he came to see me when he returned from the west."

"Christ on a crutch," the dark man swore. "That's all I need, Terian coming after Dev now."

"Terian saved Sarelle from a man named Devlin. He's loved her since he met her."

"Terian loves her?" the dark man hissed. "Why? They were never anything to one another save friends, to my knowledge."

"I don't know. He said she was kind to him, and no one had been kind to him before."

"Bullshit," the dark man said flatly, hissing. "She must be a good lay. But when did she find the time to fuck him? She was busy enough with Theo and Danial."

"He was never with her like that," I said, grimacing. "They never did anything."

"I don't understand these romantics," the dark man hissed disdainfully. "How can you love a woman you've never lain with that much?"

"Who are you?"

"Lash," he said, focusing again on me. "My name's Lash. And you are Sundown, Dev said."

I began to cry again. After I sobbed for another few minutes, I managed to pull myself together again. "Thank you, for taping me back together," I said, wiping my eyes with a tissue. "I'll be okay. I'll take a few days off from work. And I won't go to Davy's again."

"I've never said this before," Lash hissed, gripping my arm hard. "But you are right. I am tired of seeing this happen. It's a waste, and it's evil." He cupped my face in his hands and looked at me, his flat eyes revealing no emotion. "Get out of town. Leave tomorrow, or the next day. As soon as you are able to move, and drive."

"I can't. I don't have my car, it's at Davy's."

"It's not," Lash hissed. "I brought it back here last night, on Dev's orders."

That was a relief. Lash's next words were not.

"But you need to sell it anyway, and rent one instead. Because plates can be traced."

"I can't rent a car, my credit's too bad. I don't even have a credit card."

"Take a bus then. I'll even buy you a ticket."

"Where? Why?" I asked, confused.

"Anywhere at least a state away. Because you would already be dead, like that other woman Cassy, if he didn't want to draw it out."

Foreboding filled me. "Draw what out?"

"Your death," he hissed softly. "You remind him very strongly of someone he can't touch, can't hurt at all, someone who he hates and yet is obsessed with completely."

"Sar," I breathed.

He nodded. "He'll send me back to bring you to him in a few days, when he thinks you're healed. He knows where you live and where you work. So leave, and don't forward your mail. Don't forward your calls. Disappear."

"Why?" I stammered.

"Because if you aren't here, if I can't find you easily, he'll be angry, but he'll forget you soon enough. There are a lot of women with long dirty blonde hair. There are a lot of women with hair like hers that won't be missed."

"He can fuck off," I said hotly. "I'm not going to consent again."

"Dye your hair for the first six months at least," Lash interrupted. "Any color but the one it is. Cut it shorter too, to your shoulders or above. A large part of the attraction for him is your hair, because it resembles hers. You can't do anything about your face, but I don't know how closely you look like her."

"You speak like you don't know her."

"I've never seen her, or met her," Lash said with a shrug. "But I've heard of her and nothing else for months now, ever since the night he first got a taste of her blood. He's obsessed with her blood. He says it tastes of summer, and he won't let it go. It reminds him of another woman's blood, a woman he knew long, long ago."

I shivered, thanking God I wasn't Sar. I'd envied her for so many months, but I pitied her now. *After what he did to me, what will he do to her, given half a chance?*

"Your blood isn't like hers, Sun. Yours is normal human blood, or he would not have let you leave Hayden," Lash continued. "So there is no reason he would pursue you cross-country. If you get away, and you don't look like you do now for a while, you'll be safe."

"Why don't you come with me?" I offered. "We can both get away."

Lash looked at me in surprise.

"He's evil. You stay with him long enough and you'll become the monster he is. And you seem to be a good man."

41

"I'm not a good man," Lash said, narrowing his flat eyes. "Don't think that of me, because I dressed your wounds. You thought that of Devlin when you saw his pretty face, and that's why you're in this mess, because you were stupid, and trusting. I'm neither good, nor even human."

Not human? I felt a shiver, but pressed on. "You're no monster, not like he is."

"I am a monster," Lash hissed angrily. "You have no idea of the things I've done. I've killed more people in my life than he has killed in his, and he's four hundred years old. Hundreds of people, thousands. I don't even remember their faces, none of them. They don't haunt my dreams. I don't think about them at all, or care that I killed them. And maybe that's the surest sign I am evil."

He let out a breath. "It's way too late for me. I'm sorry for you, but he's my friend, my only one left. He was there when I needed him. He's done more for me than anyone ever has, ever. I'm not going to abandon him now, no matter what he's done, not when he needs me most of all."

"I'll go," I ventured. "Thanks for warning me. But why do you care what happens to me?"

"I don't," Lash said casually, standing up, and adjusting his whip. "But I want him to forget her, and get back to what he's good at, which is Ruling. He is nothing now, he who was Ruler for over two hundred years. It is my reputation alone that is keeping Hayden from being burned to the ground, but that won't last much longer. We need to be in power again, because we aren't getting any respect, and some of his best fighting men have left. Soon, other younger vampires or hunters will find out that Devlin's much weaker now than he was, and come for him. He's got a lot of enemies. I'm good, but not good enough to fight off crowds looking to kill him by myself. And if he dies, I'll—"

Lash abruptly stopped talking, then went to the door and opened it. "I'm a killer, Sun. I'm going to Hell when I die," he hissed sadly. "Maybe saving your life will take away one less beating I'm scheduled for."

Then he was gone.

* * * *

The next few days passed in a haze. I got better almost immediately, the wounds healing without leaving scars by nightfall, as Lash said they would. But the memories remained. I had dreams every night of what had happened to me, and the worst was that I remembered how good it had felt, being with him, and part of me wanted it again, wanted that pure euphoric rush. I knew it must be the drug he'd given me, and worried it was addictive. *Had Devlin been counting on that, planning on my wanting him so much I'd let him do anything to me he wanted?*

Frightened of that possibility, I packed my bags that night, paid up all my outstanding bills, and told my boss I was quitting Hotcakes. I got a ride from a stranger to the bus terminal, and went to the counter. Sure enough, there was a ticket waiting for me in my name, paid for, that would take me anywhere in the United States. I cashed it in, grateful but uneasy at my debt to Lash. Without his help, I wouldn't have had enough money to get away, as I'd had to forfeit not only my apartment's deposit but also fork over an additional few months rent for canceling the lease almost a full year early. While I could have just left in the night without paying anything, that was too shitty. My landlord had watched out for me for years, made sure I was never robbed or bothered, and I couldn't do that to him. I'd had to sign my beater car over to him to cover that bill, though. In return, he'd said he'd make sure all the other bills that came addressed to me were paid, until the value of the car was used up. That was fair enough for me.

After years of staying in one place, I was suddenly adrift with almost no money, the only certainty that I needed to leave town. All my carefree loner idealism was reduced to the fact that I had no family and no real friends to turn to, no one I could call to come and get me, no one I could hide with, or even spend a night on their couch.

I have no one. My life isn't carefree, it's empty.

That cold truth messed me up, to put it mildly. In my highly emotional state, I decided to go back to Montana. I knew it was a mistake, almost before the destination left my mouth at the ticket center. But I wanted to be near my mother, even if only to have the comfort of being near her final resting place. Besides, how much worse could my father be, now that I'd met the devil himself?

Chapter Seven

The bus ride was long, hot, and dusty, like I'd dreaded. About halfway there, I reconsidered, but I had no money for changing my mind. So I kept going. Finally, I found myself in Janesville.

I got off the bus, and went first to the cemetery. My mother's grave was overgrown with weeds. Saddened, I spent a few hours pulling them out, scratching my hands on briars, and cursing my father, who couldn't be bothered to come here once in a while to honor her after all he'd done to her. But he'd never respected her in life. Why should I expect him to do it when she was dead?

When I was done, I stole a small bouquet off a new grave five rows over that had a ton of other flowers. *Fuck them. No one would miss this one.* God damn it, I had no money for flowers, but I wasn't leaving there until I'd given some to my mother. It was late summer here, so all the scraggly wild ones were long since withered in the blistering heat.

I kneeled down before her stone. My father had been cheap in that, too. It said only Geraldine V. Law, and the dates of her birth, and death. No "Beloved Wife."

No "Beloved Mother."

I'd taken crayons once, and written "Beloved Mother" on the stone. But when I'd come back the next day, it had been scrubbed clean. Later my father had spanked me. Groundskeepers couldn't fucking weed a grave, but God forbid a stone had "graffiti" on it.

I took a Sharpie from my pocket, and wrote "Beloved Mother" on the headstone. "It's the best I can do," I whispered. "I'm sorry it's not more, Mom."

I sat there for a while, and gathered my courage. Then, I went off to see my father.

The trailer looked even smaller than it had the last time. To my surprise, it was also abandoned. There were some cracked picture frames, some beer bottles, and enough condom wrappers to make me realize high school kids were using this as a pad to fuck. But no Dad.

I headed to the local bar. His local bartender would know where he was, even if no one else did.

I asked around. By seven, the night bartender came on, and pointed me in the right direction. I hitched a ride with a decent guy, who took me to where my father was living now.

Jesus, that man is lucky. I walked up a long stone paved driveway to a house so new I could almost smell the cedar planking on the wraparound deck. There, lying next to an Olympic sized swimming pool, sipping a Bud Light, was my father.

He looked at me, and did a double take. "Sunny?"

"It's me, Dad," I said, forcing a smile. "You win the lottery?"

"Yeah! Well, kind of," he said, giving me his most affable and heart-melting smile. "I met Sheryl, and she's rich!"

She must be in a coma, or a hundred. Or both.

My father got to his feet. He'd kind of gone to pot in the years I hadn't visited. Sure, his face was still good, and his body wasn't bad, for a man in his late fifties. But he was overweight, and he didn't wear it well. "Come and meet her, Baby Girl," he said, putting his arm around me. "I want you to meet her."

He brought me inside, and to say the place was opulent was doing it a disservice. It was so over the top that it almost looked fake. There were chandeliers, polished wood, and paintings on the light-hued walls that had to be originals. And mirrors; there were fancy mirrors everywhere, on every wall, and of every imaginable size.

"Do you like it?" a sensuous voice asked politely.

I turned to see a small woman in her late forties, heavily made up. She was fully dressed, and the clothing was expensive. To my surprise, she wasn't ugly; she was very pretty, even with all that thick makeup.

"This is my daughter," my father explained. "Sunny, this is Sheryl."

"A pleasure," the woman said, offering an insincere smile.

I detected right off she was either pissed I was here, or ill at ease. "It's good to meet you."

"Are you staying?" she asked politely.

"Would you mind?" my father asked her, before I could say anything. "Usually when she visits, she stayed at my place. It won't be long."

The latter was true. But the first part was a lie; I'd never stayed with him, ever. *Why is he lying?*

"A few days aren't a problem," Sheryl said, after a pause. "But I'll need you exclusively for the weekend, darling."

"Then I'm there, babe!" my father said enthusiastically.

"I'm going to bed," she said, her eyes flicking to me and then away. "You probably want some time with Sun tonight."

"Nah," my father said, predictably. "We'll catch up tomorrow, or the next day. I've been waiting all day for you to leave your office, hon." He put his arm around her waist. "I need some loving."

Sheryl smiled, and after they showed me to a guest room, they quickly left.

I lay in bed for a while, wondering about this odd turn of events, which were just as strange as the ones that had prompted my return. How had my father gotten this woman? I guess I'd find out in the morning.

* * * *

The next morning, there was no trace of them. I found a message on the counter that they'd gone off to play some tennis at the country club, and would be home after having drinks there, and some lunch.

I spent the afternoon by the pool, and then ate some food and drank a bottle of wine. It was peaceful here. So what if it wasn't my home?

I went to bed that night without seeing my father, or Sheryl.

The next day was the same. And the next. It was always something, a luncheon they were invited to, or a play they already had tickets for. Finally, on Friday, I managed to get my father alone, while Sheryl was out running errands.

"Dad, how did you meet her?" I asked.

He grinned. "I was trucking near South of the Border. And there she was, lost, looking for a small town in North Carolina."

"And so she took you home with her?"

"No! She took me to dinner, and we had a few drinks—"

So, they'd had sex.

"—and the next morning, she'd said she'd had a good time with me.

46

Then she said she'd love it, if I'd come and live with her. She said she had enough money to take care of us in style. But she'd been divorced, and it was messy, and so she'd prefer it to be casual with us. And I told her that scene seemed like Heaven on Earth to me." He paused. "But I told her this town was home to me, always had been. So she said she'd live here, and a few days later, she bought this house."

Weird. I nodded. "That sounds amazing."

"So here I am!" he said triumphantly. "And six months later, I'm still loving it!"

"So you haven't cheated on her?" I said pointedly.

My father lost his happy look, and his pissy face came on. "No, I haven't. She gives me whatever I want, whenever I want. So what if she's older than the women I usually took to bed? I'm not young myself anymore."

Good for him. "I'm just surprised."

"So am I," my father said, looking happy again. "I never thought my train would come in like this. And it sure beats driving trucks. Your old man gets stiff now from sitting behind the wheel more than an hour, Baby Girl, and it's not the good kind of—"

Spare me your sexual talk. "What's the catch?"

I expected my father to give me a sarcastic line, or say something funny, which were his two usual responses. But he just looked a little crafty.

"The catch is that she's got cancer," he said in a whisper, as if we would be overheard. "She's got only a few months to live. That's where she really is now: at a doctor visit. She says she feels weaker every day. When she goes, I'll get it all!"

I wanted to vomit on him. "Do you care about her?"

"I like her," he said with a shrug. "I'll miss her in bed. She really gets into it. But I'll find someone else quick enough, rich as I'm going to be. And Baby Girl, the next one's going to be in her early twenties."

I'd heard enough. "Dad, I have to get going tomorrow."

"Sure," he said, taking a swig of beer. "Come back in a year or so, Sunny. We'll have a blast, throw a huge party! Your old man's hit it big!"

I gave him a hug, packed my bags, and hitched a ride out of town the next morning. I felt bad for Sheryl, sure. But she was old enough to know better, and I wasn't her daughter. And I trusted my father just far enough to be sure he wouldn't hurry her passing.

* * * *

I spent the next few months in Nevada, working at a strip club outside the Las Vegas strip. I was able to save enough money to afford a small apartment, and I spent a lot of time there thinking about what I wanted, when I wasn't working as many shifts as I could.

After some self-imposed solitary, I finally decided on a few things for myself.

I wanted to go back East. I missed the green, and the hills. It seemed like a desert here in comparison.

I wanted to see if Terian was okay. I missed him, and maybe...maybe somehow we could make it work. Yes, we had a lot that we'd have to overcome, but I wanted to try, damn it. I still loved him, and if he still loved me, we had a chance.

Lastly, I wanted never to see my father again.

* * * *

A month later, I took a bus back east. I got a job in another strip club, and a new apartment. This one was near a park, and I spent a lot of time there that first week, enjoying the greenness of everything.

In addition, I finally took Lash's advice. I'd never cut my hair, though I had darkened it to a light brown. Now I dyed it a dark brown, and cut it in a many-layered style, with short bangs. It made me look different enough that I doubted I'd be recognized. But I kept it long, at least the back of it. *Old habits die hard.*

Having successfully accomplished my first goal, I attempted the second thing on my list. But Terian seemed to have dropped off the face of the earth. His old cell phone number was disconnected. The website he'd sold his magical potions on was no longer valid; it was up for lease.

I went to some of the places we'd visited together, and asked about him. But no one remembered seeing him for months. One night though, I did catch sight of Sarelle.

I was on the corner waiting for a bus when I heard a voice say, "What do you think, Sar?"

I looked over discreetly as a voice dissimilar to mine said, "I'm okay either way, Danial."

She was in a car behind the wheel stopped at the stoplight. There was a dark man beside her, so finely featured he was almost beautiful. Her face, her build...God, she looked enough like me to be my twin sister. *Thank God I cut my hair.*

"We don't have to make a decision now," Danial said, looking over at her. "You've had no signs. There's no rush."

"Please, let's not talk about it," Sar replied, sounding tired. "I want to get home to Elle. She's probably turned cougar, and slipped out her window again by now, sure something happened to us."

Who is Elle? Theo's daughter? Sar and Theo's daughter? Why isn't she with Theo?

"She's probably giving Cia a hard time," Danial said with a laugh. "She wanted to go with us."

"*Macbeth* is too old for her."

"Theo wouldn't think so."

Sarelle didn't respond. When the light changed, they drove off.

I sat for a while thinking later that night. Sarelle was back to spending time with Danial. But Theo and he were friends, right? That was normal, to escort a friend's wife to a play as a favor. Maybe it had been innocent, but maybe not. The important thing was Danial and Devlin were brothers. How long would it be before Devlin decided he'd waited long enough for the real thing?

Didn't matter to me. As *far as I'm concerned, that bitch has it coming.*

Chapter Eight

Months passed. Christmas came and went. I sent my father another card, and got one from him in return. Sheryl still seemed to be going strong, and I said a loud "Good for her!" as I tossed his card in the garbage.

When it got to be Valentine's Day, I finally gave into the feeling that had haunted me for months. I'd been in Sar's shoes with Devlin. I felt so angry with her for a long time over how much Terian had loved her, but that wasn't her fault. Devlin was obsessed with her, from what Lash had said. I owed it to her—one woman to another—to warn her, to let her know that he hadn't forgotten her, even if time had gone by.

I tried looking up her number in the phone book, but it was unlisted. *Fuck.*

I tried online at the library, with the same results. *Motherfuck.*

Then I remembered that note of Terian's I'd kept, the last one. He'd written her number on the bottom, because he was going to be out at her house having dinner. *He wanted me to be able to reach him, and his cell was recharging...*

After an hour of sifting through my clutter, I found it. I dialed the number with shaking hands.

What would I say to her? She didn't know me at all. What if she hung up on me? By now, she knew I'd rejected Terian's offer of marriage, she had to know why, too... *Shit. I have to do it.* Maybe I'd luck out and get her machine.

I dialed the number, and no one answered. Not even a machine. I tried back for the next two days, and got nothing. Shit, she must have moved. *What else can I try?*

Danial's company, Solutions, Inc. He would know where Sar was, if they were friendly enough to go see plays together and Theo worked there with him. I could just talk to Theo, tell him what I knew, and that would be enough, and I wouldn't have to talk to Sar at all.

I dialed the Solutions, Inc. number listed in the phone book on one of my breaks that next night, and a man answered. Well, I assumed it was a man, though from what Terian had told me of Danial, it was probably really one of those werefoxes that were his guardian army.

"Hello, this is Solutions, Inc. Can I help you?"

"Hi. I need to speak to Theo, please."

"He no longer works here," the man said a little sadly.

What the hell? Has he been killed? I couldn't make myself ask. "Is Sarelle McGarran there?"

"Sure, but she's outside with her daughter."

I felt shocked. *Sar had a baby? When? Is it Theo's? Does he mean Elle?*

"I am to notify Danial, or the chief of security before anyone talks to her, on their orders."

I didn't want to talk to Danial. Terian had always painted him as little better than Devlin, and I'd heard of what he'd done to Sar when he'd found out about her and Theo, and later, with his brother.

"Is this Kat?"

Who was Kat? *Shit, I am in over my head. Maybe I should hang up.*

"Hello?"

No, I have to tell someone. What if Devlin hurts her because I said nothing, because I was too afraid? That wasn't happening, not if I could stop it.

"Give me the chief of security," I said with a sigh. "Whoever replaced Theo, I can speak to him."

"Sure, let me get him. He's out there with Sar and her daughter."

I felt an inkling of something unsettling as I waited. Then I got the shock of my life.

"This is Terian. Who is this?"

I couldn't speak. I couldn't form any words. Because Terian was there. He had somehow replaced Theo as Danial's head of security. Suddenly, it all clicked into place. I hung up, and began to cry.

He'd been outside with Sarelle. Theo was dead. There was only one reason Terian would have gone back to work for Danial.

The phone rang. I picked it up before I thought.

"Who is this?" Terian said in a menacing tone. "Answer me, or I'll put a bolt of lightning through this phone to kill you where you stand."

"It's Sun," I said softly.

There was silence.

"What is it?" he asked tenderly. "Are you okay?"

I'd expected him to be angry, or standoffish. It hurt me worse to know he still cared about me. My bitterness rose up in me, making my tone cold and hard as steel. "Where is Theo?"

"Dead," he said with a sigh, "at least presumed. It's been more than a year."

"And you're working for Danial."

"Sar and Elle needed me. They need protection. Danial offered me Theo's position—"

I felt a wave of relief. Elle was Theo's daughter, I remembered.

"—Sar's pregnant now, and it's been a difficult pregnancy—"

I almost threw up. Danial couldn't have children being a vampire like Devlin. He had to be sterile, too. If Theo had been gone for a year, the baby had to be Terian's. Hate welled up in me for Sar, who had the love of Theo and Danial already. She didn't need Terian's love. I doubted she loved him at all, and here she was having his baby! I'd been hurt by Devlin because of her! *It should be me there having Terian's baby, not her! I'm the one who deserved that! She has enough!*

"Sun?"

Bitch! I was tired of her taking everything that was mine. *Sick and tired.*

"Sun, why did you call?"

"It was nothing," I whispered. "I just wanted to…" *Shit, think of something. Anything.*

"Wanted to what?"

I had to say something. The truth would do, though I'd be damned if I'd admit to Terian what Devlin had done to me. "I just wanted to make sure that Sar was okay," I said lamely. "I had this dream—"

"What dream?" Terian said, alert.

I remembered he was a big believer in the power of dreams for some reason. "Nothing. She was in danger, and there was a blond man hurting her with gold eyes. It was bad. I woke up screaming. So I tried her at her house, but no one answered."

"Don't worry," Terian assured. "Sar lives here now. Elle does, too. Devlin hasn't come around here for a good while, since the big fight with me that night. He and Danial talk, but Danial's forbidden him from coming to even see Sar, though after the baby's born, Danial said that might change."

I felt a wave of sickness, and fought it down.

"But he's done nothing in close to a year, Sun. I don't trust Devlin either, but he's been nothing but polite when I've seen him. He knows Danial's more powerful, and so he stays in line."

I remembered Devlin's treatment of me, and what Lash had said. *Devlin's only biding his time. He hasn't forgotten Sar at all.* But I was angry and hurt. *I did my part. It's not my job to save Sar.* "That makes me feel a lot better," I agreed. "I'm glad to know I was wrong."

"Is there anything else you wanted?" Terian persisted.

"Like what?" I retorted sharply. "What else would I want? You seem to be getting along just fine."

"I thought you might miss me," Terian shot back angrily. "But forget it. You clearly don't." He hung up.

I replaced the pay phone in its cradle, and walked back to my car. Screw work, I couldn't pretend to feel or act sexy, not after that. I needed a drink, and to not be alone. So I drove to the nearest bar and had a few shots, trying to convince myself that I'd done the right thing.

There's no way to make him see Sar is still in danger without admitting what had happened to me. And I'm never going to admit that to anyone, ever.

It was midnight when I got up to leave, but before I turned around, I heard a familiar voice ask for some scotch. I turned to see Lash sitting down at the end of the bar.

I looked in fear to see if Devlin was with him, but there was no one else in the bar at all. Unnerved, I drank down my shot, and headed for the door. *Devlin might be just outside.* I didn't want a repeat performance. I'd finally stopped having those wet dreams that drug he'd dosed me with had inspired, those dreams that made me long to be under his hands again, sickening me with my own twisted desires.

53

Lash saw me as I tried to slip by him to the exit. He nodded to me, then looked away.

Well, if he was going to acknowledge me, I'd just ask him. "Is he here?" I whispered. "Is it safe to go out this door?"

"No, and yes, respectively," Lash answered, sipping his scotch. "I'm meeting someone here in a few minutes for business. I wanted a drink first, so I came early."

I sat beside him on a stool. "Thank you, for what you did," I whispered, my eyes cast down.

"You're welcome," he said, then sipped his drink, draining the glass.

"Give him another one on me," I said, handing the bartender some money. "I owe him one."

"Thanks, but you don't," Lash commented with a faint grin. "Now get out of here, Sun. You don't want to be here when the shooting starts, and it's going to start in about five minutes. I'm not meeting a client, I'm meeting a mark, though it's going to be a surprise to him, I'm sure."

I went to leave, then turned to him with determination. "If I need to find you sometime, where do you go?" I asked bluntly. "And I mean not with Devlin."

Lash looked at me curiously out of the corner of his eyes, obviously wondering why I might want to find him. But he didn't ask that question. "I prefer no crowds, Sun, but Devlin's often with me if I'm out. I usually only go alone to The Tavern," he hissed at me. "Most Thursdays. It's my one night off, and no one else is usually there. But you don't want to be around me when I'm drinking. No one does. I get mean."

"So do I," I said, getting up. "We'll make a good pair."

Lash said nothing; he just turned back to his drink as I left.

* * * *

Months passed. I showed up most Thursdays at The Tavern, where Lash and I would have a drink or two. For the first month, we didn't talk. But over time, we began to. He never talked about himself, but he liked to talk sometimes about the weather, or TV shows, sometimes different current issues, depending on his mood. I found myself beginning to like him, and to look forward to our weekly talks. It was nice to be with someone who didn't expect anything from me, and who wanted nothing from me, not my body, not my attention, not even for me to fill the silence we were sharing with words. I didn't have to be sexy, or entertaining, or anything but what I was. It was a little freeing, because I'd never had that before from a man, not ever.

Lash was something like my first real friend, sad as that sounds. I'd never had someone to talk to, other than the other strippers in passing, and I'd never been close to any of them. I'd spent most of my childhood alone in the company of an ever-changing list of adults who never stayed for long and traded that for a list of lovers that had basically done the same thing. Terian had changed all that for me, made me see there was another world out there, a better one. Maybe I couldn't have that, but that didn't mean I had to live an utterly solitary existence, either.

This went on for the next few months, until it was nearly fall. Lash never said he'd be there the following Thursday, or that he was looking forward to seeing me, but he was always polite, and most nights he bought me a drink or two. After that first night, he had always refused my offer of buying him drinks, saying he was the man, and men were the ones who bought drinks. But I understood in time from the way he talked, and the things he said, that he was a much older man than he looked, so I wasn't surprised he was a sexist. That was one of the things I liked about him, actually.

Soon, the days were turning colder, and I was thinking of getting out my sweaters. *Maybe it's time I moved on. What am I staying around here for? For Devlin to catch sight of me one night? For Terian to decide his life with his one true love isn't worth it, because of what we were to each other once? Yeah, right.*

That cool September Thursday night, Lash dropped a bombshell on me. While sitting at the bar, he said out of the blue, "I won't be here next week, Sun. Dev is moving our operations overseas for a little while. I don't know how long we'll be gone, but it will be at least a few months, maybe even years. We can't stay there long, or Samuel, the Ruler there, will notice us. Devlin's got business there that has to be dealt with. Well, so he says, but I think really he just misses Anna, and wants to go where they spent their honeymoon, so to speak. I don't care. In fact it will be better to be where it's warm, with winter coming."

"Who is Anna?" I got out. I was floored that he was just springing this on me with no warning, then I reminded myself that we weren't exactly friends. He had never invited me to drink with him; I'd sort of invited myself.

"The only woman Dev ever really loved," Lash said, finishing off his scotch, and standing up. "The one with blood similar to Sar's. She's been dead a long time. Anyway, I wanted you to know I wouldn't be here."

"Thanks," I said, not sure what else to say.

Just like that, Lash threw down some money on the counter, and left. I sat there for about five seconds in shock, and then I got up and went after him.

Chapter Nine

He'd already made it to his truck as I banged out the exit door to the parking lot. But he heard me coming, and turned around with the door open, facing me with a little surprise. "You want something?"

"To say good-bye." I stepped into him, and kissed him hesitantly.

Lash pulled me close in an instant, and kissed me back hungrily, his mouth moving on mine. Then he drew back from me, an intent look in his eyes. "Why'd you kiss me?" he asked, curious.

"I felt like it." My response was defiant, though I was smiling.

"There anything else you feel like doing?" he asked with a grin.

"Maybe," I said, grinning back, and leaned into him to kiss him again.

He held me away from him, his hands clasping my wrists gently. "You know I'm snake," he cautioned. His forked tongue darted out to scent the air. "And you're human. You really want me wriggling around inside you, Sun?"

I shivered when he said it like that. But it had been a long time for me, and I just didn't care that he wasn't human. I wanted to feel loved, just for a while. "Yes." I went to kiss him again.

Again, he held me off. "Get in," he said gruffly, sliding behind the wheel. He opened the door for me from inside, then started his truck. I climbed in beside him. Five minutes later, we were at a nearby motel, and Lash was inside the main office, getting us a room.

I was surprised that he hadn't just asked to come home with me, but he'd said nothing more to me after telling me to get in his truck. I guessed this was more chauvinism, that since I had said I'd be with him, he owed me at least the price of a bed to have me in. I wasn't sure how to feel about that. On one hand I liked that he felt that way, as most other men I'd known, Terian included, had just assumed that they were welcome in my bed, and had never offered to take me anywhere, not even to their own beds. Yet part of me was glad of the hotel because I remembered too well the one male I'd known who'd taken me to his bed, and how much of a mistake that had been. Lash came out of the office, and motioned to me. I got out of the truck, locked the door, and followed him a few feet to the door of our room. He unlocked it, pushed the door open, and then turned to me. "You sure, Sun?" he hissed. "I won't ask again. You walk into that room, there's no changing your mind. And you won't be walking out until its morning."

My heart began to race, fear tingling up my spine at his proclamation. I looked him over: his cold eyes, and the well-used weapons at his belt. *How well did I know him, really? Well enough to do this?* "Promise me right now you won't hurt me?" I asked in a small voice. "That you aren't…like him."

"I won't hurt you," Lash hissed, eying me as he leaned up against the doorframe. "You'll be walking out, not need to be carried out. The only wounds you might have tomorrow are ones you ask me to give you, or soreness from normal wear and tear. I don't go in for that."

I wavered for a few seconds, and then thought, *screw it*. Lash had protected me. If he'd wanted, he could have had me any way that he liked while sharing me with Devlin. Instead, he'd saved me with a bus ticket, for no more reason than it had been the right thing to do.

I pushed past him, and walked into the room.

Lash was right after me. As soon as we were both through the door, he locked it behind me. He turned and grabbed hold of me, kissing me passionately as he pushed me down on the bed, pulling off my jeans as fast as he could. I was as eager for him as he was for me, and I helped him, crying out a little in my arousal. He pushed down his jeans, holding me down with one hand, baring his erection, as he pushed aside my underwear, and got himself into position. Suddenly he let out an irritated hiss, drew back from me, and quickly slid on a condom from his back pocket. The second it was fully on, he was on top of me, shoving himself into me as fast as he could, grunting with each thrust, his hands under my buttocks as he pistoned in and out of me. I moaned, feeling his thick hard length filling me like no one had in so long. I wanted it to last, but a few seconds later he let out a long hiss, then went limp on me.

Lash withdrew from me right after he came, pulling off the condom, and throwing it away. He stripped off his jeans, put his weapons within reach of the bed, and took off his sweater, though he left his T shirt on. I took that time to pull off the rest of my clothes, and toss them aside. Lash crawled back across the bed, and took me in his arms.

"I broke up with my lover yesterday, when I told her I was leaving," he hissed softly, kissing my face gently. "We'd been together in our other forms, but not as humans. She was bent out of shape I was leaving, and that I hadn't told her until then, and so she refused to. I needed it bad, Sun, I apologize for not waiting for you."

"It's okay," I replied, hugging him. "I've been there myself. But I hope that this isn't the end."

"Of course not, I'm a weresnake. Just give me a minute, and I'll pleasure you, I promise," Lash hissed with a lecherous smile, still kissing me. "Tell me what you like, while we wait."

"What?" I said, furrowing my brow.

"What you like in bed," Lash said easily, giving me a serious look. "I want you to enjoy tonight, Sun. All women are different, they want different things. So tell me honestly what you like, so I can make it good for you. I won't judge you, whatever you tell me. Just tell me the truth."

"Sex," I said uncomfortably, not sure what he was asking. No one had ever asked me that question before, ever. "Regular sex."

"What positions?" Lash hissed gently. "And do you like oral sex? 'Other' sex? Any particular place you like it, besides the bed? You want me to talk dirty to you, or say nothing? What turns you on?"

I felt myself blushing. No one had been so frank with me ever, asking about what I wanted or needed to feel satisfied. But I thought it was nice he cared, even if the way he was asking me was a little blunt. "Any position, and the bed's fine," I said, blushing slightly. "You can talk or not, whatever you like. But just regular sex." I actually would have liked some oral sex quite a bit, but I remembered his tongue was forked like a snake's, and there was just no way I could face it, not at all. *And what about his fangs? Shiver.*

"Got it," Lash said, nodding once. "Would you mind if I didn't wear anything?"

I gave him an irked look out of the corner of my eyes.

He sighed. "I will if you want me to," he said reluctantly. "It just feels better if I don't. And if you want me to, I'm going to have to leave to get some, because I've only got another two in my wallet, and they are probably expired by now, or damn close to it. I'm lucky that one didn't break on me."

"Aren't you worried about catching something?" I interjected.

"I've been with my current lover for more than a year," Lash said with irritation. "I trust Lys, and I know she never—"

"I meant from me!" I said exasperatedly. "You don't know my sexual history."

"Have you been with anyone since Devlin?" Lash said with a steely gaze.

I shuddered in his arms, just hearing that name. "No," I got out finally. "I haven't been able to bring myself to be. I haven't wanted anyone for a long time, except...except—"

"Except him," Lash supplied very softly.

I shuddered again.

"I thought not, Sun. That's the way the drug works on most women. I'll bet you had dreams too, dreams of him—"

"Can we not talk about that?" I interrupted. "Please, Lash?"

"Sorry," Lash hissed apologetically. "My point is that knowing that, I know I'm safe being bare with you, because I had your blood tested. Because you were clean then."

I narrowed my eyes, suddenly irritated. "Why'd you do that? You said a vampire couldn't give me anything."

"Because he wanted me or another were to join in the next time he was with you," Lash said bluntly. "I know Kev had you that night and the condom broke when he did."

I let out a cry, struggling hard to get away from him.

"Stop, shh! Relax," Lash said calmly, restraining me easily. "That's one of the reasons I helped you get away. I don't want any woman who doesn't want me. He was being an ass though, and wouldn't drop it. Anyway, I took some of your blood, and tissue when I bandaged you up, and Dr. Camlyn said you were safe, completely clean. Kev said he was, but I made him get a test anyway to make sure. I don't trust that bastard. I never have, he's too much of a fucking deviant, the things he likes to do."

"But why trust me, when it's been months since that test? I could be lying to you now."

"Are you?" Lash said, grabbing my face and making me look into his flat eyes.

"No," I said honestly, staring back at him. "But how about you? Why should I trust you?"

"You shouldn't trust me about much, but you can trust me about this," Lash hissed, his eyes boring into mine. "I got tested today, because I always get tested between lovers. I prefer not to wear anything, and I know damn well that can be risky. I've had lovers lie to me; tell me they were safe when they weren't. But I've never given anyone anything to my knowledge, not ever. It's my prerogative, when I have permission." He paused. "We are both clean. So yes or no?"

I nodded. "Yes."

Lash leaned in and kissed me again, rolling his body on top of mine. A second later, he penetrated me, his bare shaft stroking me slowly and deliberately. Aroused, I ran my fingers up over his back, then went to move to his chest, to slide them under his T-shirt. He stopped me gently with a shake of his head, moving my hands back to his shoulders before he resumed kissing me. I thought it odd, but left it alone. He probably had a scar there he didn't want me to see or touch.

Lash took his time with me, until I was panting and moving under him, straining to come. He clearly knew how to please a woman, and before long I felt myself shaking as my orgasm broke over me. It had been a long time for me, and it was such a relief, so satisfying as it washed over me, to know I could still feel that feeling, that it wasn't just something that I used to know and never would again. *God, I felt like that for so many months...*

Lash came a second after I did. This time, I felt his climax as he spilled himself deep inside me with a long satisfied hiss. With that familiar shudder within, his muscles tensing, then relaxing completely, something broke in me. I began to cry softly.

Lash drew back from me, though he didn't pull out of me, or let me go. "What is it?" he said gently, looking at me intently with his flat eyes. "Was it because it had been so long for you, Sun?"

It wasn't just because it had been so long since I had a lover of my own. It was because it had been so long since I felt like my lover cared about my pleasure, as well as his own. None of the men I'd been with in my life besides Terian had. *Terian and Lash are the only ones in my life who've ever even made the pretense of caring about me, caring that I was satisfied, or that I enjoyed the sex at all.* I'd been used or objectified so often by everyone else in my life, my clients, my bosses, my father, my lovers, and even my mother a little, as a shoulder to cry on. No one had ever really cared about me, the me I was, or my happiness.

Well, one man had. One man had wanted to give me everything he had. Terian had wanted to marry me. *Now he's with Sar...* I let out another sob.

"Sun, say something," Lash hissed again, his snake eyes looking into mine. But for once, I didn't find them cold, though they held no expression. "What's wrong?"

"Please hold me, please," I whimpered.

He did, sliding his arms around me, and fitting my head under his chin. I cried a few more tears, but in a while, I began to feel better.

Lash was still holding me in his arms, waiting for my answer to his question. And there was no way I could tell him the real reason I was crying. It was just too pitiful, and I didn't want him to pity me. Horribly, something else hit me then like a bolt of lightning, and I swore mentally.

"Shit, I'm such an idiot," I said, lying back with a grimace and wiping my tears away. "I only thought about catching something, but not about—"

"There won't be a child," Lash interrupted, hugging me. "I can't, even if you can. So don't worry, Sun. Don't cry over that."

I looked at him. "You sure?"

"Very sure," Lash said, grinning. "You can trust me about that, too."

"Then come here," I said, crooking a finger.

I didn't need to ask him more than once. We had sex all that night, until the early hours of the morning. Lash was far more skilled than I thought he would be, and I enjoyed his body, and the ways he'd used it to make me feel oh so good. He went to lengths to make sure every time was as good as it could be for me, asking me if what he was doing felt good to me, and stopping when I asked him to. That touched me, especially as he refused my hesitant offer of oral sex, saying if I didn't want that from him, then it wasn't fair to ask me for it.

He felt no different to me from other men, and I wondered several times during our passion why he'd made such a point of him being weresnake. He kept his tongue in his mouth, but I felt his fangs sometimes in his kiss. The feeling wasn't much different from a regular man's teeth. He didn't bite me or anything, not even when he sucked on my skin. With the areas he was teasing with his mouth, I was sure he was going to draw a little blood just by accident, but there wasn't even a scratch. In fact, the only differences at all between him and a human man was that he never got soft after coming, and he never pulled out of me after he was done. Even when we rested between bouts, he stayed close to me, holding my hips to his so that he might stay sheathed. I thought that odd, but guessed he liked the sensation. *Maybe it's a were thing?* I wasn't sure, as he was the first were I'd ever been with, to my knowledge.

"Why do you like it?" I finally asked sleepily, sometime near dawn.

"Sex?" he hissed with a grin, hugging me. "Duh. It feels good. I sometimes feel like I live for it, but maybe that's just my snake side talking."

"No, being in me, after."

"After sex?"

"Yeah."

"It feels good, too," he hissed with longing. "You're so warm inside, Sun. I'd put my whole body in you if I thought I could find a way it would fit."

"You feel good in me, too," I said languidly, snuggling against him. "I like laying here and having you there inside throbbing gently." I ran my hands down, clasping his rear. "I like that you don't get soft."

Lash held my hips, then moved closer, sliding his penis in to the root, drawing a long groan from his lips. He held me close, keeping my hips tight against his. "Then you don't mind if I stay where I am?" he hissed softly in my ear. "I like how it feels, being held by you like that."

Unable to resist, I squeezed him with my vaginal muscles.

Lash went completely still, his entire body tensing up rigidly, his eyes closing. He stayed like that, unmoving, as if bracing himself.

Did I somehow hurt him? "Sorry," I whispered, "I—"

"Please, do it again," Lash hissed eagerly. "Please, Sun, please for me, do it more?"

Surprised but pleased, I squeezed him again. Lash let out a long, loud hiss. I began to do it in rhythm. Lash began to shake in my arms, hissing almost continuously.

I did it faster. Lash again grasped my hips, straining closer to thrust himself in as deep as he could, holding himself there, his body pressed so tight to mine there was not a hairs breadth between us. A moment later, he squeezed me in his arms so hard it cut off my breath, a loud yell tearing out of him. His hips began spasming lightly, his dick pulsating in me as he began to come. His climax lasted a long time, groaning loudly every time he shot himself into me again, every squeeze of my body around his dick teasing out more semen. Finally, he softened, his body going limp.

"Fuck, that was great," Lash hissed in utter satisfaction. "I didn't know humans could do that, only weresnake women." He pulled back slightly, slipping out of me, then gave me a gentle kiss. "Thank you, Sun. It means something to me that you did that for me, though you must have thought it was pretty weird."

"Not a problem," I said, hugging him. "I'm glad you liked it."

"I fucking loved it," Lash said, a smile splitting his face from ear to ear. "Even though I'm too soft now to stay in you and my ears hurt, it's a small price to pay."

Hearing his confession, I thought it was probably good I'd been quiet during my climaxing. "Good."

Both of us were exhausted. We dropped off to sleep in a few moments, holding one another.

Chapter Ten

I awoke about ten a.m. Lash was awake beside me, gently running his hands over my naked flesh and hissing softly. It felt strange to see him next to me in bed in the light of day, me naked, and him still in his T-shirt. But I hadn't been drunk when I told him yes and it wasn't bad at all, waking up with him.

I reached out and hugged him. "Hi."

"I liked being with you," Lash hissed hesitantly. "Did you enjoy me, Sun? Honestly?"

"Yes," I said, flashing a smile. "You were great. Better than great."

"Good," Lash said with finality, getting up from the bed. "I wanted it to be good for you; as good as I could make it."

He began putting on his clothes. It hit me then that he expected me to do the same. We'd fucked, but now that the night was over, he was just going to leave.

He noticed me staring as he buckled his belt. "What?" he said curiously.

What indeed. It wasn't like I was in love with him. But maybe that was better, not to love a man I was lovers with, to just like him as a friend. In fact, maybe that was the best.

"Why don't you stay, and not leave?" I asked.

He stopped moving, his eyes flat and unreadable. "We need to be out by noon."

"Come home with me?" I asked hesitantly, feeling foolish and a little lame.

Lash gave me an incredulous stare. "Sun, you want more? I thought for sure you'd be rubbed raw by now, being human. My body heals itself like nothing, but yours—"

"I just don't want you to leave now."

"Why?" he asked, slipping on his weapons.

Because I want there to be more than this. More than just good sex, and leaving each other, and then finding someone different to do it with all over again the next time I wanted sex. Terian had ruined me for that. I just hadn't known it until now.

"Are you going to answer me or not?" Lash probed, curious.

Blushing, I cast down my eyes. "I like you. I liked spending last night with you. I don't want you to leave. I want there to be more."

Lash grinned widely, surprise on his face. He came over and kissed me gently. "Then tell me where you live now, and I'll come by tonight. I'm off work at ten. But I have to go now, Sun; I have to be at Hayden by eleven-thirty."

I gave him the address, and got dressed. He dropped me off in his truck at my car, and told me with a grin he'd see me tonight.

I got another odd twinge watching him drive off. After he left, I sat for a while by myself and thought about things.

I was asking for trouble. Lash had told me he killed people. He was best friends with Devlin, the world-class asshole. Just that should have been enough to have me running. Instead, I was beginning some sort of relationship with him. *What the fuck is wrong with me?*

But he wasn't bad. *He just isn't.* He'd helped me get away from Devlin. He'd listened to me, and talked to me, and he'd never once made a move, though clearly he'd been interested in me all along. When we'd been together last night, he'd been almost certainly the best lover of my life, screw that he wasn't human. So what if he wasn't the most handsome man I'd ever been with? So what if he was older than me by a few years? I wanted to try to have something with him if he would agree to try with me. That meant I was going to have to ask him if he wanted to try. But hell, what did I have to lose? If I didn't ask him to stay, he'd leave for sure.

Fuck it. I'll ask him tonight.

I returned the hotel room key, and went into work about noon. Work sucked royally, being the afternoon and early evening shift with almost no clientele to speak of, but I got through it. At quarter to nine, I left work, picking up a pizza on the way home. I was still eating some of it when Lash arrived.

I let him in. "Want a piece?" I tempted him with a smile.

Immediately, his face closed down and he bared his fangs. "No, I want to fuck," Lash hissed, grabbing hold of me roughly. "You didn't ask me here to eat, Sun. I'm here for a repeat of last night, so let's fuck."

Taken aback, I led him to my bedroom. In a few seconds, I was on my back, my jeans around my ankles as Lash pounded himself into me. But he stopped almost as soon as he'd begun. "What is it?" he hissed worriedly. "Doesn't what I'm doing feel good to you? Did you reconsider during the day? Do you want me to leave?"

"It does, and no, I didn't, and I don't," I replied awkwardly, touching his arm. "I'm just a little nervous, because you were kind of fast tonight with me. I thought we could work up to the sex—"

"Don't be nervous," Lash said eagerly, beginning to move again. "You feel wonderful to me, Sun, just like you did last night. Relax and enjoy yourself. Let me do the work. I'm sorry, I should have been slower. I'll take my time, until you're as worked up as I already am. God, I've been thinking about you all day. I couldn't drive here fast enough!"

I had to grin at how his mind worked. When he leered back at me, I kissed him, wrapping my arms around him.

True to his word, Lash took his time, drawing out the stimulation, stroking me with his hands, kissing me, rubbing my clit, his deep thorough strokes making me whimper with longing. It went on and on until the feeling built up so much I felt as if I was going to shake to death, I wanted it so bad. Like a clap of thunder, the climax hit, engulfing me, making me scream as I writhed under him. Lash groaned, his body going rigid on mine as he came, his arms squeezing me, his hands gripping my breasts possessively.

When we could talk again, Lash pushed his upper body up off of mine with his arms. "Same as last night, Sun?" he asked with a leer. "Or you want something different tonight? So long as I get to be in you and come, I'm up for anything you want to do."

It's now or never. "Lash, I want you to stay here, and not go with Devlin to South America," I said, flushing. "Tell me, is there something I could do so you'd agree to stay here with me?"

Lash blinked once at me, then got up off me with a sigh and began

67

pulling on his clothes, moving towards the door.

I pulled my jeans up, and followed him anxiously. "Lash, why are you going now? What's wrong? Am I not supposed to like you, after spending the night with you, and all those months talking?"

"Because I can't stay here with you, I have to go with Dev," he said, his back to me. "He needs me, Sun, more now maybe than he ever has. And it goes without saying I can't take you with me, much as I might like to. I can't risk that Devlin wouldn't hurt you again, when he gets in one of his moods. Dev is not over Sar, not at all, no matter that that stupid Theo thinks he is."

"Theo's alive?" I said in shock.

Lash looked over at me, grimacing. "Alive and married to Sar," he hissed with distaste. "She's such an idiot to be with him, after what he...well, never mind that."

"What about the baby?" God, Terian must be a wreck.

"Theoron?" Lash said, and shrugged. "I'm sure he'll stay with Danial like he has been, that's his father."

I let out a squeal.

Lash whipped around, taking a step toward me. "Jesus, Sun! What is it?"

"I thought it was Terian's baby," I blathered. "I thought all this time that they were together, he and Sar."

"No," Lash said, looking at me strangely. "Sar went after him once when she was pregnant, I heard, but he rebuffed her. It was some kind of vampire thing, because of the bloodlust, Dev said. Danial is Theoron's father through some sort of magic spell Terian made. Terian's never been with anyone. As far as I know he's been alone this whole time, the last year and a half."

Oh God. I've been an absolute idiot. I shut my eyes and put my face in my hands.

Lash sat down beside me. "I gather it's not important to you anymore if I leave or stay," he said bitterly. "Because you still love Terian."

"Lash—"

He patted my knee. "Don't worry about it, Sun. This works out better for both of us."

68

"I still want you to stay, you ass! I care about you," I said angrily.

Lash's arm darted out and he pulled me close, kissing me more deeply than he ever had. In the kiss, his forked tongue slipped into my mouth, and licked me. It felt a lot like a large, warm, live worm moving around in my mouth. I shivered before I could stop myself.

Lash pushed back from me, scowling. "You don't," he hissed angrily, disentangling himself from me. "You're human, and I'm snake. You can't care for me, because as soon as you feel how different I am from you, all you can think of is getting away from me as far away as you can."

"Come back," I said, reaching for him and trying to be brave. "Kiss me again. It's not that I was disgusted, it's that your tongue feels so different, like nothing else I've ever felt. And I wasn't expecting it. You never kissed me like that before."

"No, I'm leaving now, Sun," Lash said angrily, heading for the door.

After all he'd done for me, I wasn't ending it like that between us. I went after him, putting my arms around his neck, and bringing his lips hard down on mine. Lash kissed me back, then moved to draw away. I licked his mouth with my tongue, probing gently at his lips. Instantly, his mouth opened on mine, his tongue caressing my lips, then sliding deeper.

Though I felt a mental shiver, I didn't pull away. In fact, I kissed him harder, willing myself to relax, telling myself his tongue was just a part of him, and it wasn't going to hurt me. I hesitantly licked at his tongue, and he licked me back, his tongue winding around mine. I brought his tongue into my mouth, and sucked on it gently, caressing it with my tongue and lips. The sensation was strange, but not unpleasant. I teased and prodded, telling myself what I was doing wasn't that odd, it was just a different kind of oral sex.

Lash sighed in satisfaction. When I took his hand and moved to draw him back towards the bed, he came with me eagerly. There was no more talking between us that night, though there was a lot of kissing, moaning, and gentle caresses.

* * * *

The next morning, we lay there in bed, hugging each other. "I can't stay here, or take you with me, Sun," Lash hissed regretfully, "Even if

69

you still wanted to go, which I suspect you don't, last night notwithstanding."

"You're right, I do still love Terian," I said grumpily. "Damn it to hell."

"Then talk to him," Lash advised, stretching happily. "He seems reasonable from what I've heard, though I've never met him face to face. He must still care about you, to not be with a woman in all this time. That or he's really gay, and he's harboring a crush on Theo."

I wanted to remark that not all men went from one woman to another like stepping stones on a path, but held it in. He'd get testy for sure.

"I've got to go," Lash said with a little groan and a lot of reluctance. "We are supposed to leave on Monday at first dark. It's Saturday morning. Fuck, I've got so much shit to do."

"You sure?" I said teasingly, kissing his neck. "I don't have to work tonight, so I could stay in bed for another ten hours or so."

"You must be part were," Lash said in awe as he got out of bed. "I never met a human woman who liked sex as much as you do."

"You must have not known many human women then," I replied, laughing.

He laughed too, but his eyes were sad. "Not many," he said almost inaudibly. "Mostly other weresnakes."

"I need to ask a favor," I said quietly, changing the subject.

Lash looked at me expectantly.

"Can you keep it to yourself that we were intimate? I don't want Devlin to know I'm back here, even if he is leaving."

"Sure," Lash said, nodding. "But it's not really him you're worried about, is it? You never asked me to keep it to myself I was meeting you for drinks these last months, though I knew not to say anything to him. You just don't want Terian finding out about you and me, now that you know he's available."

Damn, why couldn't he be oblivious like every other man I've ever known? "That, too," I said, nodding. "He won't understand. He's never had sex with a friend; he's just not that way." That was an understatement. What I'd done casually with Lash would be appalling to Terian, with his strict moral ways, even with Lash being more than a friend to me.

"Then it never happened," Lash said flatly, reaching for his pants. "No one will know but you and me."

I got up and hugged him. "It was good with you, both nights," I whispered. "Don't think I regret it, because I don't. I'm glad I was with you, that we were together. And I still wish you were staying, and not leaving. I'll miss talking with you."

I hugged him close. *Fuck it.* "I'll miss what might have been between us," I said very, very softly.

Lash hugged me, and let out a breath. "I'll miss you, too," he hissed tenderly. "You've been a good friend, Sun. You were the best human lay I've ever had. That's saying something, all the years I've been alive."

I laughed and he did, too, as we located our clothes here and there around the room.

"So are you going to call him?" he said, pulling on his clothes.

"I don't know," I said with a shrug. "What should I say?"

"Tell him you want him, that you missed him, and you're waiting here in bed naked for him to come to you," Lash advised, buckling on his weapons. "It'd work for me and most men I know, if a woman called them and said that. It will certainly work on a half-demon. They like sex as much as weres do as a rule, though maybe not as much as weresnakes."

My grimace became a smile against my will. He had a good sense of humor, Lash did. "Okay. I'll do that."

"But shower first and wash your sheets, before you call him," Lash hissed in warning. "Or he'll smell my scent on you and be pissed off. Demon's noses are as good as weres and snake scent is the strongest, especially the scent on you now from being with me all night."

I nodded, appalled. Like I'd call Terian up as soon as Lash was gone. *Men...* "Got it."

Lash came over to me, tilting my head up. He gave me a last kiss, then a hug, caressing my cheek gently.

"Going to call me an angel?" I said, figuring he wouldn't get the old reference from a Juice Newton song more than thirty years old.

To my surprise, he smiled knowingly, baring one fang. "A morning angel," Lash hissed with affection, then kissed me one more time. "I

71

most likely won't see you again, though I hope to someday," he said gently. "Take care of yourself. I hope it works out with Terian and you."

Then he was gone, the door closing behind him.

Chapter Eleven

I called Danial's business again that night, and left a message for Terian with a woman who said her name was Monica. Although I waited a week, Terian did not call back.

In anger, I went again to the bar where I'd met Lash all those weeks, hoping for another night with him to ease my despair. Though I stayed until closing, he never showed.

I was debating calling Terian again when I got a Fed Ex delivery. It was a first class plane ticket from my father, which could only mean one thing. But instead of the jubilant note I expected, I found this:

Sunny,
Please come to me when you get this. Sheryl's dead, she died last week. I need you, Baby Girl.
Love, Dad

My father had never said he needed me in his life before. *Weird and also very strange.* I told my boss I'd be back in a few days, and got a cab to the airport.

* * * *

I rented a car at the airport, and drove to the house that had been Sheryl's. I wasn't surprised to see a "For Sale" sign on the front lawn.

I next drove to the lot where the old trailer we'd lived in used to be. Sure enough, there was my father. He was sitting in a lawn chair in a bathrobe, drinking a Bud Light. There were several empty cans at his feet.

"Baby Girl," he said happily when he saw me. "You came!"

"So where's all the cash, Dad?" I said mockingly. The trailer behind him was a newer one, but it was still a wreck, and clearly at least twenty years old.

"She left it to her two daughters down south," he said angrily. "She left me a measly ten grand! Ten grand, for a year and a half of my life! Bitch!" His expression cleared. "But at least she left me the house. I'll sell it soon. It should bring a half mil easy, or so the realtor tells me."

"Then why do you need me?" I said angrily. "Your dreams have come true. You don't need me."

"Because I'm dying," he said sadly.

I gaped at him in shock. "Dying?"

"She didn't have cancer," he said bitterly. "She had AIDS; got it from her philandering husband. She told me she bruised easily, that she had diabetes, that's why all the drugs and the marks on her skin."

I grabbed onto a nearby tree branch for support. *This is poetic justice, sure, but God...*

"Anyway, the doctors say I could live a while, but I'll need help—"

"So you thought of me?" I interrupted flatly.

"Sure," my father said. "You're my daughter. I need you."

"So what?" I said nastily.

My father gaped at me for a few moments, then became enraged. "You know all the nights I had to deal with your kid shit? So many nights I wanted to be out, and I had to be home, because your mom was in one of her depressions, and couldn't get past the bottle to give you yours—"

"I don't remember that!" I yelled back at him. "I remember you fucking Natalie! I remember her crying, and you leaving and Mom dying—"

"So what if I had sex with her? She wasn't any blood relation to me! It's not like I had sex with you!"

With a disgusted shudder that ran down my spine like icy water, I backed away from him. "You abused us all. We turned out the way we did because of you."

My father held out a hand. "Now calm down, honey. I'm telling you, your mom was cold, and she never wanted me, not after you were born. And Natalie, she'd been having sex long before she came to stay with us—"

He was saying my foster sister had wanted what he'd done to her. "Don't say another word!"

"Sunny, I need you! Please, I'm sick and I really need you!"

"What about when I needed you?" I whispered. "What about all the times I was alone, with some woman you left me with? Do you know one of them locked me in my room for a day, because she was tired of me asking her to play with me?"

"Sunny, if I'd known—"

"You did know!" I screamed. "You didn't care! You never cared! You only ever cared about yourself! You still only care about yourself!"

"Honey, that's not true!"

"Good-bye, Dad," I said, wiping away my tears. "You won't see me again."

"Baby Girl, I need you! Don't leave me here alone—"

"You'll find someone," I said, walking away from him without a backward look. "You always do."

* * * *

I kept to myself for the next few months. I picked up the phone several times to call Terian, but always put it down. That woman named Monica had surely given him the message. He just didn't want to talk to me.

But I did make a vow to respect myself a little more. I hadn't slept with anyone since Lash, and I decided to keep it that way, turning down all offers from my appreciative patrons, even the ones that would surely have been pleasurable. I'd had enough of sex that didn't mean something. I'd had enough of being with men to whom I didn't mean anything. I'd lived a lot of my life viewing myself as just someone trying to live. That was no longer enough; I wanted a good life, one that made me happy, with relationships that mattered. I wanted friends I could count on, and a place that was a home, not just a place to sleep. Maybe I'd never have a white picket fence, or someone to wake up with and share a good morning smile. But I deserved that as much as anyone else did. It was time to go after that happy dream, and try to make it my reality.

* * * *

At Christmas, I didn't send my father a Christmas card. He didn't send me one, either. That wasn't a surprise. I did drink a bottle of wine by myself though, and got trashed. But hell, I'd been good for months. I deserved a little downtime.

For New Years, I went to the bar where Lash and I'd met all those nights, and toasted him. I hoped he was having a good time down in South America. At least he wasn't freezing his ass off like I was. All that week, I built up my courage to make a second try to contact Terian. The next day, January eighth, I decided to finally call him. Again, when I called, the person who answered said he wasn't in.

I was done being nice and leaving messages. "Listen, Asshole, I need to talk to him. Where is he?"

"He has guard duties," grumbled the gruff man who'd said his name was Brian.

"When will he be back?"

"Around four, or so today."

"Will you remember to tell him, or should I call back then?"

"I'll tell him," Brian growled back. "But call back if you want."

I hung up, realizing I needed to get to work.

I got done around seven, and went back to my place. On my machine was a message from Terian.

"Hi Sun." Pause. "I was glad to get your message. I tried calling you at your old place, and stopped by, but they said you'd left town more than a year ago. And when I stopped by your work, they said you'd left town, too—"

I'd asked Hunter and the other guys to tell that to anyone asking for me, in case Devlin ever came looking for me. I'd never thought Terian would come looking for me. *Shit.*

"—I'd like to see you, if you want to get together. Dinner, maybe? Call my cell, it's always on."

Terian stated his cell number number, then paused, and whatever he was going to say was lost, because he paused too long this time and the machine hung up on him.

Shit. It's now or never. I called, aging years from sheer tension as I waited for each ring to go through. Then Terian came on the line. "Hi," he said awkwardly. "How've you been?"

Tears came to my eyes, hearing his voice after more than a year. I couldn't get any words out.

"Sun?"

"I'm here," I rasped finally. "It's just really good to hear your voice."

"I'm glad to hear yours, too," he said tenderly. "Are you free for dinner?"

"Yes," I said immediately. "Where do you want to meet?"

"How about our old diner? You know, the one we always used to go to?"

"Sure. When?"

"I don't get off work until eleven," Terian said, regretful. "And there have been a lot of problems here, Sundown. Sarelle's Oathed to Devlin now, and to Danial as well."

Holy Shit. That poor girl. "What about Theo?"

"He's leaving her. There's another woman."

I felt very guilty for wishing bad things on my perceived rival, and didn't know what to say. "That's awful."

"I'll tell you more about them when I see you. Wait for me?"

"That's okay. I'll see you then."

"You sure you don't need a ride?"

"I've got a car."

"Is it the one, um, you had before?"

He meant the one he'd helped me buy. "No. I had to sell that more than a year ago. But I bought another one. It's pretty beat up, but it's a pretty blue color—" *God, I'm rambling and sounding like an idiot.*

"You can tell me shortly," Terian interrupted pointedly. "I mean I want to hear everything, Sun. I'll see you then. Take care."

We hung up, my next concern what to do with myself for hours. I watched a movie, and then went for a walk, and was too restless to enjoy either. Finally, I decided to go get a drink at the Tavern, hoping it would bring me luck.

When I got there in my car, I got another surprise. Lash's truck was there in the parking lot.

I sat there for a few minutes in utter shock, staring at it. I decided to wait there, because unless I was sure I wanted to talk to him, I couldn't get out. He'd scent me. *Besides, what if he's with someone?*

I felt jealous suddenly and pushed it away. We'd been together more than three months ago, and he'd never called me once. Well, sure, he didn't have my number. But he was such a smart guy; he'd have found it, if he wanted it. He knew where I lived; he could have stopped by when he'd gotten back in town. He hadn't.

Definitely better to stay here. For all I knew, he was killing someone in there.

In a half hour, Lash's dark silhouette came striding out of the bar, the telling clue a slight swagger always present in his step. I couldn't see his face, but I'd known him long enough to know his singular walking style. He went to his truck, got in, then backed up almost to my car. With a squeal of tires, he drove off.

I waited until his taillights faded, then went inside. When the bartender came to me, I ordered a scotch.

"You're Sundown, aren't you?"

I nodded, immediately ill at ease.

"Got something for you." He reached under the bar and handed me a folded sheet of paper.

I tucked it inside my shirt, trying to act casual. "Thanks."

He nodded. "That guy you used to meet for drinks a while back showed up tonight, and asked if you still came in here alone. I told him sure, sometimes," the bartender said, pouring my drink. "So he said next time I saw you, to give that to you if you were alone. And if you weren't, to toss it out."

I nodded and sipped my drink nonchalantly, trying not to give away my anxiety. In spite of my best efforts, I inhaled my scotch in record time, then left a few minutes later. While it was too early to meet Terian, I couldn't stay there.

I drove for a while, wanting badly to read the note, and also not wanting to.

What if it says Lash wants to have a relationship with me, now that Devlin has the real Sar to keep him occupied? Or maybe he just wants some sex, and since he's back in town, he thought he'd look me up? It hadn't been just a friendly hello, or he wouldn't have made being alone a prerequisite to the bartender giving me the note.

78

Sundown

Deep down, I knew it wasn't the latter or just about casual sex. But I told myself it was anyway as I pulled over to the side of the road. I took the note from my pocket, and burned it unread in my car's ashtray, blinking back tears as I did it.

Then I went to meet Terian.

Chapter Twelve

Terian was on time, like always. He told me over dinner the whole story of what had happened the two years we'd been apart, and of the new ongoing drama that was the Theo/Sar/Danial/Devlin three-dimensional love triangle. It was hard to believe some of what he said had happened, but I took his word for it. In return, I told him what had happened with me and my father, leaving out only Lash, and what had happened with Devlin. While I felt bad not telling him everything, I justified that by telling myself the cold truth could only hurt him, if not cause more trouble if he either sought revenge against Devlin, or felt jealous of Lash.

Afterward he followed me home for a drink. At first, we were both reserved and kept our distance, careful of one another and unsure. Then the alcohol kicked in. The moment we accidentally touched, our passion ignited with a roar. Terian's lips met mine in a punishing kiss, his arms going around me, pulling me close. I kissed him hungrily, all those lonely nights of wanting him determined to be satisfied.

He made to get up, but I'd waited long enough already. I pulled him back down on me, my hips rising to meet his, my hands going down his back to cup his buttocks through his jeans. Terian's lips broke with mine, his head ducking to kiss my neck, then moving lower as he pulled down my low cut top, exposing my lace brassiere. With a tug, he pushed it down, revealing my breast, his hungry mouth fastening on the left as his hand cupped the right, squeezing possessively.

I moaned, my hands fumbling for his belt, anxious to free him. With a snap, I popped the button, then tore down the zipper. I reached in, my hand grasping his throbbing erection. Terian stiffened his back with a cry, then moved back, attacking my jeans. He tugged, but despite his efforts, they did not come off.

Damn stretch jeans. "I'll get them," I panted, standing unsteadily. "You get ready."

We both stripped off our jeans, his taking longer than mine. By the time I'd helped him get them off, he'd finished putting on the condom. I pushed him back onto the couch, straddling him. With a shift of my hips, I impaled myself, throwing my head back with a groan.

Terian grasped my hips, chest heaving, and began to move me. I grabbed his hands, then held them down to the couch. I used my hips, moving him in and out of me with long deliberate strokes. Terian groaned, then jerked, his blissful expression delightful to watch as he strained upwards.

I kissed his neck, then took some skin in my mouth, sucking hard. Terian broke loose of my hands, grasping my breasts, squeezing. With a snarl, he pulled my upper body closer, burying his head between my breasts, his hot tongue stroking. His other hand grabbed my rear, pushing it down hard against him.

His stiff penis slid in another few inches. I jerked, letting out a sharp cry. Terian took my nipple in his mouth, sucking hard as he drove into me again and again.

I screamed, the climax washing over me like a tidal wave. The pure feeling expanded, filling me completely, freeing me utterly. Terian yelled, his lower body contracting again and again as he clutched me tightly to him.

We held each other, sweaty and panting, completely sated.

"Do you mind if I spend the night, Sun?"

Only he would ask, after all our history together. For the first time, my normal sarcasm was absent in my reply. "No," I said, kissing him lovingly as I blinked my moist eyes rapidly. "I want you to stay."

* * * *

The next morning, he asked me formally to move in with him. I agreed immediately. To celebrate, we made love again.

"Are you okay to keep going?" Terian asked suddenly with concern, stopping his movements. "I don't want to hurt you. And we've been at it all night."

"It's okay. I've gone longer than this." *Stupid!* I bit my lip, before I said anything more.

"With who?" Terian growled. "No human man could have lasted this long."

"A were," I whispered. "That's how he referred to himself."

"What type?" he growled, his eyes glinting red.

"I don't know," I lied. "I never saw him be anything but human," I added.

"Fine," Terian said roughly. "You've known the staying power of a were. But demons have the most staying power of any being, and faeries are a close second. I could go for days, and not stop."

That admission was simultaneously scary and exciting. "Faerie?"

"I'm half-faerie," Terian said, blushing slightly. "Turns out my mother isn't dead, and my father's alive, too. But that's another can of worms, Sun."

"It's okay," I consoled him, touching his cheek gently. "I've learned a lot about accepting things I can't change, in the time we've been apart."

"So have I," Terian said in an old, slightly bitter tone. "So have I."

* * * *

I moved in with Terian the next day, and quit my job. It was a nice change to not have to get up for work in the afternoon, or stay up every night until after midnight. With that simple change, there was a deeper feeling of me finally being on track to a real life, not living on the fringes of one. That first morning when I woke up and actually saw a sunrise as the first part of my day instead of its end was the beginning of an awakening for me.

My life had been a certain way for a long time. I hadn't been happy, but I hadn't felt I could change my direction. Maybe I thought I hadn't deserved more than getting by. But I did deserve more, a lot more. And so did Terian, for giving me a third shot at some happiness. Determined, I turned my focus to my new home and partner, and got busy.

I did a fair bit of cleaning that first week, as Terian was messy and something of a book hoarder. His lab was always neat, but his large bedroom—our room—was a mess, and so was anywhere he spent time. But once I got that straightened out with the help of some large bookshelves with metal shelving, plastic bins, and upscale labels for the rest, keeping order was easy.

Meeting Sar was less time consuming, yet still a lot harder. It didn't help that Theo had mistaken me for her when I was kissing Terian one morning in his lab and blown a gasket. He'd come through the lab door shouting about betrayal, breaking the door lock in the process. While he'd apologized over and over after seeing I wasn't Sar, and replaced the lock himself that very afternoon, his sudden rage had made me wonder if all the weres living there were as tightly wound as he was.

After all the time I'd cursed Sar for being a bitch, she was...well, nice. She smiled when she saw me, and welcomed me. It was in her tone that she meant what she said about hoping we'd be friends. Still, that gold bear of ownership around her neck gave me a chill. And along with friendliness, Sar's tone also had an intensity that told me she had already formed some opinions about me, at least a few of them as negative as the ones I harbored for her. That if I hurt Tears again—the nickname she and everyone else here called him—she'd make me sorry.

That was understandable. I still wasn't willing to completely let go of my old negative opinions of her, no matter how nice she seemed. Besides, I was happy living in Danial's guard quarters, talking with Cia and Janice, and keeping to myself. I didn't need to hang around with Sar, especially where I might run into Devlin. Cia had told me when I'd inquired discreetly that he almost never came to Danial's compound. When he did, it was always to the main house to visit Danial or Sar.

As the weeks passed, I even began sitting in on some of Elle and Theoron's lessons. I'd never cared about books, never even finished high school. But I enjoyed learning about history and art when there was no pressure on me to have to take a test. Bill, the man tutoring Elle and Theoron, asked me finally if I wanted private lessons. I agreed at once, arranging the next day for a session three times a week. Everyone here was always talking about books they'd read, or referencing something in history that had once happened. Shit, Terian seemed to know about every battle that had ever been fought, and was always going on about how amazing some of the early commanders had been, even when they'd been fighting with only bows and arrows. I wanted to be able to join the conversation, to know what they were talking about, and to be able to say something, when they asked me what I thought.

I walked into the kitchen that second week, and Cia was baking some kind of cookies that smelled heavenly. When I asked her if I could help, she just smiled and told me to pull up a chair. That day we baked two kinds of cookies, mint chocolate chip, and ginger molasses. In the weeks that followed, we became closer, as she taught me how to cook and bake. I'd always bragged that talent in the kitchen wasn't necessary if you had talent in the bedroom. Yet along with my new surroundings was a new sense of not only wanting to fit in, but the desire to take a chance on some of the things that I'd always sneered at as not being "my thing". I hadn't been happy with who I was, not deep down. So why hold onto that person's beliefs and values?

Letting go of that old chip on my shoulder was the beginning of healing for me. I'd never sought any reasoning for my way of life, or even felt it was necessary to understand why I did the things I did. But as I began to feel valued by the people around me, I understood finally it was because I was finally standing up for myself. I'd always been very vocal about not letting anyone screw me over, and making sure that I got my fair share of whatever I wanted, whether it be orgasms, tips, or anything else. Yet I came to understand that my attitude hadn't ever really gotten me something I'd yearned for my whole life: true admiration born of respect. There was a difference between someone giving me a fair deal because they were made to, and someone willingly sharing things with me because they wanted to spend time with me, or thought I'd earned them through an equal share of work.

With that newfound sense of self, I finally was able to look towards a future. I'd always lived day-to-day my entire life, my mantra that tomorrow would take care of itself and the present was all that was important. I saw now much of that attitude had been because I had never been able to see a tomorrow that was filled with something better than today. Cliché as it was to admit it, I hadn't known anything was missing in my life until Terian had shown me how much more was out there. Hesitantly, I secretly began to consider a future of getting married, maybe enrolling in a short college program, or getting some kind of part-time job with Solutions, Inc., like Sar had. Hell, maybe I could fill in for her on the days she wasn't here, as that seemed to be most of the week these days. With Danial growing the business, Terian said there would be a lot more work coming in.

I was finally happy, really happy. I had a home, a committed man that loved me, and real friends. I wasn't going to mess that up for anything.

* * * *

A few months later, I got a letter from a lawyer, telling me my father was dead. In spite of everything he'd done and how much I hated him, I still went to pieces.

Terian was wonderful, holding and comforting me until I managed to pull myself together. We arranged travel to meet with the lawyer, fortunately having already planned to go west to try to track down any remaining members of Terian's foster family.

Terian's "can of worms" was not that big, but it was supernatural: a demon Titus was his father, and his mother was a faerie called Leri. Titus had apparently wanted a child, but Leri hadn't, or at least Titus hadn't checked with her before casting a spell to make a pregnancy possible. Leri had dealt with her bundle of joy in the worst possible way: hiding it from Titus until she gave birth in secret, then foisting the child off on an unsuspecting human whom she'd bespelled. It was obvious that Terian's feelings for his mother resembled mine for my late father. While I couldn't fault him for that, I did understand Leri's panic; most women who got pregnant by a demon died giving birth. I didn't excuse her for her actions, but I trusted Titus even less. *Another reason I was not rushing into marriage anytime soon, with those kinds of potential in-laws.*

Our trip was a good one. Terian did find the sister of his beloved brother—well, the man he'd thought of as his brother. When he came back from meeting with her, he'd clearly been crying. But he seemed so much more at peace than he had been, almost like he'd been given a reprieve from the gallows.

On our way home, we stopped in Janesville, and met with the lawyer.

"Your father didn't leave you anything," he said in a solemn tone. "He said you betrayed him when he needed you most. But he didn't leave a will, and so the money comes to you, as next of kin."

"I don't want it," I grated out, full of old wrath. "Draw up papers to donate it to the state program for children."

"Which one?" the lawyer asked, clearly taken aback. "There are dozens."

"Pick one for abandoned and orphaned children," Terian said, putting his hand over mine and squeezing. "One that gets them together with new families, and gives them a chance, even when they think there isn't one."

I nodded, pressing my lips together tightly and blinking a lot to control my emotions. The lawyer said he'd do it, and send me some papers to sign in a few days.

Later, we went to my father's old trailer. Once again, it looked abandoned, with all the signs that it was being used for sex by the local teenage crowd.

"Want me to incinerate it?" Terian offered, a blue ball of his mystical fire appearing in his hand. "Just say the word, and it's done."

"No," I said slowly. "Leave it. My father liked sex more than anything. Maybe this is a good way for him to be remembered."

Terian clearly thought me crazy for that thought, but he just held my hand, and together, we walked away. We had one more stop to make, before catching our plane home.

When I got to the cemetery, my mother's grave was overgrown again. Terian helped me weed it, and before long, the patch of earth in front of it was bare again.

"We need to plant some flowers," I said in dismay. "I forgot to bring any."

Terian looked around. "Grab me one of those wild roses, over there," he said.

I grabbed one. Swearing when it jabbed me, I broke off a piece with a flower. It was a pretty variety, kind of pink and pale orange. I handed it to him, and he stuck it in the earth.

"It's better than nothing—" I broke off, gaping in shock. Terian was murmuring something, and the rose was growing before my eyes, branches and greenery springing forth. Soon it was a foot tall bush, covered with fragrant blossoms.

I stared at the beautiful roses, touched to the point I couldn't speak. I had known for years that Terian could wield magic, but this was the first time he had ever done some for me. "Thank you," I finally managed, blinking back tears.

"The roses will last," Terian said, giving me a smile. "I helped the flower grow deep roots, Sun. It'll be able to get water when it needs it."

Only one thing more was needed. Blinking rapidly, I got out my Sharpie, which I had remembered this visit, and wrote "Beloved Mother" on the stone. "Mom, this is Terian," I said. "He's my guy, and I'm finally happy. I might not be back for a while, but—"

"I can teleport you, Sun," Terian reminded me in a whispered tone. "We can come back whenever you want."

I'd forgot. I shot him a grateful look, and went on. "Dad's dead, maybe you already know that. Anyway, he donated his body to science, to try to help find a cure for what he died of. Maybe he wasn't the bastard we both thought he was." I paused. "I wanted you to know that. And I hope you can see Terian and I, and that you're happy for me." I wiped away sudden tears. "Because I finally am happy, with him. He helped me find my way to a great life, instead of just a life."

Terian took my hand, and we began to walk away.

"Why do you write on the stone?" Terian asked. "Did your Mom and you have some inside joke with Sharpies?"

"No," I said, smiling at his naïve assumption. "I want the stone to say what I wrote. And it doesn't."

"I can fix that," he said lovingly. "Cover your eyes."

He turned, and lightning shot from his hands, striking the headstone. I covered my face with my arms as stone chips exploded outward with a sharp crack.

Terian gently took my hands away from my face. "How's that? It's a little jagged, I'm afraid."

He'd rent the stone with the lightning. Now "Beloved Mother" was there in scrawled letters, beneath my mom's name.

I gave him a hug and a kiss, more unshed tears in my eyes threatening to spill down my cheeks. "It's perfect. Thank you."

"Anytime," he said, kissing me again. "Now let's go home, Sun."

Chapter Thirteen

I decided I'd better walk to the main house, and call Terian on his cell. He'd probably already left, but he was going to be so pissed off when he realized he'd forgotten the meeting plans. He'd have to stop with Theo, wherever they were in route, and teleport back to the house to get them. At least if the plans were at the great room, it would be easier for him.

I walked up the drive, and saw his truck was missing. He and Theo had already left. *Fuck.*

But there was another truck there I recognized, one I didn't expect. More unsettling, I also recognized the man in the front seat.

Lash got out when he saw it was me. "Hello to you, too," he said, grinning a little. "I heard you and Terian are back together. I'm happy for you, Sun."

I couldn't stop gaping at him. It was so odd seeing him here like this, knowing what we had been to one another. Especially after Terian had been so repulsed by Sar being with Devlin and then later with Lash. How would he feel knowing I'd been with them both, too? Especially knowing I'd been the one to initiate sex with Lash? Not good was my guess.

"Would you rather I pretend I don't know you?" Lash hissed, his face losing its friendliness.

"No," I said biting my lip. "I'm sorry, Lash, I just don't know how to act. It's been a long time since I saw you. Things are so different now."

"Only nine months ago," Lash said with no expression. "But it's a lifetime ago, Sun, for both of us."

There was a nasty scar on his face. "What happened?" I asked, reaching out to touch him,

He grabbed my hand before I touched his skin, pushing it away. "Demon attack. His blade had poison."

I knew enough now about werepoison to know it inhibited healing. "Does it hurt?"

"Only when I smile," Lash said, and smiled, his scarred skin twisting a little to bare one fang.

"What are you doing here?" I asked worriedly. "It's day, Devlin can't be here."

"He's not," Lash retorted. "Devlin had a fight with Sar. She left without her sushi. I brought it for her, so it didn't spoil—"

There's something in his tone when he talks about Sar.

"—and she let me borrow a DVD I needed to return. You've heard of *South Park*, Sun? It's these kids, but they don't talk like kids—"

"Not you, too," I said in disbelief.

"Not me what?" Lash hissed in confusion. "Do you not like *South Park*?"

"Not that, her," I said angrily. "Sarelle. The woman it seems everyone wants, sooner or later, even fucking weresnakes!"

Lash bared his long fangs and hissed at me, in that moment looking angrier than I'd ever seen him. "I don't know what you mean."

"You're in love with her, too."

"She's just been nice to me, that's all, and—"

"Don't lie to yourself! You like her! You probably fucking love her!"

"Fuck off!" Lash hissed at me loudly, leaning back on his truck, and crossing his arms over his chest. "It's not your business what I do, Sun, or who I do it with."

"You fuck off! Theo and she are happy, don't go chasing after her."

"Shut up and get out of here. Right now, Sun! You have no claim on me!"

"Stay away from her Lash, or I'll—"

"You'll what? Tell everyone you slept with me?" Lash said loudly.

I cringed, hoping there was no one around to overhear.

Lash saw my fear, and seized on it. "There is nothing you can say without admitting we were together. And it wasn't just once! You asked me for more the next night! You want your demon to know that? That you couldn't get enough of me? That I had you so much that night that my sack was empty, because all of my seed was in you, every last drop? That hardly ever happens to male weres, especially snakes, but you did it to me, Sun. You drained me dry."

I flushed bright red, horrified. "Shut up!"

Lash kept talking. "You think he'll still want you in his bed, knowing you were with me? That it wasn't just sex—you all but asked me to live with you? That you spent the night with me even knowing he was alone, that he would have wanted you back? That you only got back together with him after I left the fucking country? Shall I tell Terian all that, my morning angel?"

I flushed a deeper red, and dropped my eyes, cowed. "Please don't say anything."

"Then leave, Sun. Now," Lash hissed urgently, looking at the house. "Sar's coming. I don't want her to see us together. She's not stupid; she'll see I was your lover. It's all over your face."

I broke and ran, sobbing. The front door opened as I rounded the corner of the garage, Sar's surprised voice asking Lash what he was doing here. A moment later, she went back inside to tell Danial she and Lash were going to lunch.

I debated going after her and trying to convince her not to go with him. Spending time with that infatuated snake was just going to make things worse between Theo and Lash. It was obvious Lash wasn't going to listen to me, but maybe she could. But I was angry all over again at her for always being the one everyone wanted. Instead of intervening, I stayed where I was, watching them drive off together.

As soon as they left I returned home. Then I called Terian, telling him about the forgotten plans. He appeared in the great room in a second with a relieved sigh, taking the plans from me. "Thanks for this. I'll be home about two or so," he said, giving me a kiss. "Theo and I'll stop for lunch someplace, but we'll be back right after. Want me to bring you anything?"

I wanted him to bring me some revenge, because I was still smarting from Lash's words. The easiest way would be to send Terian and Theo to the same place Lash was headed to with Sar. Theo would go ballistic. Everyone knew he hated Lash. If Theo knew they were together, he'd go after them and separate them, whatever it took. The hard part was arranging the chance meeting without saying it flat out like a tattletale.

Where had they headed? Lash had mentioned their shared taste in sushi. But I couldn't ask for raw fish. *Gag and yuck.* I couldn't ask Danial the name, either, though he had to know. Fuck it, without knowing for sure, I couldn't point Terian the right way, either.

"Sun, what is it?" Terian said with concern, interrupting my thoughts. "Are you feeling okay?"

"Bring me some Chinese food," I said with a shrug. "Some lobster fried rice?"

The nearest place to eat was Alan's Creek. Lash and Sar had likely headed there for lunch. All the eating-places there were on the same street. It was the best I could do.

"Sure," Terian said. "I hope I can convince Theo to go there instead. He wants to get sushi at some new restaurant in Alan's Creek, because Sar brought some to him the other day." He made a face. "I said I'd go before I thought about it too much."

I gave him another shrug, wicked glee radiating through me. "Make the best of it. I'll make you a sandwich when you get home, if that stuff tastes too awful."

He flashed me a smile. "You're on." Then he disappeared.

Maybe it will work. Maybe it wouldn't...

"The game you're playing is a dangerous one, Sundown," a low voice said.

I turned to see Danial at the top of the stairs, his eyes glinting red. "I don't know what you mean." I blushed, hearing myself repeat Lash's words.

"I think you do," Danial said as he glided down the stairs, baring his fangs. "And as it involves Sar, it involves me. You wanted Terian and Theo to go where Lash and Sar are, to find them together. Why?"

I went to leave but he grabbed hold of me, and squeezed my wrist hard. I cried out in pain. "Stop, you're hurting me."

"I'll hurt you worse, if you don't answer me," Danial growled. "Why?"

"I heard that about you, that you were just like your brother," I retorted, deeply bitter.

Danial dropped my wrist, snatching his hand back, sudden understanding breaking across his face. "When?" he asked softly.

I closed my eyes, and didn't answer him.

"When, Sundown? Back this past fall? When did Devlin have you? Because I hear in your voice that he did. I'm guessing it had to be before he left for Rio, before being with Sar. They are Oathed now, and Dev would not risk breaking that, not for you."

I flushed, and then realized belatedly he didn't know about Lash at all; he was only asking about Devlin. "Back when Devlin was weak, over two years ago," I admitted. "When he was angriest at Sarelle. You know why he came on to me. He's your brother. You must know what he wanted to do with Sar; what he did with me, pretending I was her…"

I trailed off as cool arms encircled me. "I wondered why you mostly kept to yourself at the werecompound, and didn't ever spend much time here," Danial said quietly, hugging me gently. "I thought it was Sar, or me, maybe. But you were afraid of running into Devlin."

"Yes," I confessed, trembling. "I don't ever want to see him again, I'm so afraid of him."

"Don't be," Danial assured. "He has the real Sarelle now. No matter that they fought recently, nothing has changed between them. He would not even lay a finger on you now, Sun. Not for Terian's wrath, or mine, but because he doesn't want to lose her. He does love her, in his way. He was obsessed first, it's true, but that obsession has turned into love."

I stayed quiet. Maybe Devlin was his brother, but he didn't know him well, if he thought Devlin could ever love anyone.

"Do you want me to say something to him?" Danial offered. "My word is law, at least in America, even to another Ruler. I can forbid him from coming within sight of you, if you like."

I've already managed to avoid Dev all by myself. I'd be all set, if only my fear was rational. "No," I replied, pulling out of his grasp. "But thank you."

"You're welcome. Now explain your actions," Danial said, his dark eyes on mine. "Why send Terian and Theo to where Lash and Sar are? You want them found together for some reason, even though you must know it will cause a fight, a bad one, no matter that it's just lunch."

"Because it's not just lunch. Lash cares for her, I think," I said.

Danial said nothing, though he looked uncomfortable.

"You knew?" I accused. "Why did you let her go with him, then?"

Danial sighed. "Devlin said they had been together again a few days ago, and that he thought Lash had feelings for her, by the way he acted afterwards. He said not to worry, that he had talked to Lash, and Lash accepted that the situation was temporary, that when The Lust ended, Sar and his sexual relationship would be over. It's not what I'd prefer her to do—being with that repulsive creature—but it's not her fault, Sun. It's not as if she wanted to be. She must sate The Lust when it occurs, or she becomes wild. It is better Lash is with her, and not one of the other guards. I know she hates having to be intimate with him. But that is a small price to pay for Devlin to have a child of his own—"

I didn't hear the rest of what he said. I wasn't even focused on him enough to be pissed off that he made it seem as if wanting to be with Lash was utterly disgusting. All I could think about was that Lash had been with Sar. *More than once. Worse, he already wants her just like the rest of them do.* I'd heard it in Lash's words; he wanted her bad. He cared about her after knowing her for a few months, more than he'd ever cared about me, me who he'd known for years now!

My anger reached a fever pitch at how Lash had treated me in the driveway. It was safe to say that his best-ever human lay was no longer me. I wanted to kill someone. *If Sar ever asked Lash not to leave the country, he'd fucking just roll on his back and tell her sure, and was there anything else he could do for her besides that, like maybe kill Devlin. Bastard! Slimy no good bastard!*

"Sun, why are you so angry?" Danial inquired coolly, touching my arm gently with his hand. "You're shaking with rage."

I went still, because under that cool tone was wrath, and also more coldness, coldness enough to stop my heart with an icicle dagger. This was Dev's brother, with the same blood in his veins. Danial wouldn't hesitate at all if he thought his Sar was in any kind of danger. He'd hurt me—hurt me bad—if he guessed how much I hated her right now.

I tried to calm down. "It's just that Sar seems happy with Theo. They went through so much shit to be together. I want their relationship to work. Lash is trying to split them up, I think."

"Is it really that, or that you are jealous?" Danial asked searchingly.

"Jealous of Sar? That she is desired by all of us, and you, who looks so similar to her, are not? Or are you angry with her, that Devlin hurt you because you look like her, and you thought it unjust, and want her punished?"

God, he seemed to be reading my mind. "I'm not jealous!" I said heatedly.

"You surely are," Danial said. "I know that particular tone in your voice. I've heard it often enough in mine this past year. But I'm warning you now, do nothing again to cause any more fights—"

His grip tightened on my arm in a flash. I let out a cry of pain.

"—or I'll wait until Terian is away for an afternoon, and tell Devlin you are missing him." His tone turned malicious, and dark as night. "I know the potion he probably used on you. All he needs to do is sing to you, Sun, and you'll want him more than anything else, do anything he asks for without a thought." He grinned widely. "And Sar has given him permission for oral sex with other women."

I jerked my arm free of his with a curse, and ran into the other room. I wiped at my angry tears as I listened to his feet on the stairs walking back to his study.

Chapter Fourteen
A few weeks later

Where the hell was Terian? While he was not coming home tonight, he still hadn't called to tell me the hotel where he'd be staying. Maybe it had slipped his mind in all the chaos. Terian was headed out alone on a trip he should have been going on with Theo. Now a trip that should have taken a day was going to be an overnight.

Nagging doubt gnawed at me, that my fiancé had possibly had a setback. Last fall, Terian had finally done a little too much dark magic, and his waning tenuous control had shifted from his faerie half to his demon side. The effect had been all the more traumatic as the sudden shift had happened in the middle of sex. *Sudden burning heat, taloned hands holding me down, and my lover's fanged visage grinning down at me with red eyes of lust.*

Stop, Sundown. You know Terian's father Titus took magical steps to stop a regression after he helped Terian find his way back. There'll be warnings now, and you'll never be caught by surprise like that again. And Terian's sworn off the dark magic. He's regained complete control.

I wasn't resentful of his being away overnight, even if I sounded like it. The reason for Theo staying home was the death of Devon, Theo's only son, the little cougar everyone had loved. He'd been so happy all of the time, even when he got into things, and knocked over lamps, and made a mess. He had been the best of Sar and Theo. His loss had hit us all hard. Everyone had been crying at the funeral, even me.

Sar and Theo had just buried Devon that morning. How horrified they'd both looked, and how lost. Sar had looked so old, and worn out. When I'd hugged her and told her I was sorry, for the first time I'd really meant it. She was a shadow of the happy woman she had been back in the spring, when I'd met her for the first time. She'd gained some weight after having the twins, and the years were showing on her, like they hadn't before she'd given Lash her blood. But I'd heard that she was mortal now, that saving Lash from death had drawn the vampire taint from her blood and her body. What I'd seen had confirmed it.

I called the main house from my cell, hoping to get Theo. No one answered. I swore, then put on my jacket, and drove over there. Going inside, I noticed spots of blood on the floor. There were also bloody footprints going down the stairs. I let out a shriek.

"Sun?"

It was Elle. She'd been crying.

"What happened? Whose blood is this?"

"Sar and Theo fought," Elle got out, crying again. "He tried to force her to be what he was, but she said she loved Lash and she didn't want to be a cougar."

I sat down and hugged her, thinking I was in a crazy world. Terian had told me Titus was breaking Theo and Sar's famous true love bond. I guessed this fight was the end of them.

At that moment, I finally put my envy of Sar to rest. Why had I ever been jealous of her, anyway? All the men in her life were so bad to her, so what if they wanted her? I didn't envy her Danial, with his constant distantness and violent tendencies, or Theo, with his possessiveness and abusive way of shouting at her the minute he didn't get what he wanted. And Devlin was just completely insane for her. Terian had told me tearfully one night in a drunken binge back last spring that Devlin had raped her not a week after Lash and I had been together, as soon as he had had the opportunity to get her alone where no one could help her. And that it hadn't been once, but time after time. I pitied her, because even though she'd fought him tooth and nail the whole way this past year and a half, hell, since the day she first met him years ago, Devlin had still possessed her in the end. She'd had his child, she was Oathed to him, she was living with him at his castle, and I didn't need anyone to tell me that no matter what might happen, Sar was never, ever going to get free of him.

I was the lucky one, who should be envied. I had Terian, a man who was devoted to me, and despite what we'd gone through, he loved me. He loved that I was having his baby, and he hadn't mentioned Sar to me once since he'd recovered his human self. There was only he and I now, and we were a family. Best of all, Devlin had forgotten me completely.

Then Elle's words finally fully registered. "She said she loved Lash?"

"Yes," Elle said sniffling. "She said she was in love with him, that she had saved him with her blood, and that he'd been going to make her weresnake like him, that she wanted him to—"

God, she must really love him to say that. I'd liked him, wanted him, and even then, just his kiss with that forked tongue of his had scared me. Sar knew what it would mean to be turned, that he'd have to bite her, and how everyone would look at her after. She knew she'd lose Danial and Theo, and maybe even Devlin, though maybe she wanted that. So she must truly love Lash. *Weird, but romantic and sweet in a way, too.*

"Will my mom be okay?" Elle asked. "She got away, I saw her teleport."

"Shh," I said, hugging Elle. "Sar will be fine, Elle. She's tough. A lot tougher than you or me."

Chapter Fifteen
A few weeks later

I had gone to Davy's with the express purpose of giving Gary an invite to the wedding reception. He was one of my friends from way back, and I wanted him to be there. But when I got to Davy's, the place was trashed. Worse, it was quiet; almost as quiet as it had been that night I'd first met Lash and Devlin. Instead of no one being around, there were broken tables everywhere, and unconscious forms laying around here and there, all men.

I knew who had done it. His name was in bullet holes down one wall.

I went to the back room with the pool tables, and there was Lash, at the far end of the room, sitting at a table. I hadn't seen him since the spring. He looked much younger, but there was no mistaking it was him. He ignored me, smoking, and drinking heavily.

I sighed, then went and sat down at the other chair at his table. "Tell me what happened."

"No," Lash hissed, taking another swig of scotch.

"Sar and you fought?"

Lash looked at me in surprise, then anger. "How do you know my business? Does everyone already know she broke up with me? We just got together a week ago."

"Terian told me you two were an item," I said flatly. "Remember Theo's best friend? My fiancé? He saw you together one day last week in Hayden's kitchen. He said she'd been making you breakfast."

Lash grimaced, and said nothing. He took another drink, finishing the bottle. He pushed it off the table, but it didn't shatter when it hit the floor. He looked annoyed about it, but didn't get up.

I got up, walked to the bar, and got another bottle of scotch. I brought it back with a shot glass, and sat down.

He poured himself most of the bottle, then made as if to hand it off. "You joining me?"

"Sure."

He gave me a recriminating look. "You're pregnant."

"One won't hurt," I said defensively. "I intend to drink during the wedding toast. Besides, the baby's tough. He's part demon, remember?"

Lash made another grimacing smile, but he poured me a shot. We clinked glasses, and sipped. I hadn't had anything strong in a long while. My eyes teared up almost immediately at the bitter alcohol taste, and I put down the glass. *Serves you right for being a bad mom. Now pour the rest out when he's not looking.*

"So what happened?" I asked again.

"Why do you care?" Lash hissed, baring his fangs. "Who am I to you?"

"Someone who cared about me when no one else did," I replied. "Someone who saved my life, and got me out of town, when a madman was after me. I'm sitting here because you did what you did. I'm going to be a mother and a wife and I got a chance to, because of you. And you were more to me than that once, too, you ass."

Lash considered that, then threw his head back and took a long drink. I poured my shot remnant out discreetly on the floor, then pretended to do the same.

"I didn't do it for you, I did it for me," Lash said, lighting up another cigarette. "I told you that. Go home to your demon fiancé. Leave me to my misery."

I stared at him, raising my eyebrows just a bit.

"I thought if I could save just one," Lash hissed softly, his flat eyes revealing nothing. "Maybe it would change things. Maybe I wouldn't be damned."

"You aren't damned."

"I am! Sar doesn't want me because I'm a piece of shit killer! Everyone knows it! Everyone!"

"She loves you."

"She doesn't! She told me to stay away from her!"

"Lash, don't be an idiot! She left Theo for you—"

"She didn't! She left him because he attacked her!"

"She did! Terian said she did, that he knew she loved you most of all her lovers! All of them!"

"He's wrong," Lash hissed sadly. "She loved Theo and Danial, but not me. She told me she'd never be with me again. She told me to stay away from her." Lash took a deep breath and let it out. "I've had enough, Sun."

I felt a cold chill. His next words were worse

"I'm going to drink until I can't feel anything anymore," Lash hissed softly. "And then I'm going to finish it."

"Women get mad and say things they don't mean! Don't be an idiot."

"She shouldn't have found me, and saved me! She should have stayed here, and I would have died, and that would have been that!"

"But she didn't! She loved you enough to almost give her life to save you—"

"How do you know all this?" Lash hissed. "Titus said he erased the memories of anyone else who knew."

"He will, after the baby comes," I said, patting my stomach. "But he can't safely, until then. So I know what really happened, not the whitewashed version."

"It hurts too much," Lash hissed, agony in each word. "It hurts too much to care for someone, and have them take themselves away from you. I had no idea it would still hurt this much. I'd forgotten how much it hurt."

"That's always the same," I said shrugging, thinking of Terian and myself, and the times we'd fought and broken up, and how glad I was that was over with now. "You must have hurt her too, with what you must have said to her when you fought."

"I know I did," Lash said guiltily. "I feel awful for that, too. The things I told her…I didn't mean them."

"So apologize."

"She won't take me back," Lash hissed in sadness. "She doesn't want to be a snake for me—"

"Did you ask her?" I interrupted.

He shook his head.

"Ask her, jerk," I said. "You may be surprised. What do you have to lose?"

"My dignity, my pride, and my self-respect. And that's all I have left."

"So it's better to die than to say you were wrong? Than to tell her you need her like that, and give her a chance to say she'll do it?"

"You're young, you can't understand! I've lost the one woman who maybe ever really loved me because of who and what I am! And there's nothing I can do about it. She's human and I'm not. I can't not be a weresnake. And I can't go back and erase the last hundred years! And what other woman do I have that's my own, that belongs to me? None. Who else do I have that really loves me? Who else did I ever have? Who else will I ever have? No one! There has never been any woman for me like her. Not in my whole fucking life."

God, he sounded just like I did, back when I'd broken up with Terian. I reached out and took his hand in mine, making him start. "You aren't alone," I said softly. "I'm your friend, Lash. And I know for a fact she loves you more than her life. It doesn't matter that you aren't human, not to either of us."

Lash covered my hand with his, and squeezed. He gave me a sad smile. "It was okay for a long, long time to be alone, to have Dev, and nothing else. I stayed in this life so long for him, because I knew he was as lonely as I was, despite all the women he had throwing themselves at him. I knew he needed me with him, because a big part of the reason for his evil was he was so lonely. But he has his child now, and he's got Sar. He doesn't need me like he did. And I got a taste of something so sweet with her, I can't go on living and never taste it again. I can't go back to being alone, to being by myself again, to just fucking women when I get the urge and knowing they don't care about me at all. Not after how being with her made me feel. Not after how she made me feel."

God, I knew what he was talking about. I'd felt the same way after loving Terian, and being loved by him. I understood right then that Lash loved Sar, loved her completely, and that she most likely loved him the same way.

"Go home to Hayden," I said, exasperated. "She loves you like you love her. Say you're sorry, and that you need her as a snake. She'll forgive you, and be with you like you need her to, and you can be happy—"

"Get out," he said curtly, not looking at me. "I don't want you to be here when I do it. I'd rather you remembered me this way, not covered in blood. And there's going to be a lot of blood Sun, I heal too fast now for there not to be."

"Lash, please," I begged. "Don't do this."

"Go home, Sun. There's nothing left to say. I've made my decision. Respect it, and leave."

I got up, went over to him, and hugged him hard. "Don't do this."

He let out a surprised hiss, then hugged me back. "I wish you the best with Terian. I'm sorry for what I said to you that day at Danial's house. I want you to know I never told anyone about us—not Sar, not Dev, no one. I wish I would have seen you get married. I'm glad you're getting a happy ending."

"We can both have a happy ending, stupid! Come with her to the wedding! Stop being such an ass!"

"I can't," Lash hissed, and then grinned when he realized what he'd said. "But think of me sometimes, okay? Maybe say a prayer for me, when Terian isn't around to get hurt by it?"

"Okay," I said, getting to my feet. "I'll go." Gary's invitation could wait. I had to get to a phone.

Lash grabbed me hard, and gave me a deep kiss, stroking me with his tongue. It felt strange to me, just like before, but I made myself kiss him back.

He drew back from me with a soft aroused hiss. "I'm mated to Sar, even though she said it was over. If I wasn't, I'd ask to have you one last time right here, Sun. I remember how good it was with you. But you're pregnant, and love Terian and so you'd probably say no, anyway."

"I'm engaged," I said, giving him a smile. "Sorry."

Lash made a face, then sat me down on his lap, holding me. "I'm the one who is sorry," he hissed gently. "I shouldn't have left when you asked me to stay, or I should have taken you with me. I understand things better now, from knowing Sar. I'm sorry I didn't give you the chance to try. It was easier to say I had to go, because I couldn't face trying again and have it not work out with a human."

"It's okay," I said, feeling uncomfortable. "You did what you thought you had to."

"Could you have loved me?" Lash hissed, looking up at me, his face sad and worn. "If I'd given you the chance to?"

"In time, yes," I said honestly. "I already loved you as a friend. It wouldn't have been far to go to love you as more than a friend."

"Kiss me good-bye, then," he said longingly. "Kiss me one last time, my morning angel."

I kissed him for all I was worth, and then got up, blushing. As I got up, Lash grabbed one of my hands, and touched his lips to it briefly. The act was quick, but I was struck by it, that he who could be so cold and brutal and nasty had some of the gentleness of Terian, at least when he wanted to.

"Goodbye, Sun," Lash hissed. Then he looked away from me.

I nodded, and left, letting the door swing shut behind me as I walked outside, then flipped open my cell phone and began dialing. The inside phone at Davy's had been ripped out of the wall. And the ancient one outside was partway under Lash's Hummer, where he had driven it up into the side of the building.

There were two rings, then a click. "Hayden."

I took a deep breath. "Devlin, please."

"Who is this?"

"A friend of Lash and Sar's. I must speak to Devlin."

"He's not in at the moment. Can I take a message?"

"Listen, this is a fucking emergency! Now get him on the line!"

"Hold on. I know where he is. I'll patch you through to his cell phone."

There was silence, and then that beautiful voice, one I hadn't heard in years.

"Yes? This is Devlin."

God, please let him not sing. "Lash is at Davy's. He fought with Sar and she told him they were done. He's thinking of killing himself, once he's drunk enough not to feel the bullets. Get here as soon as you can."

"Who is this?" Devlin hissed. "If this is a woman of yours, Ulysses, you'll rue—"

"It's Sundown, Devlin. But maybe you've forgotten my voice? It has been years."

There was utter silence. And despite my bravado, I felt an old chill creep down my spine. I forced myself to keep talking.

"Get there ASAP," I said. "You have maybe forty-five minutes to an hour, tops. Because he's going to do it, if someone doesn't stop him."

"Why are you trying to save him?" he asked curiously. "Why do you care, Sun? I didn't think either Sar or Lash were your friends. And after what you and I—"

"I care about *them*, both of *them*," I said quietly, making a point. "Get there in time, or he's going to kill himself."

"I'll leave immediately for Davy's, as soon as I find Sar and get her to teleport us. I thought they were...well, never mind, I didn't know they had fought. I thank you for your help." He paused. "And I'm sorry," he added quietly. "For what I did to you, that night all those years ago."

"You'd do it again in a heartbeat if Sar wasn't your own now, if she'd have gotten away from you!" I rasped, shaking in rage. "You weren't sorry back then, and you aren't now."

"You're right, I'm not sorry," Devlin purred, his voice instantly losing its sad tone. "I should be, I know, but I'm not. I loved having you that night, pretending you were her. It was some of the most satisfying sex I ever had, and that's saying something. You brought my happy thoughts back, Sun."

"It was the worse sex I've ever had," I lied harshly. "It was pathetic."

That seemed to piss him off, for some reason. "You came screaming your little heart out, Sun! You enjoyed it."

"Because of a drug, not anything you did," I said, laughing cruelly. "You're supposed to be this great lover, Dev, and you didn't even kiss me! Not once! You relied on a drug to give me pleasure. It wasn't any skill of yours that made me come. I'd have come for anyone under that drug. Anyone! Do you really have any skill yourself in bed?"

"I do!" Devlin choked out, mortified. "I—"

God, this is fucking satisfying! "You're nothing but a cad, and everyone knows it! Sar knows it! She'll never love you, not really!"

"She does love me!" he shouted, desperation coloring each word. "She does! She's giving me her Oath in two days!"

"She loves Lash," I whispered maliciously. "She loved Danial. She probably loved Theo, at least a little. But she'll never love you. Because she can see right through to the core of you like I can. What she sees is rotted and black with evil!"

"She does love me," Devlin said morosely. "But you're right. She loved them more. All of them." His voice strengthened. "But it doesn't matter. I love her, Sun. More than anything. I thank you, for telling me about Lash. I'll go there now with Sar. I know Lash, and it will take him a good while to work up the will to do it, being were by birth. He'll need another hour at least to get drunk enough." Devlin paused. "Can I do anything to repay you? I am sorry about hurting you. It was wrong, and despite my enjoyment of you, I admit I shouldn't have done what I did."

Yes there is, you bastard. "I never want to see you again in my life," I grated out, emphasizing each word. "But now we're bound into the same circles, with me marrying Terian. So that's what I'd like you to do for me. You see me at a gathering, or a party, or anywhere socially, you leave. I don't care what reason you give, or how. But leave. Never come within sight of me again. Don't come to the wedding. And I never want to hear your voice sing to me again. Not ever."

"As you wish," Devlin agreed. "I will do that, I promise. Good-bye, Sundown."

"Go fuck yourself, Devlin."

I hung up.

Chapter Sixteen
A month later

I reached out my hand, enjoying the giddiness that admiring my wedding gown sleeves brought me. *Silly isn't ever a word I used for myself, but today, that sucker fits. But screw it, even with all Terian's promises, who would have thought that I'd be here now, actually getting married? Not me.*

"Sundown," my soon to be father-in-law Titus called from behind me. "It's time. Are you ready?"

I took one last glance in the mirror, forcing my worried frown to become an anxious smile. My ivory dress was perfect, the long tulle skirt dotted with sequins and beads like a ballerina's that I'd admired long ago as a child. My long hair was up in a mass of waves and a bun, with a tiara and veil to crown me. My shoes were high heels I'd probably be kicking off right after I said "I do", but they looked fabulous with the dress.

"I'm coming," I called, adjusting my veil down over my face.

The morning was still dark, the winter sun just below the horizon. But dawn was approaching, and I hurried to join my uncle John at the back of the outdoor tent for my walk down the aisle.

So strange, that after all this time, I actually have some family relations. John was my father's brother, but one I'd never known until he'd called Solutions, Inc. a few weeks ago, having tracked me down through the lawyer's office who had handled my dad's will. There hadn't been any huge emotional outpouring like in a WE channel movie, but I had gotten to know a little more about my grandparents, and why my father had been the way he was. John was ecstatic to see me, thrilled at my new life, and eagerly asked to stand in for my father to walk me down the aisle. He unfortunately also had a lot to say about my

106

grandparents, plus a few cutting truths about my mom's alcoholism. I hadn't wanted to hear that last part, because the mother I remembered had been the only parent I'd had to hang onto as a child. But hearing history I'd been too young to fully remember, brought some long-buried events back. While I didn't want that, and was still processing how to handle most of that new information, I was grateful to have him with me at the wedding, which was populated almost exclusively by coworkers and associates of Terian's. The only others I knew that were here to witness my big day were Cia and the werefoxes.

But you'll see other relatives soon, for the first time. John's family had flown in for the event; in fact, his oldest son's wife was one of my bridesmaids, his three grandchildren were my flower girls and ring bearer, and his son was one of the groomsmen. While my father and mother hadn't ever been big on keeping in touch with extended family, John was. He'd asked for us to come for a visit after the honeymoon, so I could introduce my new husband to the family, and also get to know them myself.

Terian hadn't been too keen on this, and had simply told John we'd visit that day, between the wedding and the reception, then taken John's hand in his and demonstrated teleportation. John had handled the experience well for someone with no previous supernatural experience, though he'd asked a lot of questions that Terian hadn't been eager to answer. After John had left for his hotel, I'd sat down with Terian. "Do you not want to meet with them?"

Terian looked up at me quizzically. "Do you?"

"I'm not sure," I admitted, biting my lip. "I've never really had family, though. I would like to at least meet them." I touched his hand, then grasped it in my own. "You have family here with your mom and dad."

"I'm okay with us going there after the wedding for a quick visit," Terian said slowly. "But I don't think they should come to the reception. Even without Danial there, there'll be a lot of questions about the other attendees." He squeezed my hand. "You're part of a world they aren't part of, Sun. It's kind of like Sar's family and friends she had before Danial; she had to let those friends go, and now only sees her immediate family. I don't want you to be disappointed."

"Sundown!" Titus boomed. "It's time!"

I pushed away my worries, and headed out to the hall. Peeking around the corner, I saw most of the guests were here, and Terian, Theo, and Theoron, Sar's son with Danial, were up with the justice of the peace in front waiting. My flower girls were fidgeting in line, as their mother tried to keep the ring bearer from throwing his pillow and ring on the floor. Jenny was talking with Cia, and both of them gave me smiles and excessively huge eyes to say I'd missed something shockingly hilarious, and that they'd tell me as soon as we three girls were alone.

John gave me a huge smile, then hugged me. "You look beautiful," he exclaimed. "Are you ready?"

"As ready as I'll ever be," I joked, taking his arm in mine.

Titus patted my back, then took his leave, cueing the music as he headed down to the front row where Leri waited. Nervous, I fidgeted as I saw the first flower girl start on her path, a million worries flooding my mind.

Am I making the right decision? Yes.

What's our life going to be like together? Probably not like John's life with his family. Will Terian still love me when I'm old and he's still young? He's never been anything but true blue so far.

What about Sar? I peeked around the corner again, as the second flower girl began walking. Sar was indeed there, close to the back, with Lash at her side and her daughter, Elle. *She's got Lash, she's not a problem for Terian and me anymore.*

What if Terian loses control and goes all demon again?

I took a shaking breath, as Cia went down the aisle. The reason I was pregnant now was that Terian had "gone to the demon-side" back in the fall. He had lost control to his demon half during sex with me. The experience had been terrifying. Although I hadn't been permanently harmed, I'd gotten pregnant. All of Terian's talk about the potency of demons hadn't been macho bullshit. Terian had fought back over the next months and regained control, with Titus's help. As soon as my love knew I was pregnant, he'd proposed with the same ring he'd offered me before years earlier. This time, I'd said yes.

As Jenny began walking, John turned to me, concerned. "Are you okay, Sundown? There's still time to change your mind."

I looked at him aghast, then pasted a smile on my face. "I'm okay."
When had his wife left? Shit, we're next to walk down the aisle!

"You look terrified," he whispered. "If you don't want to get married, you don't have to."

Terian and all the other weres can hear that he's asking me this. John, you mean well, but it's too late for do-overs, not that I'm looking back ever again. "I want to," I assured him, taking a deep breath. "I'm just nervous."

The music suddenly stopped, then the wedding march began loudly, and I heard the loud grating sound of many chairs pushed back as everyone got to their feet. John nodded, then began walking and I matched him step for step as we strode into view. Cameras began flashing immediately, and I smiled widely, my eyes catching Terian's form waiting for me. I kept focused on him until we were down at the justice of the peace where John was hugging me, and then pushing back my veil.

As the justice of the peace said the traditional bit, I clasped Terian's hand tightly, and tried to breathe.

"Have you the ring?"

Theo handed the ring to Terian, who placed it on my finger. "I promise to love you, cherish you, keep you safe, and do my best to make you happy as long as you live," he said solemnly, slipping the ring on my finger.

I blinked back tears, then felt Jenny nudging me with Terian's wedding ring. I took the ring with trembling hands and put it on his finger. "I promise to love you, cherish you, and do my best to make you and our child happy, as long as I live," I said, my voice breaking as soon as I said the word child.

"I now pronounce you man and wife," the justice of the peace said with spread hands. "What has come together today let no force put asunder."

Light had been building in the sky, and as he intoned the words, the dawn broke, the light of the new sun searing my eyes as I looked at it. Then Terian kissed me and I forgot about everything but him, and the possibilities of our new life together.

Tara Fox Hall

THE END

SERENA

Chapter One

A normal weekday night in the diner, with me still busy flipping burgers at five minutes to closing. For us restaurant workers, ten at night meant the end of the workday, though the attached lounge was open until one a.m. The city of Rio de Janeiro loomed close enough to send us nightly traffic in Penedo, our small tourist town on its outermost outskirts, but too far away for any of the glamour or wealth of its inhabitants to fully reach us.

Don't think about that, Serena. Longing for what you don't have won't bring it to you. You've got a job to do. Just do it, so you can get home to bed.

My boss, Fred, was standing nearby, griping about the cost of beef. Then he abruptly switched topics. "Serena, I need you to fill in for Patty," he said gruffly. "She's going to be late again."

Big surprise. Patty was late for almost every shift she worked, and I always ended up working an extra hour while she had one last screw with whatever man she was calling her boyfriend this week. Yet Fred would never fire her. Patty's double D figure brought in the customers late at night, and her Latin good looks got the tourists in the mood for drinks in the adjoining lounge when she waitressed. Which was fine by me, as I always needed the extra money, anyway.

I nodded without looking at him, and finished my last orders, putting them on plates for him to take to our last customers. Then I undid my apron, and hung it on a nail. "I'm taking a fifteen minute break," I said, and headed outside to get a little air. Fast food tasted good, but the heavy grease sometimes got to my nose. I was part fox and part coyote, one of the mixed blood weres. Tonight, the scent seemed to cling to me like a second skin.

I looked up, leaning against the outside of the building, taking deep breaths to clear my head. The stars were somewhere above me, but I couldn't see much of them. The diner was located on a tourist strip, and the lights from the many nearby attractions lit up the skyline in both directions.

It would be nice to see the stars, I thought to myself futilely. Nice to be walking along some beach, and have someone to talk to...

"Jazz, get your ass moving!" a raucous voice yelled out, drawing my attention. Two men were hurrying into the front door of the diner, a third man trailing behind by a few paces.

Great. We were closing the kitchen in a few minutes, but Fred wouldn't tell these men that; he liked money too much. But he wouldn't be the one to cook their food. In short, there went the rest of my break.

I took one last look at the sky, then headed back inside. Fred was waiting for me. "Can you take care of the three men that just came in? Patty's still not here, and I need a smoke."

I nodded, and headed over to the table they were sitting at. "What can I bring you, boys?"

All of them ordered beer. I brought that to them quickly, and asked them for their food orders, hoping it would be something simple that wouldn't need to be defrosted first. They asked for another minute. I nodded but stayed there as they looked at menus, because I knew as soon as I moved away, they'd be ready to order. Customers were always like that.

While I waited, I looked them over, trying to determine where they were from. They were all wearing jeans and short-sleeved button down shirts over T-shirts. They didn't look like tourists, but they weren't dressed like local men in khakis and tank tops. Also, they were too pale skinned. Their tans were light, as if they spent most of their time in the dark. *Curious.*

The one who seemed to be the leader was tall, with short straight blond hair, styled so that the top was a little spiky. He had blue eyes of a light color, and fair skin. He wasn't so much handsome as masculine looking; his body was powerful, his upper body heavily muscled.

The man next to him was so handsome as to be almost delicate-looking. His hair and eyes were a rich color brown, like chocolate, and his hair was styled too, but in longer, loose curls hanging over his eyes and collar. He was also heavily muscled for his size, though not so much as his blond friend.

The last man had dark hair, and his skin was darker than his friends, almost swarthy. His five o'clock shadow was dark, and he had brown eyes, his expression affable.

Still, even as good-looking as this trio was, I wanted to go home. "Are you ready to order?" I asked impatiently.

All three men looked up. There was blatant interest their collective gaze almost immediately, which made me blink several times in surprise. I wasn't Patty, with her large breasts and her sultry bedroom eyes. I'd always thought of myself as plain. My skin was deeply tanned from being outside, and my body was fit, but not overly curvy. My brunette hair was long, normally falling halfway down my back in rich waves. Right now though, my hair was under a hairnet, tightly coiled up in a bun, and my body was covered in a large apron. I wasn't sexy, I just looked like a frumpy lunch lady. But their stares were telling me the opposite.

I blushed, and looked down at my pad of paper, pen poised.

The leader cleared his throat and began to give me his order. His voice had an odd faint growl to it, as if he were on the edge of action, tensed for something to happen. I shifted my weight, uneasy, but began writing.

As soon as I had their orders, I retreated to the kitchen, where I began to make their food. As I got the meat out, and began to cook the burgers, it dawned on me suddenly why they were interested. Those men were werecreatures of some kind. And somehow, they knew I was a wereanimal, too. *They're attracted because I'm a female. That's all there is to it.*

Relieved I'd solved the mystery, I settling into making the food. Patty came in a few minutes later. She went over to their table, and spent a little time flirting with them, trying to make sure that the tip she would get for bringing them the food I was making wouldn't be too small. I shook my head at her antics, but said nothing. I was used to her games.

I looked over every once in a while as I cooked, but didn't see the men doing anything interesting other than talking to each other. Were they just in town for the night? I had never seen them come in before, and I worked every night now, except Sundays.

I finished the food, and Patty took it over to them. They wolfed everything down in minutes, and then asked her to bring the bill. I sighed in relief. I am so ready to go home. I went in back, took off my apron, and grabbed my purse.

"Darlin!" Patty said, coming in the kitchen door in a rush. "Come on out! Those men you waited on want to compliment you on the food."

I gave her a look that said she had to be kidding me.

"I'm not kidding," Patty said, her eyes sparkling a little. "They want to talk to you. They're waiting by the register."

Nervous, I put down my purse, and went out to see what they wanted, wondering if this was a joke of some kind. But the three men were waiting for me at the counter. When they saw me coming, the swarthy one nodded to me and left the others, going outside. I reached the other two and looked at them expectantly. "Yes?"

"Hi," the blond one said, giving me a bold smile. "I'm Vince. This is my friend, Nick."

"Hello," Nick said, nodding. He was the handsome one with the brown hair.

"We wanted to compliment you on the food, and see if we could talk to you outside for a moment."

Butterflies were fluttering in my stomach, but I mustered a smile. Hadn't I just been hoping for someone to talk to? "Sure. Let me get my coat. I'm heading home."

"We'll meet you out front," Vince said with a smile. He and Nick left by the front door.

Patty really wanted to know what was going on by her expression, but I just gave her a winning smile, and got my things, leaving out the back door. I took my time walking to the front of the diner, feeling excited but also shy. I'd never been out with a man before, much less two at once. *Maybe they want to take me for a drink? What do I say? Do I want to go out with them?*

It might be fun to go out with a man. I decided that I'd say yes, if they asked me for a drink. It wasn't like I had anyone else interested in me. We rarely had younger single men come out this far from the city. Everybody born here went to Rio or another big city, as soon as they could afford it. This slowly decaying strip was a place for local retirees, tourists, and poorer senior citizens. To be honest, the five or so eligible decent-looking men that lived in town had never even given me a glance. Coupled together, that had led to a whole lot of nothing; I had never so much as been on a date before.

Nick and Vince were waiting for me near the entrance. When they noticed me approaching, both came over to meet me. I looked at them shyly, and didn't say anything.

"Look," Vince said softly. "We know you're wereanimal. We are, too. We have a proposition for you, if you are interested in hearing it."

I looked at him with curiosity.

"We got into town a month ago," Nick chimed in. "We've been busy, working most of the time. But even when we've been out, we haven't seen any weres. You're the first one."

"There aren't any here in town, except me," I said, giving him a shrug. "It gets lonely, sometimes."

"Exactly!" Vince added. "We have been lonely. We want to know if you'll consider being with us, for a price."

I was shocked to the point I think I stared at him for a moment with my mouth open. I knew what he meant, that it wasn't a drink he was asking me for.

"We don't mean to offend you," Nick appeased, seeing my expression. "But it was worth it to us to ask you, on the off-chance you'd say yes."

"We'll make it worth your while," Vince said gruffly. "A thousand dollars American, just for the one night. But we'd want you to stay with us 'til dawn."

I thought to myself quickly that I didn't have to work tomorrow until dusk. I could do it, if I wanted to. *A thousand dollars! That's so much money!* My rent was due in two days. I had been going to ask Fred for an advance on my paycheck to cover it. If I did this, I wouldn't have to.

"We don't want anything too…um, unusual, either," Nick said slowly. "We just want to be with a were, because even though you aren't bear, like we are, your body's more resilient than a human woman's body would be. We can't really enjoy ourselves with a human woman.

There's too much risk that we might hurt her, because we're so much stronger than human men."

I nodded. I understood that part of it now. They weren't interested in me for me. They wanted me to have sex with them because of what I was, and because there were no other weres within a few hundred miles to choose from. The thought made me a little sad, but I put it out of my mind. *You're lucky they only have you available. You need the money.*

"Will you do it?" Vince said, his words still with that growling undercurrent. "We need to know right now."

He's growling because he's so eager. An excited tremor went through me.

"Will you be safe with me?" I asked hesitantly.

"Yes," Nick said, nodding. "We'll wear protection."

I hesitated. I'd never been with a man. Never even kissed one. But a thousand dollars was more than I made in a month. Doing what they wanted would mean I could not only pay my rent, I could also take off the next months' worth of weekends, maybe even go to the beach and spend some time looking at the stars.

Under my human reasoning, my animal side was already clamoring for me to say yes. I hadn't been chaste my whole life from choice, only lack of opportunity and prospects. Faced with three hot prospects and an unbelievable opportunity, there wasn't any reason to say no. The only thing that worried my pragmatic human side was that this offer of theirs seemed too good to be true.

If they wanted to just rape me, or even have me by force, it would have been easy for them to follow me and take what they wanted. No man I'd heard of paid for something he could get for free. "Can I trust you to pay me when it's over?" I asked, unsure. "How will this work?"

"We'll pay you before," Nick said softly. "And each promise you that we won't hurt you. We just want some release. Our coupling will also be just in our human forms."

I shivered again, hearing his eagerness in his words. But this time there was no fear, only excitement and lust. "Okay," I agreed.

"Great!" Vince said, smiling widely. "There's a hotel down the block. Nick, you go there with her, and I'll go get my half of the money. I'll join you in a few minutes."

Vince took off running. A car started up down the block a few moments later, its headlights too far away to illuminate Nick and me.

"Come on," Nick said eagerly, taking my hand, and pulling me with him. We walked fast down the block, and into the lobby of the hotel Vince had mentioned, The Surf. I waited, smiling nervously as he rented us a room, looking around me at the loud seascapes painted in bright colors on the walls, and the distressed wicker furniture.

When he was finished, we went upstairs to the room. He unlocked the door, gave me a slight push inside, and locked the door behind us.

Nonplussed at his handling, which my animal side told me was eagerness to mate, I turned to face him. "Will he come in a few minutes or more like an hour?"

"When Vince gets here, he gets here," Nick said nonchalantly, all his attention on me as he approached. "But it will take him a while. He'll have to do it by scent, unless he asks the desk clerk. That's his own fault. He lost all his money on the pool games we played tonight. If he'd have been smarter, he would be here with us now."

Nick came close to me and grabbed me roughly. "I'm glad he's not here, because I want you first." He kissed me passionately.

Having never been kissed before, I wasn't sure what to do. I parted my lips in shock, and Nick thrust his tongue into my mouth, licking me, groaning. His mouth devoured mine hungrily.

His arms were tight around me, and then slid down my back to cup my rear, and pull me against him. I felt a hardness against the front of me, making my stomach turn strangely and my breathing quicken. My heart sped up and I took deep breaths through my nose, the scent of his desire electrifying.

I have no experience, what if I do something wrong?

You can do this. I was a woman; I had the right equipment. Rosa, my stepmother, had always told me that a smart woman let the man do all the work anyway. *I'll just do that.*

Nick broke the kiss, fishing out his wallet. He handed me five hundred dollars, which I slipped quickly into my purse. "Thank you," I said politely, then flushed.

Nick didn't notice my unease. "Take off your clothes," he said huskily.

I almost went into the bathroom to do it, stopping myself in one stride as I blushed even deeper. *You can't be shy now.* I took a deep breath, and began unbuttoning my shirt.

I slowly stripped off my clothes, until I was standing naked before him. By the end, my face was bright red, having never been naked in front of a man before. My lover-to-be was so busy struggling with his own clothes, he didn't notice.

Nick slipped off his underwear, and turned to me. When I saw him naked for the first time, I was shocked by how much I instinctively liked his body; the curves of it, the hard muscle, the leanness of his hips, and the dark hair that covered his chest. I also saw the male part of him, erect and tight against his body.

He pulled me hard against him for another rough kiss, then pushed me back on the bed, and laid his warm body on top of mine. I fidgeted, nervous. He hadn't put on a condom yet, and I hoped to God he wasn't expecting I would put it on him, because I didn't know how.

Nick kept kissing me, rubbing his penis on my pubic mound as he ground his hips into mine. "You're going to feel so good," he said huskily.

He got up off me, and took out a packet of condoms from his wallet. He put on one with practiced ease, and then lay down on top of me again. He took his penis, angled it down so the tip of it was against my vulva, then he bore down with his hips. As I felt his body began to slide into mine, there was a quick thrill of fear, then eager anticipation took hold of me, making me go perfectly still.

Nick slid himself into me, moaning, and abruptly reached my hymen with the tip of his penis. At that brief contact, he stopped completely. Drawing back, he looked at me, his expression one of disbelief. I bit my lip and looked up at him, not sure what to say.

He just looked down at me for a long moment. "What's your name, Sweetheart?" he asked finally, in a very soft voice.

"Serena," I replied.

"Serena," he said, nodding. "That's pretty. Well, Serena, I apologize. I didn't know it was your first time with a man."

I looked up at him, worried now about what he was going to do. *Would he not want me, because I was a virgin? Was our deal off?*

I needn't have worried. "I need to thrust hard into you, to take your maidenhead," Nick explained. "It may hurt. I'll do it fast, but I wanted you to know, so you can brace yourself."

I nodded. "Alright."

Nick slipped his hands under my rear, and held me firmly. With a forceful thrust, he pushed himself though, breaking my hymen and sliding himself fully into me.

"Ah!" I cried out, shaking under him. What he'd done had hurt.

Nick held himself still over me, and looked down at me. I looked up at him nervously, wondering what was next.

He kissed me softly, and again, my lips parted at once. This time, instead of using his tongue, he just moved his lips on mine gently. His lips felt sensuous against mine, and I slid my hands up to pull him closer to me. He kissed me harder, then opened his mouth, biting my lips a little as he kissed the edges of my mouth. I tentatively licked his tongue with my tongue, and he licked me back.

Slowly, I felt him slide himself out of me, and then back inside. He drew back from me, looking down. "Did what I just do hurt at all?" he asked, his eyes dark with desire.

I was tender there, but there wasn't any pain. "No," I said.

He smiled at me in relief, then began to stroke my body with his own. I held completely still for him, liking the feeling of him moving inside me. The sensation was so new to me, yet it felt completely natural and fulfilling. Nick groaned, and began to kiss me harder, kissing my face, my eyes, my neck. He dipped his head to my chest, and took one of my breasts in his mouth. I let out a gasp of sudden pleasure, and he sucked hard, cupping my other breast in his hand as he pistoned in and out of me.

Something was happening to me, a burning need building between us. I'd never felt anything like it before. Nick moved faster, and I began to move with him, pushing my hips up to meet his, liking the feel of him when he put himself all the way inside me.

"Do I feel good to you, honey?" he grunted, kissing my throat.

"Yes!" I gasped. "I...I never felt anything like this!"

"It'll feel even better in a few seconds," Nick groaned. "Oh, Serena!"

I didn't understand what he meant, but at that moment I didn't care. Nothing else mattered but the pleasure from our two bodies coming together. I tensed up, my body going rigid as Nick kept thrusting into me, stroking me. I cried out as utter joy suddenly washed though me.

I'm complete. I'm whole. This is so good!

I shook in Nick's arms, clutching his body to mine as my orgasm ebbed. Nick went rigid a few seconds later, then he shouted. His organ almost vibrated inside me as he pushed deep, then his hips spasmed against mine. He went limp against me with a sigh, then gave me a soft kiss.

Carefully, he held onto the condom as he withdrew from me. "God, that was good!" he said, grinning down at me. "Stay right there."

He got up, and threw the used condom away, putting on another one immediately. Rejoining me on the bed, he slipped back inside me easily and began to move again. Knowing now what was expected of me, I moved for him, eager for the warm thrill of climax. This time, we came together, holding each other tightly as he pumped his seed into me with a guttural shout. Afterwards, he threw away the condom, and hugged me close. "I'm glad you came," he said, kissing me. "I wasn't sure if I could bring you that first time, before I came myself."

So this is what Patty had meant, all those times she's talked about orgasms. I understood now why she'd been late so often. Who would want to hurry to work when they could be feeling this bliss?

There was a knock at the door. Nick got up to answer it. Vince strolled in, looking angry.

"What took you so long?" Nick said pleasantly.

"Fucking ATMs!" Vince growled angrily. "I had to go to three before I could find one with any money."

He took a sheaf of bills and stuffed them in my purse. Then he tore off his clothes in such haste I was surprised he didn't actually rend them. I marveled that his erect organ was bigger than Nick's had been, then felt a liquid rush of desire, wondering how it would feel inside me. Vince put on a condom, then moved to the bed where I waited.

"Be gentle with her," Nick cautioned.

Vince looked back at him, pausing. "Gentle? Why?"

"Because she was a virgin a few minutes ago," Nick said with a satisfied smile. "She's probably still a little tender."

Vince looked at me in awe, as he took me in his arms. "It's true, what he said?" he asked.

I nodded.

"I've never had a virgin," Vince said, obviously surprised. "Even an 'almost one'. Tell me, if I'm too rough."

He rolled on his back, and then lifted me astride him. The penetration of his substantially larger organ gave me a moment of discomfort, then it was lost in sheer pleasure as he began thrusting up into me deeply, crying out with each thrust. Vince grabbed my hips in his hands, and then he was moving me on him, sliding himself in and out of me fast. I let out moan after moan as I rode him, and before long I was crying out again as I crested the wave. As I cried out, Vince ground himself deeply against me, and my cry became a scream. "Ahh!"

Vince eased me off him, and got up on his knees. "Get in front of me, on all fours," he growled.

I did as he asked, my only thought what new pleasure he was going to show me.

He took my hips in his hands, and with a loud cry, he shoved himself into me again.

Soon he was thrusting as fast as he could, slamming himself into me. Within seconds, his penis pulsating inside me, he shouted out his release, digging his fingers into my hips. He withdrew immediately, and got up, pulling off the used condom.

I moved so I was sitting up on the bed, not sure of what I should do next. Nick came over and lay next to me, pulling me into his arms. Vince came back in a few moments, and lay on my other side.

"For a virgin, you're good," Vince complimented, his voice relaxed and cheerful. It was the first time I'd heard him speak without growling.

"Rest for a little, Serena," Nick said gently. "Sleep, if you want to. We'll mate again in a short while."

I nodded, and relaxed against them. But I was too excited to sleep, no matter that I felt relaxed, and also warm and comfortable. I felt like I couldn't believe what had happened between myself and these men I barely knew. Every caress of Nick's hands running over my body gently electrified me, making me want more. I finally dozed a little, lulled by the warmth of their bodies against mine, and the touch of Nick's hands.

Sometime later, Nick brought me close to him and slid his hands down over my body, running over my breasts to my waist to reach into my pubic hair gently. He caressed my thatch of pubic hair, and I went still beneath his hands. With a few movements of his fingers, he parted my folds, and slipped two of his fingers inside me. I shook a little and recoiled instinctively to have someone touch me so intimately.

He tightened his arm around me. "Easy," he whispered. "I'm not going to hurt you. You'll like this, promise."

I forced myself to relax as he rubbed my clit with his fingers. In a few strokes, the first stirrings of pleasure flooded me. Soon I was breathing hard in his arms as he manipulated me. Vince abruptly moved to take up position behind me, another condom already on his new erection. Nick kissed my breasts, sucking the tightening nipples. Vince pulled my hips back tight against his. With a deep thrust, he slid himself inside me again, bringing a cry from my lips. Then he was grunting, as he pushed himself in and out of me fast, his head buried in the side of my neck. Nick reached down his hand and began to rub my clit again. My orgasm began to build again immediately, my body awash in sensation.

Vince was thrusting into me very hard now, almost bruising me. Abruptly he roared, a guttural growl that seemed to shake the room. He pushed his body tight to mine, forcing my hips back against his with a flex of his powerful biceps. His body jerked again and again as he held me firmly against him, moaning over and over.

"Mmm, God!" he said in a raw tone, as he took a deep breath and let it out in a rush. "I needed that so much!"

Vince kissed me gently on the side of my face as he pulled out carefully. I felt him get up from the bed, and then Nick took me in his arms again.

"Serena," he said quietly. "I want you to try something for me. Okay?"

I gave him an unsure look, yet I nodded.

"I'll talk you through it," Nick explained. "Just do what I tell you."

I nodded again, and then Nick rolled over on his back, so I was on top of him. He took my shoulders in his hands, and then he pushed me down a little, so my head was on his chest. I looked up at him, waiting for directions.

"Kiss me," he said. "Just lightly, and work your way lower, as you kiss me."

I did as he asked, looking up at him as he watched me. Soon I was at his navel, and I was very conscious of his swollen flesh lying against his body just below my chin.

"Rest your head on my thigh," Nick said. "And give me your hand."

I did as he asked, so my face was inches away from his erection. He took my hand, and placed it on his swollen flesh.

"Hold me tightly in your hand, and run your hand up and down the length of me," he whispered.

I did as he asked, his penis flexing a little in my fingers, and he let out a groan. He took himself in his hand, and then he was rubbing the head of himself on my face. I didn't understand what the thrill was, but from the sounds he made, I knew he was getting turned on.

Nick rubbed the swollen head of his penis against my lips. "Open your mouth, Baby. I want to slide into you."

I complied nervously. Nick let out a sharp cry as he slid his erection between my lips. He trembled slightly. Though his penis was stiff within me, the skin itself was very soft, and I liked the feel of it against my tongue.

"Now, Honey, slide me in and out of you as fast as you can. Suck me hard, as you do it. But be careful of your teeth, so you don't cut me."

It was hard doing all three things at once, but I managed the best I could. Nick groaned loudly over and over as he felt my lips on him, caressing him, and his fingers went into my hair.

"When I tell you to, Baby, I want you to swallow."

I couldn't reply, as my mouth was full, but I figured he knew that.

"God, yes, Serena, just like that! Oh God!" Nick gasped, as I moved on him. I felt him began to tense a little, and he began to thrust into me, choking me somewhat.

"Now, Baby!" Nick yelled, and I made swallowing motions with my throat. I felt him spasming, and he was roaring loudly, over and over. He gave one last deep thrust into me, and I tasted a bitterness on the back of my tongue. I felt his dick vibrating, pumping his seed into my mouth, and I swallowed it down, trying hard to breathe in between swallows.

Then Nick withdrew with a last groan. I took a gulp of air in relief.

He was breathing hard, his body covered in sweat. He reached down, and pulled me up into his arms, and held me close to him. I looked at him with questioning eyes.

"You were wonderful, Serena," he said, still groaning a little. "God, you felt good! You were perfect, absolutely perfect!"

"I want to try that with her," Vince said jealously.

Nick gave me a long kiss, then he let Vince take me from him.

Vince laid me down on my back, my head up on some pillows. "Do what you did for him," he said gruffly. "I want you to know I'm going to be a little rougher than he was with you. But it shouldn't hurt you, Serena. Breathe in time to my thrusts, when I pull out of you, and you'll be okay."

I felt a jolt of fear, but I nodded.

Vince straddled my shoulders, so my head was right in front of his groin. He was erect again, his penis dusky pink with blood. He took himself in one hand, rubbing himself on my cheeks, and my lips. "Open your mouth," he growled.

He slid himself between my parted lips with a moan. Raising himself up, he leaned over me so his hands were on the headboard of the bed, and he began to thrust shallowly. I breathed as he'd said to, concentrating, and found I could get enough air.

"Suck me harder," he growled.

I sucked hard, hoping it wasn't too hard.

"Oh!" Vince cried, thrusting harder and faster.

His swollen flesh was a little too much to take. I slid my hands up to his hips in an effort to keep him from going so deep into my mouth. When he felt my hands clutching him, a tremor went through his body. He thrust even harder, to the point he was hurting me a little. Before I could react, he convulsed hard suddenly, and roared again loudly, "OH BABY! BABY! YES!"

I tasted him as he spurted into me, his organ almost dancing in my throat as he came. I swallowed again and again, timing my breathing to his movements. Finally, Vince slipped out of me with a loud sigh, his penis softening.

"You were great," he said, giving me a kiss on the cheek. "I loved feeling your hands on my hips, like you couldn't get enough of me!"

I hadn't meant it like that, but I didn't say anything. What would be the point?

Vince took me in his arms and Nick opened the bed covers up, and the three of us got beneath them. Vince held me close, his head on my shoulder. Nick did the same from the other side. Sated, I snuggled between them, feeling content.

"We need to rest for a while, before we do any more," Vince said easily. "Sleep for a few hours with us. You must be tired. You'll be safe, Honey. We'll be right here."

Exhausted, I dropped off to sleep within minutes.

Chapter Two

When I woke up two hours later, I wondered where I was. Then it all came back to me. Nick was still sleeping, his head pillowed on my breast, his arms around me.

Vince was awake, and looking at me, his blue eyes thoughtful. "Are you hungry?" he offered. "I was thinking of ordering out for pizza."

"Sure," I accepted, with a small smile. I liked pizza, but rarely ate it. Most of my money went for rent, so I almost never ate out. If my boss hadn't given me free food from the diner for half my meals, I'd probably been begging by now. I bit my lip, to get away from those bad thoughts. They wouldn't help me get less poor.

Vince shook Nick's shoulder, and my other lover sleepily opened his eyes. "We're getting pizza. You want one?" Vince said.

"Sure," Nick said, yawning. "Get me one."

Vince got up from the bed, and went to the phone. "What meat do you like on yours, Serena?" he asked as he dialed.

"Plain is okay," I said softly. I didn't want to act greedy, since he was buying mc food.

"C'mon!" Vince said jovially. "You're were, girl, you must like meat on your pizza!"

"Pepperoni, then," I acquiesced.

Nick was already asleep again beside me, snoring very faintly.

Vince ordered two everything meat pizzas, and one with double pepperoni. Then he gave them the room number, and hung up. "An hour," he said. "Good. We can sleep a little more."

Vince crawled back in beside me, and then he laid his head on my shoulder again. I dropped off to sleep, lulled by how comfortable I was.

A knock at the door awakened me. Vince got up, and slipped on his jeans. I went very still as I watched him grab a gun from the side of the

127

bed, and tuck it in the waistband behind his back.

Why does he have a gun? What do these men do?

Vince took some money from his back pocket, and went to the door. In a few minutes, he was back with three huge boxes. Nick roused himself, and put on his jeans too. Then he handed me his shirt, and I slipped it around me. I inferred from him giving it to me that he didn't want me to get dressed again, but he wanted me to feel comfortable as we ate. I buttoned the shirt, and it covered most of me, though I left some of the top buttons undone, as I'd seen women do in movies after coupling.

Vince brought the pizzas to the bed, and handed me mine. We all dug in. The piping hot food tasted wonderful. "Thanks. I don't remember pizza ever tasting so good before."

"It's the sex," Nick said, seeing my expression and giving me a smile. "Good sex makes you hungry. Food always tastes best after sex."

I gave him a smile back, and nodded, trying to eat delicately so I didn't drop any sauce on his shirt.

"So, Serena, how old are you?" Vince asked nonchalantly.

"Eighteen," I answered, feeling very young.

"We're both in our early twenties," Vince said, grabbing another piece of pizza. Nick nodded, his mouth full.

Not sure what I was supposed to say, I nodded again in response. What I really wanted was to know why they were armed. *Don't ask. You're probably better off now knowing.*

"Kev's going to be royally pissed off that he didn't come tonight!" Vince laughed, making his double meaning clear. "Jazz is sure to tell him we finally found a werewoman to hook up with after fruitless weeks of looking!"

"It's his own fault," Nick commented snarkily. "I told him to come with us, that we were going to hit a few new places."

Jazz must have been the man in the restaurant, the one who'd left. Why hadn't he wanted to join in? *Don't ask, you'll seem man-hungry. There must be some reason.*

Vince and Nick finished their entire pizzas in the time it took for me to eat two slices. They watched me finish one more, eyeing me hungrily in silence.

Serena

Wow, they want more. An excited thrill went through me, accompanied with a surge of satisfaction and pride in my newfound sexual power. "I'm full, for now," I said huskily, and set my unfinished pizza aside.

Nick slipped another condom on, then moved atop me as I lay back. He kissed me gently, then more thoroughly, as my eager lips sought his. He reached down and slipped his fingers in me, eliciting an eager gasp. "You're ready for me already?" he said, sounding very pleased, but also surprised.

"I want more," I said without thinking, then flushed.

Nick slid himself into me with a groan, and began moving. He went slowly this time, kissing me, rubbing my bare skin, and biting me gently with his human teeth. I writhed under him, wanting to feel him bring me to orgasm again. As we had before, Nick and I came together, crying out loudly as he emptied himself into me.

Vince watched us with hot eyes. As Nick rolled off me, he rolled onto me. He was much gentler than he had been before with me, kissing me, and sucking my skin between his teeth as he moved in me.

"Do you want to be on top again?" he offered, after a while.

I nodded eagerly, already pushing at him.

He rolled over in a quick movement, changing our positions while still attached. I began moving fast, grinding against him as he thrust up into me, panting hard. The thrilling feeling built almost immediately. I rocked faster on Vince, crying out, and he thrust harder, pushing my body down on his to take all of him in. A sudden climax washed over me as I screamed loudly, "Oh! Yes! Please don't stop! Please!"

Vince roared, his back arching off the bed, and I felt him coming, his body flexing over and over. When he finished, he pulled out of me, and threw away the condom. He was breathing hard, and he lay down beside me, running his hands over me again. "I love it when you scream for me like that," he murmured.

The next few hours passed the same way: sheer pleasure. I coupled with Nick and Vince a few more times each, and I went down on them both again, this time actively using my lips and tongue to intensify the experience for both of us. But the night, like everything else, eventually came to an end.

Nick shook me gently awake. "It's going to be dawn soon," he said, "We need to get back. We have to be at work at eight."

"Shit," Vince grumbled. "I forgot we had early duty."

"It's because of fucking Lash," Nick griped. "He's worried that Ruler Perseus is going to find out Dev's here in his territory, and he's paranoid."

"He is right to be paranoid," Vince said gruffly. "Perseus is bad news. Dev tangled with him once before, with Perseus getting the shaft. He'll come for some of Dev's hide, if he knows he's here. Dev's not stronger than Perseus anymore, not since that fucking brother of his drained his power along with his blood."

"Leave it," Nick said flatly. "Danial wasn't to blame. He either did it, or Dev was dead meat."

"It was all the fault of that fucking bitch!" Vince growled, furious. "Everything is her fault! Why Xavier got killed, and Gerry, and Harrison."

"Leave it!" Nick interrupted harshly. "She had a right to try to defend herself."

"I'm glad Devlin finally gave her some payback last month," Vince said, a mix of mean satisfaction and arousal in his cryptic words. "Kev was there. He heard everything that happened."

"You never told me that!" Nick said, shocked. "I thought he just saved her that night! What did he do to her? What did Kev hear?"

"Kev drove them to a hotel, because the sun was coming up, and they weren't going to make it to Hayden. Titus was off on his little vacation, still upset from breaking up with Leri, and Dev couldn't get a hold of him. And Lash and you were with the other bears cleaning up at Alphonse's."

"I know all that! Tell me what happened!"

"Kev said that Devlin drank her down, because she stupidly offered to feed him," Vince said with relish. "He waited until she was asleep, and then he undressed her. She started dreaming of her cougar honey, and Devlin pretended to be him."

"No WAY he did her as she was sleeping!" Nick said in disbelief. "I've seen him! She would've woken up!"

"She woke up right before he started to," Vince said wickedly.

"Then he forced her to let him have her. Kev said she was fighting Dev, but Dev had her anyway. Then he tricked her, made her think he was sleeping. Kev was just coming back from breakfast, and he saw her try to run from the room, and Dev grab her by her hair, and jerk her back inside."

"Then what happened? Tell me!" Nick demanded.

"Dev had her every way to Sunday," Vince said, grinning. "Kev reported she loved it. She's a screamer too, like Serena here."

I flushed red, but neither of them noticed.

"Kev also said she did something to Dev the last time, and he screamed so loud it was like an earthquake. As it was, he had to pay off a few of the hotel workers, so they all didn't get thrown out of the room!" He paused. "He said that Devlin sounded like she rocked his world."

"Get real!" Nick said, rolling his eyes. "The man's been with thousands of women. Why would this one be any different?"

"Kev said something happened," Vince said in a low serious tone. "He could hear the two of them talking all sweet and lovey, then she was yelling at him, and he began to yell back. He said he heard the shower start, and Devlin came out, and told him to call me, to have me come and pick Kev up, to give him a ride back to Hayden. Now you tell me something didn't happen, that Devlin told his only guard to get lost. What's more, you know her and that cougar are married, Nick. Yet it's been a month, and there's no sign of him coming here for a piece of Dev. Lash is worried about that too, I think. So where is he?" He gave Nick a triumphant smile.

"You think she didn't tell her husband what Dev did to her?"

Vince nodded.

"Why?" Nick said.

"Simple!" Vince explained. "She liked it! She can't say anything, or it'll look like she just had sex with him willingly, and reconsidered later, and now is saying he forced her."

"Devlin's got balls as big as church bells, to cuckold that cougar," Nick said, awe again in his voice. "Theo's reputation would be enough to make me not even look sideways at her."

"I don't think Dev did it just for the sex," Vince growled darkly. "It wasn't her blood, she'd already given him that. I think he wanted her to

131

love him, though I can't understand why."

"Twisted," Nick said, awed. "You think it was more than sex to them?"

"I think Dev got more than he bargained for," Vince said, nodding. "I think that we haven't seen the end of him and her."

"I don't see where you are getting all of that," Nick said, giving Vince a hard look. "Dev's had sex with a different woman every night since he got here, sometimes more than one. He's the same as he always was."

"Really?" Vince said darkly. "Then why did he go to a specialty jeweler before we left the States, and place an order for a choker? One with a gold bear with green emerald eyes."

Nick's mouth dropped open. He stared at Vince, his expression akin to horrified.

I had stayed silent this whole time, listening and trying to make some sort of sense of what they were saying. It was clear they were talking about a man who'd seduced a married woman and implying some kind of dire consequences, though they obviously didn't know the reasons behind what had happened. But the rest I didn't understand. *Chokers? Cougars? Sharing blood?*

"You think he loves her?" Nick uttered finally.

Vince nodded. "I think he's sending her the choker, and asking her to come to him here. She'll probably do it, too. You know how women are with Dev. They fall all over themselves trying to make him happy."

"Shit," Nick swore. "I never thought I'd ever see the day he loved any one woman. He's too much of a legend! He's always been a personal inspiration to me."

"Me, too," Vince agreed. "I'm hoping she says no. I don't want that bitch for my mistress. I'll be damned if I'm going to protect her."

"I wouldn't worry about it," Nick assured, yawning. "That cougar is not going to let his wife go without a fight, especially not to Dev. He hates him. And she'd be crazy to come. Remember what Dev did to her years ago?"

"Speaking of going, we have got to get moving," Vince said abruptly, appearing to notice I was listening. "Or we'll be late. Lash'll take it out of our hides."

Nick sighed as he and Vince got up, and tugged on their clothes. I watched from the bed, unsure of what to do.

"You can stay here, honey," Nick said, giving me a kiss on the forehead. "Checkout isn't till noon. Get some sleep, and just return the key before you head home."

"All right," I said.

Nick kissed me again on the mouth gently. "I'll see you again soon, Serena," he said with a smile, then he left.

Vince grabbed the two empty pizza boxes, and then he looked at my reflection behind him in the mirror a moment, as I sat watching him from the bed. He put the boxes down, then came over and sat on the bed near me. "Did you like spending the night with us?" he asked, his blue eyes looking into mine.

I nodded.

"Would you want to do it again?" he continued. "Same money, same kind of sex?"

Sincere, yet to the point. I considered his offer fast, knowing that if I didn't agree I ran the risk of not being offered this again. That I wanted the sex again was a simple yes. My animal side had no issue with my behavior. It was my human side that was cautioning me against a repeat performance. *Was what I did so bad?* I was sure some people would think so, but really, how different was it from what Patty did? The only difference was that I was making a lot of money besides just enjoying myself. "Yes," I said quickly, before I thought anymore and found a reason to say no.

"Would you be willing to do it for other friends of ours, too?" Vince continued. "There are at least another five werebears I know who would be glad to pay you for your time."

My eyes widened at his implication. "Are they like you?"

"They aren't all as handsome as me," Vince answered with a grin. "But we're all the same age, yes. We're all guards and werebears, so our bodies are pretty much the same, too."

He was offering to pay me regularly to have sex with his friends and him. This wasn't one night of daring; technically, this would make me a prostitute, the same girl who'd been a virgin just yesterday. The human half of me was shocked that I was even considering it, but the animal half was all for it, as long as it included sex with other fit males and possibly food. *What should I say? Truth is probably best.* "I've never done anything like last night before. But I enjoyed myself a lot. I might be interested in a regular arrangement, but I'd have to meet your friends first."

"Are you working tonight at the diner?" Vince asked.

I nodded. "Same shift as last night."

"I'll bring someone to see you, right before closing. Okay?"

"You're on," I said with a smile.

Vince gave me a quick kiss, obviously relieved. He grabbed the two empty pizza boxes again. "See you later, then," he said, then left.

I lay there in bed for a while alone, considering how my life had changed and where it might be heading. Yesterday, I'd been a virgin who'd never been looked at twice, and on the edge of poverty. Today, I had enough money to pay my rent for the next two months, the memory of a night like one of the erotic romance novels I loved to read, and the promise of more money and nights of passion to come. Yes, I knew on some level I'd sold myself, but it didn't feel wrong to me. I'd enjoyed what I'd done with Nick and Vince. Patty did the same thing with many men for free. So why couldn't I? And why not do it again, if it was what I wanted?

Not coming to any specific resolution, I ate more of my pizza, and watched a little TV. I wasn't tired, even with being up half the night. I was sweaty, though, and so took a long hot shower, dressing again in my clothes afterwards. After, I finished the pizza, then grabbed the room key and my purse, and headed downstairs to check out.

The walk home felt like a jaunt to me; my mood was ecstatic and I couldn't help smiling at random strangers as I passed them by. Once back at my apartment, I hurried to put on fresh clothes, choosing the best ones I had.

I got to the diner just in time for my shift, and took up my spot behind the grill. Fred nodded to me like he always did, then went back to his paper. The normal action made me feel strange. I felt so different inside now that I expected him to notice somehow. Yet oddly, on some level, his normal routine brought a measure of relief, too. *I'm still the same ordinary Serena I've always been, if I want to be.*

Serena

The day passed by quickly. As it got later and later, I wondered if Vince would really come again to see me. I tried to relax, but butterflies flitted in my stomach. *I want him to come. What if no one comes?*

My shift ended with no visitors or sign of Vince and the other. As I closed up, I felt a little sad, wondering if they had found another were girl who was prettier. *That doesn't matter. I have money now. And I have the memories.*

I grabbed my purse, calling goodnight to Fred. As the back door swung shut behind me, a rich, euphonious voice called my name, causing me to turn. "Serena?"

The man walking toward me had to be the most handsome man I had ever seen. He was dressed in a white shirt, and some fitted cotton pants, also white. He had on some kind of soft leather shoes. His blond hair was to his shoulders, curling softly, and a day's growth of beard covered his face, making him appear like one of the foresters who sometimes visited the diner. But his outfit and very pale skin told me he was wealthy, probably a tourist. "Yes?"

He came closer, stopping directly in front of me. "Vince told me who you were, and where to find you," he said, his lilting voice so intoxicating it seemed to be caressing me. "My name is Devlin Dalcon. Vince and Nick work for me."

So this was Dev, the womanizer that they had been talking about. "It's good to meet you."

"I can see from your expression that my men were talking about me," Devlin purred in pleasure. "I can sense your arousal."

I blushed, then looked in his face and noticed his eyes for the first time. They were an unusual golden color, almost like honey when the light hits it and shines through it.

He stared at me, his 'come hither' smile widening. I blushed deeper.

"Get to it," a hissing voice said. "We can't stand out here all night, so exposed."

There was another shorter man behind Devlin, facing away from me. He was dressed in black from head to toe and seemed to be watching the street.

"Serena," Devlin continued. "I want you to consider coming to work for me. I know what you did for Nick and Vince last night, and Vince told me you said you would enjoy doing it on a regular basis for him and Nick. He said you would consider doing it for other of the werebears in my employ. It would be easier all around if you worked for me, instead of having them pay you in cash time by time."

Does he want to be my pimp? Put off, I gave him a suspicious look.

Devlin blinked, then bit his lip, as if he were trying to keep from laughing. "I'm not suggesting this to make money off you, Serena. This is about safety and security. I want you to come and live at my estate near the beach, overlooking the water. You can take care of the needs of my male guards. No one will have to rent hotel rooms, and you won't have to worry about getting money up front, or having someone get rough with you, or not paying you."

Was he implying some of his men were thugs, that they would cheat me? "What are you offering?"

"I'll give you the same amount of money for every night, no matter who comes to you. Even if no one does, though I don't imagine that will happen often."

"What do you get out of this?" I interrupted.

"My single men have been fighting lately amongst themselves from the strain of being celibate," Devlin explained "Lash has had to break them up, and he has better things to do."

"You're God damn right I do," the hissing voice griped.

The man in black must be Lash, Vince's boss. He must report to Devlin.

"I need them relaxed, with their minds on their work," Devlin continued. "If I don't act now, things will just get worse." He paused. "I'll have a portion of their paychecks taken out to go toward your salary, for all the ones who want to be serviced by you. I wouldn't be paying all of your salary myself. Some of my men have their own mates, and they won't need your services."

"Would I pay you rent?" I asked. "What about food?"

"Room and board would be included," Devlin said. "And you will have at least half of every day to yourself, usually in the day hours, for sleeping and doing whatever you want. But most nights, you'll need to work."

"Could I see your home before I give you my answer?"

"Of course," Devlin said graciously, offering me his hand. "I want you to come there tonight with me. Right now, in fact."

Chapter Three

I hesitantly took Devlin's hand. He led me to a black four-wheel drive vehicle, and opened the door for me. I got in the front passenger seat. He closed it, then got in the back seat as the man in black settled in the driver's seat with another curse. The man started the SUV, then looked up to lock eyes with me. His eyes were cold, like the eyes of a lizard. "Put on your seat belt," he hissed. I glimpsed his fangs, curving back in his mouth, almost hooked.

Fear flooded me. I held in my scream, swallowing hard instead. *Lash is some type of weresnake. He has to be with fangs like that.* Why didn't he have normal teeth, or normal eyes? Were all weresnakes like this, or was he purposely staying partly changed to look more frightening? *Will I have to sleep with this man as part of the deal?* If so, I couldn't do it. It was all I could do to be this close to him.

"If you're done staring, put on your seat belt," he said, this time his tone holding a trace of amusement.

I did what he said, silently. Lash drove us out of the tourist section, and out towards the coast.

"Tell me, Serena," Devlin whispered in my ear, as he leaned over the seat. "Are you alone here?"

I shot him another suspicious look. "Yes."

"Wereanimals are seldom alone, especially the furry four-footed ones, as I smell you are," he answered, smiling. "And you are not mated, nor do you have a lover. I find that unusual, from what I know of weres."

He isn't were, by his scent. Maybe he's some type I've not smelled before? All I knew scent-wise was my own scent, the rusty, musky scent of werebear, and now a musty earthy scent I surmised was weresnake. "My father died," I answered, shrugging. "My mother died having me. I didn't have money to go to the nearest city, Rio. I've heard there are

138

some weres there."

"There are weres in Rio," Devlin said, nodding. "But mostly snakes, and some monkeys, a few cats."

"Fucking cats," the dark man snarled. I gave him an anxious look.

"Yet even with the distance, it is odd to me that you weren't driven to seek out a mate," Devlin whispered, still in that seductive tone. "That the longing to be filled wasn't in your blood."

His words aroused me, bringing images to mind of my night with Vince and Nick in vivid color. "I didn't think about sex," I said honestly. "There was never anyone around who I was attracted to, not even humans."

"Interesting," Devlin said absently, sitting back.

"So she's a late bloomer," the dark man said, annoyed. "Better late than never."

I flushed, as Devlin laughed.

The rest of the drive was silent. Soon we were stopping before a huge villa. I got out, my eyes wide. *This place is beautiful.* The palm trees were huge, and there were so many flowers and terraces and statues, it truly was an estate.

"Get inside," Lash hissed in my ear, giving me a little push toward the front door. Devlin was already there, speaking in a language I didn't recognize. I hurried to catch up with him, stepping quickly over the threshold. The weresnake came behind me, striding fast as he looked around us, as if expecting an imminent attack.

The place was a mansion, the bright white furniture overstuffed and comfortable, like I'd seen in that magazine *Beach Living* that Patty sometimes let me borrow. I looked up at the curving spiral staircase, and wondered how I'd gotten here. I wasn't the kind of girl who found herself in mansions. "This is just stunning."

"I'm going out to check our borders," Lash hissed to Devlin. "Call my cell if you need me."

"Watch yourself," Devlin advised.

Lash nodded, going back out the front door with a loud slam.

"Come upstairs," Devlin said. I followed him up the staircase. "This would be your room," he said, stopping beside a door, and opening it.

I walked in, looking around in disbelief. The bed was huge, king size with a canopy, and there were a few dressers and a vanity. The attached bathroom had a sunken tub, and a large shower. There was real marble on the floor, and everything was sparkling new, or at least, had been very well cleaned. Most everything was white, or grayish white, except the blue bedding. "It's beautiful," I said softly.

"Then you agree?" Devlin asked, studying me with his golden eyes. *Don't be wowed. You need to be smart.* "How much money?"

"Two hundred a night," he said. "It's less than you made last night, I know. But that will all be going into your pocket. You won't have any expenses. I'll pay for everything else you need, be it health care, toiletries, even lingerie. And, as I said, you'll have a measure of protection with me handling the business end of things for you that you wouldn't have trying to go it alone."

"Do I have to have sex with anyone who comes to me?" I whispered. "Whatever they want?"

Devlin studied me. "You don't want to be with Lash."

I nodded.

"Know he wouldn't hurt you," Devlin said quietly. "But I'll exclude him. He is the only male were here who already has a werewoman he goes to, a boa. He won't need your services."

That was a relief. A big one. I nodded.

"As far as the types of sex, I'd expect you to willingly do anything within reason," Devlin said carefully. "The bears are mostly going to want regular sex and oral sex, Serena. Nothing you haven't already done. Anything besides that is left up to your discretion."

"Agreed," I said, feeling an excited thrill. I pushed it down, feeling guilty at my lust, then told myself that guilt didn't matter. *I'm doing this, because I want to. And it's okay, because it's what I want to do.*

"Take these," he said, and handed me a packet of birth control pills. "Condoms break," he added flatly. "Take these every day, and you won't get pregnant. Then you won't have to use the condoms at all, unless you want to. While the odds of two werecreatures of different species mating successfully is low with regular sexual intervals, you're going to be having far more sex than the average werewoman, Serena. That makes pregnancy a very real possibility, one that must be contemplated."

That wasn't the only possibility. "What about, um …?"

"Diseases?" Devlin supplied.

I nodded.

"Nick and Vince got tested today," Devlin explained. "They told me they were bare with you orally. I've seen the results, they're fine, but I want you to be healthy. Some of the other men are getting tested tomorrow, and I'll tell you the names of the ones who are safe. No one is going to endanger you, at least while we're here, and you're the only were they can be with." He paused. "But we won't be here forever, Serena. So if you are worried, or ever suspect that maybe someone has something, for any reason, you can refuse anyone you like for one night, and demand he go and test himself. If the test is clean, I will expect you to service him, but if it's not, or he refuses to get tested, you tell me his name, and Lash will take it out of his hide. And you will never be with him again. I don't want anyone making you sick, Serena. That's not only bad for you, but everyone who's with you would get sick, too. I can't have that. All the men are aware of what I expect of them, so you shouldn't have any problems. But tell me, if you do, and I'll take care of it."

I was feeling better and better about this deal. I hadn't thought last night about how I could have caught something from Nick or Vince, by going down on them. I'd thought the condoms had made me safe, and I felt very foolish and naive for just letting them do what they wanted with me. "Agreed."

"Good!" he said, giving me a smile. "Go and take a shower. Then dress in the robe that is on your bed, and come to the room at the end of the hall."

I blinked at him. "You want me to start tonight?"

"I'm not paying you tonight," Devlin said, his voice purring. "Tonight is for lessons, little dove. Do as I say."

Then he shut the door behind me, leaving me alone in my room with my thoughts. As I showered, I considered my options, wondering if this was truly a path I should be on. I'd always considered myself a good girl, and also a Christian. But where had all my solitary prayers gotten me? It hadn't made me less poor, or found me so much as a good friend, much less a lover or a mate. I wanted something for myself, to be happy, not just alive. There was no one like me in town, and not likely to be anytime soon, except Devlin's men.

What am I losing by doing this? Only my job. And it wasn't that great of a job anyway. I smiled, then put my head under the spray. *Damn the consequences. I'm doing this.*

* * * *

Nervous, I knocked on the door at the end of the hall an hour later. *What kind of lessons am I going to be getting? Probably sexual positions, or S&M techniques.* I fidgeted, then made myself be calm.

"Come in," Devlin called.

I walked in to find Devlin lying reading in his bed. He looked up, then put the book aside. "Come over to the side of the bed."

He stood up, as I came to stand before him. "Is it true that you were a virgin when you gave yourself to Nick and Vince?"

"Yes."

"Interesting," he said again, studying me.

I looked back at him, feeling very self-conscious. "I needed the money," I said finally. "And I was curious."

"You're wondering why you're here," he said.

"I'm guessing it is to learn about sex, other than the very little I know," I replied.

He nodded. "I am going to pay you for pleasuring my men. I know you know only what Nick and Vince managed to show you last night. To do your job well, you need more than that. So I am going to spend tonight ensuring you know exactly what to do so they get the most pleasure, and also so you know what to ask for. Nick told me you climaxed, but there's orgasm, and then there's satisfying orgasm. A woman who has neither becomes bitter, with time. And a woman who has only the former gets bored with her lover. You have the right to ask the men you're with to give you the kind of release you like best, whether it's regular sex, or oral. Tonight, we'll find out which you like better."

I didn't say anything, though I was flushing red again at his words.

"Just because you are getting paid doesn't mean your enjoyment of the act isn't as important as your partner's," Devlin added. "I believe that the best sex is between partners who give and receive the most pleasure possible." He smiled. "First lesson: don't be shy about asking for what you want. Being someone's lover is an art. It takes honesty, and also the will to please, not just skill."

I nodded and kept my eyes on him, showing I was listening.

"Unbutton my shirt, Serena. Do it slowly, one button at a time."

I did as he asked, my fingers shaking a little.

"Now ease it off my shoulders," Devlin said.

I did, letting it fall to the floor.

"Take your hands, and run them over me. Caress me," he commanded.

I touched him gently, putting my hands in his golden chest hair. His chest was hard under my hands, though he was not as muscular as Nick or Vince.

"Sit on the bed," he said softly as he came to stand in front of me. "Take my right nipple in your mouth."

I bent my head, and sucked it gently into my mouth.

"Caress me with your tongue," he whispered.

I did as he asked, enjoying the nub harden under my lips.

"Yes," he groaned. "That's good. Now do the same to my other nipple."

Again, I did as he asked, my tongue stroking his tightening skin.

He pushed me back from him. "Undo my pants," he said huskily.

I untied the drawstring and pushed the fabric down, revealing his engorged pale erection. A jolt of fear ran through me, as I took a sudden breath. *He's huge, much bigger than Nick or Vince.* I hadn't known a man could be that big.

"Shh," Devlin assured, his hands on my shoulders. "I'm not going to hurt you. Take me in your hand."

I reached out and grasped him gently. He took a long breath at my touch, then released it. "Examine me," he said.

I looked at his hard penis, not sure what he wanted from me. *Am I supposed to tell him how magnificent it is?*

"The tip is the most sensitive part," Devlin instructed. "When you give a man oral sex, pay close attention to the tip, which is called the head. Some men will look different than I do, if they aren't circumcised. Don't be afraid, if one of my men is like that. The sex act will be the same."

I nodded to show I was listening.

"Now make a circle with your hand, and slide it over the head," Devlin said.

I did as he asked.

"Grip a little tighter," he corrected, smiling.

I blushed, and squeezed. He flexed in my hand, the movement of such a large organ making me shiver. I rubbed him lightly, stroking the length, then with a start, I realized that his body was cool, not hot like Nick's and Vince's had been. *He's too cold to be human.*

I released him, suddenly afraid, and looked up. Devlin smiled widely down at me, his twin set of revealed fangs delicately curving. *Yet he's no snake.* "What are you?"

"I'm vampire," he said. "My body is cooler than a human's body. But I enjoy sex just the same."

This is what Nick and Vince meant, when they said that woman he'd seduced had given him her blood to drink! "Are you going to drink my blood?" I whispered fearfully.

"Yes, when we have sex later," Devlin affirmed, nodding. "But only a little of it. And you'll find my bite pleasurable, Serena. This is not a horror movie. I'm not a monster out of legend."

I looked up at him unmoving, still afraid. "Do I need to take this off?" I fingered my cross, a gift from my father on my first communion.

"No," Devlin said, chuckling. "Your symbol of your faith holds no terror for me." He touched the cross briefly, then leaned closer, so his face was near enough to kiss. "That it would keep such as me away is just a story to make Christian believers feel safe, my dear. But be warned, there are many old and terrible things walking the world, and they are seldom in the shadows, or so terrible that you would know them on sight. And most will not even hesitate to do as they wish, no matter how much you believe."

I shuddered. He reached down, cupping my face. "I most likely won't be with you again, after tonight," Devlin said softly. "It's good if you are a bit wary of me. I don't want you to fall in love with me because of what we are going to share. Women, especially very young women, can confuse sex with love, and I don't want you to love me. We're going to have sex, but that's all. And after tonight, I expect you to call me 'Devlin,' or 'Dalcon,' nothing more informal than that. Now tell me that you understand that."

I nodded, and Devlin began speaking, as if he had never stopped giving instruction. "All men are different. Some will want you to stroke them in different ways than others. But all of them enjoy a woman's mouth on them. I'm not sure what Nick and Vince asked of you. So I want you to do to me what you did to them, and show me."

"I'm afraid to," I said honestly, daring a glance up into his eyes again. "I almost choked with them, and they were much smaller than you."

"I have something that will help with that," Devlin said. "Reach in the drawer beside the bed."

I reached over, and took out a tube. "Squirt some in your throat. It will numb your muscles."

"Will I be able to breathe?" I asked worriedly.

Devlin laughed richly. A shiver went down my spine at how his laugh caressed me. "You'll be able to breathe just fine. It wouldn't be very good for me if you passed out from lack of oxygen, Serena."

I blushed, doing as he asked.

"Give it a few moments to work," he murmured. "Stroke me with your hand, while we wait."

I ran my hand over his stiff flesh, sliding it up and down the shaft of him, and he began to breathe faster, flexing again and again. The head of his penis dripped out a little fluid, lubricating him, so my hand moved on him easier.

Devlin's eyes were hot now, as he watched my hand stroking his erection. "It should have taken effect by now," he said in a sultry tone. "Go down on me, Serena."

I did what Nick had asked of me, first rubbing my face on him, then taking him into me, sucking him hard.

"Not so hard," Devlin corrected gently. "At least, not at first. That's for later, at the end. Caress with your mouth, kissing, and teasing a little. Run your tongue over the head, and slide my organ slowly in and out of your mouth."

I did as he asked, and after a few tries, he told me that was right. "Do that for a while, until the man begins to try to push himself into you," Devlin added. "At that point, he's ready for you to begin moving your mouth on him, what is called 'deep throating', or 'giving head'."

I took Devlin into my mouth, and slid him all the way into me. I didn't gag, so I knew the stuff I'd swallowed had to have had the effect he wanted.

"Put your hands on my hips," he commanded.

Remembering Vince, I did. Devlin took my head in his hands, then gently moved me on him. When I found the right angle and rhythm he wanted of me, he let me go. "AHHH!" he groaned. "Very good!

I moved on him, sliding him in and out of my mouth slowly, as he groaned over and over. Yet as the moments passed, I waited for him to come, and he didn't. He just sighed and groaned intermittently as I stroked him. I kept moving, not knowing what else to do.

"You'll feel a man's organ begin to throb, when he's ready to come," Devlin groaned suddenly, as I moved on him. "I'm nearly there."

Almost immediately, I felt his penis begin to spasm a little. "Move faster!" he commanded.

I hastened to obey.

"Take a deep breath," he hissed.

I gulped air, as he withdrew slightly. Then he plunged himself all the way into my throat, holding my head so I couldn't move back, and I had to take all of him. I shook in his arms, fighting a little even as I told myself it was okay, I had air, because he had warned me.

"AHHHHH!" he shouted, his cock spurting cum into my throat. Yet he was so deep in my throat I tasted nothing. He jerked, his body convulsing as he held me tightly, his penis still completely within me. I began to fight him when I ran out of air, and soon after, he was slipping out of me. I coughed a little, taking in a deep breath gratefully.

"Very good!" he said with obvious approval. "I think you deserve a reward, my dove. Stand up."

I stood shakily, and he undid my robe, pushing it off my shoulders so it fell to the floor. "Your body is too thin," he said, looking me over. "I want you to eat more, and put on a few pounds, Serena. Women should be curvy."

I blushed, as he pushed me back on the bed. "Lay down," he said.

I lay back. He leaned over me, studying me for a few seconds,

146

saying nothing. Then he began to kiss me, starting with my toes. Working his way up my body, he caressed me with his hands and his lips, licking me and running his fangs over me, pricking me gently. I'd never felt anything so good in my life. I was writhing by the time he lay next to me, and took me in his arms. Then, finally, he kissed me on my lips, and it was the best kiss of my life, even though his lips were cool. I parted my lips at once, and he thrust his tongue into my mouth, licking me sensuously, his fangs pricking my lips as I kissed him back.

When he kissed my throat, I tensed a bit, wondering if he was going to bite me, but he trailed down to my chest instead, and gently suckled me. I cried out over and over as I felt his mouth on my breast, biting and teasing. Then he moved to my other nipple, and gave that some attention, too.

Then he was moving lower, and I looked down at him, wondering what he was doing.

"Relax," he said, not looking up. "Cry out, if what I do feels good to you." Then he was parting my legs, and sliding his face in to kiss me on my opening. I gasped, and then I felt his tongue in me, and his mouth sucking me gently, as he thrust his tongue into me over and over. His fangs brushed me slightly, but they didn't prick me. I cried out, thrusting my hips up, trying to get him deeper into me. *He feels so good!*

Within seconds, that familiar feeling was building, and I began to jerk, crying out loudly as I climaxed for him. "Please! Please! Yes! OH! Oh! OH!"

Devlin gave me a final kiss, and then he moved up my body again, kissing me as he crawled up me. I felt him rubbing his shaft on me, and then he pushed himself a little inside, and I looked up at him in fear.

"Don't we need to use protection?"

"I can't get you pregnant," he said somewhat wearily, as if he'd said it hundreds of times before. "Or give you a disease. My body is exactly as it was four hundred years ago. And the virus that lives in my blood keeps me healthy."

I was skeptical, but he'd been so careful to tell me he didn't want me getting sick, I believed him. "Okay."

Devlin pushed hard, and slowly he got himself most of the way inside me. Before he was all the way in, I felt his penis hit something deep inside me. There wasn't room enough inside me for all of him. I held very still, not knowing if there was something I should be doing. *Can I make more room inside me somehow?*

"I am probably the largest man you'll ever have," he said, prideful. "Most men will not be able to reach your cervix, which is at the end of your womanly opening. If the man is long, as I am, you may feel them touch it, when they are as deep inside you as they can be. Know it won't hurt you, if they hit against it as they have sex with you. Some women find it pleasurable. I very rarely don't touch a woman's cervix, when I make love to her. I like the feeling, and I believe other men do as well."

Then he began to move, and I forgot everything but how he felt. He touched all of me at once, sliding over all of me, inside me, caressing me with his organ. I cried out over and over, shaking in his arms.

"I feel good, don't I?" he whispered.

"You do," I moaned, my head lolling with each thrust as fresh waves of pleasure rocked me. "God, yes, you do."

He moved a little faster in me, as my excited body lubricated me, my climax cresting close again. Devlin began to thrust harder into me, the orgasm rising up beneath me like a tidal wave. He was panting now as he worked himself in and out of me, our bodies covered with sweat. The cresting wave of ecstasy broke over me with a crash, and I came screaming loudly, as he drove himself into me hard. A few seconds later, he gave a harsh cry and I felt him spurt as he came, his movements slowing.

We lay there for a moment, him still atop me, and then he moved back from me, looked down at me below him, and gave me a smile. "I think you like regular sex better, Serena. But the choice of what you ask your lovers for is up to you." Devlin kissed me again, and began moving in me leisurely again, stroking me over and over.

I loved the feeling of him inside me. Nick and Vince hadn't felt like he did, and I knew it had to be because he was so much bigger than they were. No wonder that woman he'd seduced that day had enjoyed it. I'd thought her a little wanton, for being married and enjoying another man's touch. But how could any woman not love the feel of this man inside them?

Devlin brought me several more times screaming, and each time, he came as well. I didn't understand why he didn't need to rest, as Nick and Vince had. Maybe it was because he was vampire?

Finally, he withdrew from me, and lay by my side. I was exhausted, and I wanted to sleep, but I didn't know if I should. Were my lessons done?

I looked over at him. He was looking at the ceiling, his arms folded behind his head, a scowl on his face.

I wondered if he was thinking of that woman Nick had talked about, the one he supposedly loved. Deciding he had to be, I felt bad for him, that he loved her, and she wasn't here with him. He probably would much rather have spent the night in her arms than in mine. "I'm sorry she's not here with you, instead of me," I said without thinking, and then I flushed crimson. *How could I have said that! Good going, Serena!*

Devlin started and gave me a sharp glance. "What did you say?" he growled.

"I'm sorry," I said quickly. "I shouldn't."

"Repeat what you said!" he growled. "Immediately, Serena!"

Hesitantly, I repeated it.

"How do you know of her?" he said quietly. "Did Vince say something?"

"He said there was a woman who belonged to another man," I whispered. "And that you had been with her, loved her. That he thought she...mattered to you."

"Vince should learn to keep his mouth shut," Devlin growled. "I'll have Lash remind him of that tomorrow."

I said nothing, just tried to be as quiet as possible and not move. I didn't want Lash giving me any reminders.

"Your words are kind," he said finally. "I wish she were here with me, too. I miss her very much."

"Does she know how you feel?" I murmured.

"She knows," he said darkly. "But she doesn't love me. She loves her husband, the dolt!" He paused, and then swore. "I gave her the best sex of her life! Me! And she chooses to live with that Neanderthal!"

"I'm sorry," I said again, not knowing what else to say.

"So am I," Devlin sighed. "I don't want to feel this way anymore. I want to be free of her. But I think about her all the time, no matter how many other women I'm with. No matter how good the sex is. I think about the things she said to me, the way she looked at me..." He trailed off, and let out a deep sigh. "I think about going back to her, stealing her away in the night, and making her come be with me. But I'd just be killed. And she'd hate me anyway."

"Did you ask her to come to you?" I whispered.

"Yes," he sighed. "She hasn't replied. She hasn't written to me, or e-mailed me, or called me. My brother gave her some presents from me, and told me she liked them, though she burned a book I sent her."

Who was this woman? What was her hold on him? She must be a living goddess, to possess him so, him being so handsome, and charming.

"But I sent her a token of mine," he continued. "I know she must have gotten it, yet she doesn't contact me! I don't know if she's thinking about me, like I'm thinking of her, or if she's burned it like the book. I keep hoping she'll call, but it's been a month now." He paused again. "I'm losing hope."

"Send her a card, or flowers, or an e-mail," I suggested. "Ask her if she's thinking of you. What can it hurt?"

Devlin looked over at me, and nodded once. "You're right," he sighed. "It can't hurt. I'll send her a card tomorrow."

"You really must love her," I murmured.

"I do," he said, his honey-colored eyes tormented, "though it would be better for everyone if I forgot her, as she seems to have forgotten me."

"I doubt she's forgotten you," I whispered. My human impulse was to take his hand or rub his arm as a comfort. Yet my animal half warned that this apparent weak moment was not one where he would welcome casual touching by any female other than his love. "I'm never going to forget our time together, and it was just sex. She's probably thinking of you just as much as you are thinking of her. But she's got a husband to consider. She may be thinking of how to break it to him that she's leaving him. Or she may think you've moved on, because she hasn't heard from you."

"Why are you being so kind to me about her?" Devlin said, looking over at me searchingly. "What does it matter to you how I feel?"

"You've changed my life," I said quietly, still trying to be submissive, understanding instinctively that it was what he wanted from me. "I was living in a tiny apartment, scraping by and working every day with no affection or sex. Now I'm going to live in a mansion, and spend a good part of every day in bed, enjoying myself. I'm shocked how fast my fortunes have changed."

"I understand your gratefulness," Devlin said with apparent satisfaction. "Your life will be much more to your liking, I'm sure. I hope you'll be happy living here."

Devlin rolled over towards me, and took me in his arms. "I'm going to bite you now," he said, lust in his golden eyes. "Roll over on your stomach, Serena."

I rolled over obediently, bracing myself with my upper arms. Devlin moved atop me, and slid into me with a hard thrust of his hips, going deep enough I felt the press of his scrotum against my moist inner thighs. I groaned at the deeply satisfying sensation of his organ stroking my already wet channel, as he began to move in quick hard strokes. Together we strained for release, our pants like gasps of sheer need. He brought me screaming once more, my cries nearly howls as I felt some of my control over my human form lessen, fur sprouting on my forearms as my teeth sharpened and lengthened. At once, Devlin bit down hard on the side of my neck. He took deep long pulls in time to his thrusts, his swallowing interspersed with muffled groans.

There wasn't any pain at his bite, just a rush of pleasure that intensified the orgasm to the point I thought I was going to die. I shook all over, jerking under him, my screams turning to animal howling, then back again. As my orgasm ebbed, Devlin came again, his arms squeezing me hard as he bore deep one last time.

Devlin took one long last pull, then held his mouth over the bite, kissing it gently. He moved off me to my side, licking his lips thoughtfully. "You taste interesting. What mix are you?"

"Coyote and fox," I replied, flushing. "I'm a half-breed." Hesitantly, I felt the side of my neck he'd bitten. There was only smooth unbroken skin, and no pain. Somehow, he'd healed me.

"Ah!" Devlin said, sounding surprised and pleased. "I'll be wanting your blood again, then. I haven't tasted that particular mix before."

"Of course." *What other response can I give?* Asking if I'd be paid for that too made me feel churlish. *If he starts asking for it every week, then I'll address it.*

"You should go to your room now, little dove," Devlin said dismissively, kissing my hand. "You need to sleep. And I'm sliding into a malcontent mood, something I'm afraid is quite common lately. It's better if you go."

You don't need to tell me what I can already scent. I got up, and wrapped my robe around me. "Thank you for the lessons." *And the easy exit.*

"You're welcome," he said seriously, sadness in his honey-colored eyes. *He's thinking of that woman he loved, missing her.*

I shut his bedroom door behind me, thinking if that was what love was like, I was better off not ever feeling it.

Chapter Four

The next day, Nick came to my door at ten in the morning, and asked me if there was anything I wanted from my apartment. "I have the day off," he explained, grinning. "And I'm very happy you took Devlin's offer. So I'll help you bring your stuff here, if you want."

Belatedly, I realized today I'd have to officially quit my job at the diner. Already that seemed like a life so far removed from me that it was hard to imagine I'd ever lived it. *And thank God for that.* "Sure," I said brightly. "Let me get dressed."

Slipping my clothes from the previous night back on, I followed Nick outside to a waiting Jeep-like vehicle with no license plates and a few flattened boxes in the back. Vince was already there behind the wheel waiting, and he gave me a grin when he saw us. "I have the day off, too," he said. "I'll drive. Where to, Serena?"

I gave them directions, and soon, we were at my apartment. I was embarrassed as I let them in. Next to the estate they called home, this was a practically a closet, all of the furniture hand-me downs from neighbors that I'd picked off the curb on garbage day, and almost all the other décor items that I'd bought cheaply at flea markets. "Here it is."

"What should we start bringing?" Nick said, looking around a little curiously. "Do you want the furniture first? We may have to make multiple trips."

"None of the furniture is mine," I stammered, casting my eyes around at all the junk, which looked so cut-rate next to the furnishings of my new home. *None of this fits in my new life.* "I don't have much. Just the books, and the few plants there on the kitchen windowsill."

"I'll get those, then," Nick said, nodding. Vince and he began to load the books into their boxes, while I packed the plants in one large box, wrapping them in my threadbare towels to protect their clay pots.

Then I did a quick sweep of the apartment, choosing just a few clothes and other personal items. It only took an hour to pack up everything I owned, and load it in their vehicle.

My landlord came to see what was going on, and I explained to him that I was moving out. He said he was sorry to see me go, and gave me back my deposit, after inspecting my apartment to make sure I hadn't taken any of his furnishings. *Like I'd want them where I was going.*

As I walked down the stairs, it sank in finally that I wouldn't be coming back here again. Small as it had been, that apartment had been home for years now for me. *Since Rosa had left, and Father had died...*

"You okay?" Vince said, slipping his arm around my shoulders.

"I'm okay," I assured. "It's just been a lot to take in." I forced a smile. "Canids prefer routines. We're wired that way."

"That's normal for us weres," Vince said easily. "Your life is changing. It was a shock to us when we moved here, too. But we got used to it. You'll be fine in a couple days."

"You'll like living on the beach," Nick added, as he opened the Jeep door for me. "There's no one around at night. We like to become bear, and lay on the warm sand, and play in the water."

"You can join us if you want tonight, if you want to change, too," Vince chimed in, turning in his seat to look at me. "We never asked, but what canid are you? You smell kind of like a fox. I admit, I'm dying to see you in your fur."

I bit my lip, and looked at him.

Both of them saw my unease, and waited, watching me.

"I can't take my animal form," I said finally.

They gaped at me. "Why not?" Nick asked gently.

"I'm a half breed," I whispered. "My mother died having me. My father gave up trying to help me change when I was a few years old. He said there was something wrong with me."

"Asshole," Nick said in anger, then added quickly "Sorry."

"There's nothing wrong with you," Vince said with surety. "You should be able to assume at least one, if not both, of your parent's animal forms. Have you tried any by yourself?"

"No. There wasn't anyone around to show me what to do. And my father almost never changed form at all." I smiled bitterly. "He was too busy doing his own thing."

Vince looked inward, pondering. "I can ask Kev, he's turned women before."

"Really, you don't have to."

"We can show you how we do it, if you want to try," Nick said gently, reaching out to clasp my hand with his. "It's not healthy for a were adult not to change at all. It fucks with your mind, the doctors say." He flashed a smile. "Though not using those exact words, of course."

"I'm afraid to," I admitted.

"We won't press you to do something you're not comfortable with," Vince affirmed. "But if you want to try, we'll do our best to help you."

"Okay," I agreed, mostly so they'd drop the subject.

As we drove to my new home, I thought more about why I had never felt the urge to change form. *Was it tied to sexual maturity? Would I want to change, now that I was having sex?* My father had always said the animal side brought its own problems, that the human half of us weres was more than enough to deal with. For the first time in my life, things were going well. I didn't want any new problems raising their heads.

* * * *

Next, Vince, and Nick drove me to my job, where I spoke to Fred. He was sad to see me go, and told me that if I ever needed a job, to come back and see him. Patty was there, too, and I gave her a hug goodbye. She was plainly jealous of me, because neither Vince nor Nick responded to her charms and their attention was centered fully on me. Being desired made me feel good after years of being the unnoticed wallflower.

Afterwards, we went out for meat pizza, for which Nick said it was his turn to pay. Evening found us back at Devlin's estate, where the boys helped me unload the car and carry the boxes upstairs to my new room. We'd no sooner shut the door behind us after the last load that there was a knock on it.

Nick went and opened the door, revealing two men standing there. One was brown-haired, with brown eyes, though he wasn't cute as Nick was. The other was Asian, with jet-black hair, and dark eyes, though his skin was lighter than mine, like buttercream.

"Hi," the Asian one said. "Name's Brock, and this is Justin. You must be Serena. We got tested today. Are you free for the next two hours? And do you mind if we see you together?"

I looked at them, and tried to think of something to say. *Holy shit. What have I gotten myself into?* But Vince beat me to a reply. "Serena's seeing us for the next hour," he growled. "Then she needs an hour to rest, and put her things away. Come back at seven."

Justin growled, showing blunt but long fangs, and Brock took a step toward Nick.

Suddenly, a whip cracked loudly. Everyone jumped, especially Brock who let out a yell.

"That hurt!" His forearm was dripping blood from a long cut, which scabbed over quickly, then began the multi stages of rapid healing.

"Knock off that shit!" Lash said, his hissing voice hot with anger as he pushed in front of Brock, looking at the four men in succession. "There's enough of her to go round, if you don't abuse her. And I have orders from Dev to fuck up anyone who does. Got it?"

"We got it," all of the men said, in low voices.

Lash gave us all another hard look, then strode off.

"Fine," Justin said, grabbing Brock's healing arm. "We'll come back later. Come on, let's take a swim." They walked off together, Brock still growling about how it wasn't fair.

Nick shut the door, and came over to me. "You're going to have a busy night, so we'll be fast," he said eagerly. "For a week or so you're going to be so in demand you'll be tired of sex probably. But after that, most of us will be more 'once a week' kind of guys."

"Speak for yourself," Vince growled, kissing my neck. "I'm an 'every day' kind of guy. And I intend to take full advantage of a live-in lover."

I turned and kissed him. Nick began to undress me, as I lost myself in Vince's embrace.

* * * *

Nick was right, to put it simply. That night, I met Justin, Brock, Matt, and Gerry. The next night was Lars, Van, and Harald. I was also very embarrassed to see the sole mated wereman Jazz, at my door, until he said that he was there only to send a message for the one single guard who hadn't seen me yet, asking me to reserve two hours for him that night near dawn. "His name is Kevin, but he goes by Kev."

I agreed, relieved. From what the other guards had said and I'd overheard, Kev was the most trusted of Devlin's guards next to Lash, the very guard he'd sent on a mission into Rio the night I'd met Nick and Vince. Something to do with checking on the vampire Perseus's whereabouts, according to Jazz. He'd been gone for three days, but was due to return that night.

"Devlin said to tell you Kev will bring you health info tonight, when he comes to you," Jazz finished. "And to give it to Devlin tomorrow night, in the early evening."

Weird. Devlin had okayed all the men himself before they came to me for their first time, and I hadn't seen any paperwork for them at all. This one he must really trust, to not want to see the paperwork before giving permission. *Could there be some relation, with their names so similar? Obviously not a blood relative, but maybe an adopted son?* It was too soon to ask, and my gut feeling was that I was off base, anyway. "Okay."

Jazz left, and I went back to reading my romance novel, trying not to laugh at the heroine who was so smart about everything except her dealings with the man she loved. *Is this really how relationships are?*

Someone knocked at my door. I answered it. A husky-looking man stood there, almost the definition of tall, dark, and handsome. If possible, he was more muscular than Vince was. *Yow.*

"Hi Serena," he said casually. "My name is Kevin. But call me Kev, I like that better."

"All right," I said, nodding. "Please come in. What do you want tonight?"

I still felt a little odd, saying those emotionless words up front. But I'd learned in a very short time that getting expectations out of the way made my work easier, and more enjoyable, too. The other option was to get into bed and discover it through trial and error, something that I didn't have the energy for at that moment.

"I like regular sex, and oral sex," Kev answered easily, entering my bedroom. "But I like other stuff too, and I'm willing to pay you extra, if you let me do that to you."

Great, another one. What is that, over half now? Some of these bears were kinky, or at least wanted to try out things that they'd seen in porn movies—mostly bondage. Until now, I'd said no to all of them, telling them until I knew them, and trusted them completely, normal sex would have to be enough. But this was different; Kev was Devlin's close friend. I'd already refused Lash, and Devlin hadn't been happy about that. *Dare I refuse Kev's request?*

No. "Will what you want me to do hurt at all?" I said flatly. "I don't do pain."

"You might be uncomfortable, if you've never done it before," he said, sitting down on the bed beside me. He was noticeably trying hard to be less frightening, which only made me more uneasy. "But it shouldn't hurt. I'll agree to a safe word, also, if you want one."

"Safe word?" I echoed.

"I want you to act out a fantasy of mine I've had for a while. I want you to be someone for me, and say certain things. But I admit, doing something like this, it's easy to go too far, and forget it's a fantasy, not reality. So I'll tell you a word, and if you say it, I'll agree to stop what I'm doing immediately. That way, you really have complete control over the situation and won't feel scared."

I was scared already and he hadn't laid a finger on me. "Why would I feel scared?"

"Because I want you to fight me, and pretend I'm raping you," Kev said bluntly, his eyes glittering with lust. "And about halfway through, I want you to decide you love it."

I felt a little sick at his admission. Yet I'd been reading up on sex games in a book borrowed from Devlin on his orders, and what Kev was asking me to do wasn't unusual. Men often fantasized about this, that once a woman who didn't want them felt their touch, their object of unrequited desire would change her mind completely. "Who do you want me to be? I'll need some idea of what she would say."

"I'll tell you what to say," he interrupted eagerly. "I know the scene by heart, at least what she said, anyway."

I felt a sudden chill. *He's reenacting something he overheard but wasn't part of.* "You want me to be that woman of Dev's?" I blurted.

"Yes," Kev said abruptly with zero shame. "But you don't need to know any more than that, not even her name. I don't care about her. I just want that fantasy, because since I overheard them I've been fantasizing about it over and over."

If he wasn't going to call me by her name, what name was he going to call me? "I don't go in for swear names," I said, grimacing. "Not even if I am canine." One bear had called me a dirty bitch in the throes of his orgasm, and I'd thrown him out. He'd apologized, but I wasn't sure the news had spread.

"No names of any kind," Kev promised. "Especially no insulting ones. I just want you to be the female to my male, and sate my needs."

He's twisted, but he's acting professional. I can be professional, too. "Fine, then," I agreed, looking him in his eyes for the first time. "Now tell me the whole scenario from start to finish, so I can do what you want me to correctly."

Kev's eyes were a beautiful dark brown color, almost like the polished oak of my dresser. Yet the intent look in them scared me a little, in spite of their attractiveness.

* * * *

A half hour later, we began.

Kev came in, slamming the bedroom door behind him. I sat bolt upright in bed in a simple nightgown, pretending terror. "What? What are you doing here?"

Kev said nothing, he just began growling and taking his clothes off, almost ripping them in his haste. Then he dove onto the bed where I cowered, shaking.

"Please! Don't do this!"

"You know who I am!" he growled loudly, pulling me under him, and holding me still, pinning me with his body. "And why I'm here. You're going to get what you deserve tonight!"

"Please! No! Stop!"

Kev flipped me onto my stomach, sodomizing me with a possessive growl. He was not gentle, and I let out a real gasp at the sudden penetration. Yet he hadn't hurt me, though I'd never done this kind of sex before. The lubricated condom he was wearing helped.

"Feel that?" he whispered, ramming into me as fast as he could. "Feel me taking you!"

"Stop, please!" I cried, feigning fighting him weakly. "Please don't!"

"No one's done this to you before, have they? I'm your first!"

"Yes!" I cried truthfully, then switched back into character, continuing to struggle. "But please don't! Stop! Stop! No!"

Kev shuddered, and I felt him come. He gave a jerk, then swiftly pulled out of me, and stripped off the condom. Quickly, he entered me again roughly, but in the normal way. "I'm going to have you, girl!" he growled. "Every way I can think of! And you're going to come for me!"

"No! No, I won't!"

"Yes, you will!"

Kev began stroking me, and he knew what he was doing. While the anal sex hadn't been that enjoyable, his large organ felt wonderful, his touch reminiscent of Devlin's encounter with me. I felt the climax coming, but tried hard to hold it off, enjoying the sweet torture that I both desperately wanted to end and also wanted to last as long as possible.

"No! No! I don't want you! No!" I lied, my desire ratcheting up a notch because I could smell his desire for me, and knew he must also be able to smell mine. I was practically swimming in lust, I wanted to come so badly. Every motion of his body inside mine threatened to push me over the edge and I fought myself to hold back, knowing I was fighting a losing battle.

"You want it! You're begging for it! I can feel how much your body wants mine inside you, fucking you!"

God yes, it does. "No," I managed to gasp. "I...I...oh...mmmm..."

"Admit it! Say it! Say you want me to fuck you! That you want me to take you!"

"No," I managed once more, then felt the climax I'd been holding at bay shred my will. I surrendered wholly, my long groan of pleasure becoming screams. "Yes! Please fuck me! Take me! Don't stop! Please don't stop!"

Kev shivered all over, then began guttural roars, his fingers shifting to blunt black claws and back as he began to come. We finished together, shouting, clasping each other as hard as we could, our animal nails parting skin that healed before a drop of blood could be shed.

"Now for the last part," Kev growled, pulling me to my feet in front of him at the edge of the bed. "Get on your knees, woman. And show me some appreciation for your orgasm!"

I got on my knees, and bent my head, taking his unflagging erection in my mouth. He let out a scream, as I stroked him hard and fast with my tongue, sucking sensuously.

"Taste me!" he groaned. "Taste yourself on my skin, how much you liked what I did to you!"

I stroked him faster, deep throating him. He climaxed hard, shouting, pushing me down to take all of him in as he released everything he had left into my throat. After only a few jerks, Kev slipped out of me, collapsing back onto the bed, as I got to my feet. Tired and breathing hard as I was, I still got my robe and put it on.

I was creeped out by what he had said and done to me, no matter that he hadn't hurt me at all and I'd really enjoyed the game. He had been so turned on by my performance that the entire fantasy had taken only about ten minutes. *How long has he been thinking about this? Was Devlin's woman really the reason, or was that just the catalyst that finally made a secret smoldering desire so powerful that it became an undeniable obsession?*

I sat at the edge of the bed, but didn't touch him. After a few minutes, Kev took a deep breath, and sat up. "That was great," he said in a relaxed tone. "You were just like I wanted you to be. Will two hundred extra cover it?"

I hadn't expected that he'd effectively double my take home nightly pay for only ten minutes worth of fantasy. *If they're all as generous, maybe bondage is worth considering.* "Yes."

"Will you do this again for me?"

"Yes," I assented. "I enjoyed myself. But not any rougher than you were, okay? And the safe word stays the same."

"Agreed," Kev said, handing me two hundreds from his wallet.

"One other thing," I added, making sure I had his attention. "Keep this to yourself for now. I don't want anyone getting any more ideas than they've already asked about. I don't mind doing this for you, because the extra money is good, and you didn't hurt me. But in all honesty, I want you to know that I don't think I can do this night after night."

"I'll keep it to myself," Kev confirmed. "Most of the guys are pretty straight-laced, so they shouldn't ask for something like this. Our time won't always be like this, either, when I come to you. I'll want just oral sex usually, with occasional regular fucking now and then. But I'd like this once every few weeks, if you don't mind. I'll let you know when I want it, and I'll pay you extra those times, like I did tonight. That fair?

"Yes."

Kev walked closer to me, and gave me a gentle kiss on the cheek. "Thanks, Serena," he said, and then he left, closing the door behind him.

Chapter Five

Life went on like that for the next month. As Nick had said, once the men got used to me being available to them, their demand for me every day slackened. In fact, Vince was the only one who came to me every day without fail. Matt and Nick were close seconds, coming to me every few days. I got to know those three faster because I spent more time with them than the others.

But where Matt and the others were only around me when they wanted sex, Nick and Vince seemed to want to spend time with me, even when they knew we weren't going to have sex. We sometimes sat in the sun, working on our tans, or swimming in the ocean. Some nights we'd sit on my balcony, drinking beer (or harder stuff, for them), though we never drank very much, only one drink a night at most. Sometimes Kev joined us, though that wasn't often.

I wondered about the drinking, as I sensed that they wanted to drink more than they did. But I didn't figure out why they were so restrained until a night in mid-October.

I'd come in from the beach. It was later in the day, almost sunset. I'd seen Devlin's daily woman come in before me, and hung back, not wanting to talk to her. I knew after that night I'd never see her again. Once he spent the night with them, they were never asked back. I didn't understand where they kept coming from, but decided it was some arrangement that Kev had set up when he was in Rio.

Once in a while, I didn't see a particular woman leave. That she hadn't left at all occurred to me. That scared me a little, but I told myself that I'd just missed them leaving. If Devlin was killing them, I didn't want to know. Cowardly as it was, I wanted to keep my head in the sand and mind my own business, because for the first time in my life, I truly felt happy. But after that night, I couldn't deny the truth any longer.

I'd gotten to my room, taken a bath, and was just settling in bed. With no appointments that evening, I was looking forward to some uninterrupted reading. Then I heard screaming. Bolting out of bed, I threw open my door. *It's coming from outside.*

I grabbed my bathrobe, and crept downstairs. The screaming continued.

I got closer to the side where the courtyard was, and saw the source of the screaming. Vince and Kev were there holding Gerry, as Lash whipped his back raw.

I watched for a few minutes in horror, and then Lash abruptly coiled his whip up. "Let him go," he hissed.

Vince and Kev dropped Gerry, and he lay there sprawled in a small pool of his own blood. He was healing, but not as fast as he should.

"You fall asleep again, or get drunk again at your post, or any other time again, and I'll whip you until you're dead," Lash hissed coldly, looking down at him. "It'll take you a long time to die that way, Gerry. I know, because I've had to do it before." He paused. "Don't make me do it again."

"I won't!" Gerry said in a raw squeal. "Please, I won't!"

"Take him inside," Devlin ordered, coming into view. He was dressed in white again, his fair skin and light clothes almost shining in the gloom next to his black dressed guards. "See to his back."

"We'll patch him up," Lars said, lifting Gerry. Vince went with him.

Kev turned to Lash and Devlin. "You need me to take her back to the city? You're usually not out here so fast, Boss."

"I'm done with her," Devlin said with finality. "Lash will take her where she needs to go, Kev."

I felt a shiver, and didn't breathe, knowing my worst fears were confirmed. *The woman he was with tonight must be dead. Had he needed to kill her, to drink enough blood to sustain himself?*

"Okay," Kev said, turning away. "I'll keep his watch while he's busy. I'll call you, Boss, if anything happens." He walked over and picked up a discarded huge semiautomatic rifle with a scope that was leaning against a tree and strode out of sight.

Lash turned back to Devlin. "Thanks," he hissed. "It's past time for me. But I didn't want to ask you."

"I know," Devlin said carefully, his usually casual, easy manner of talking oddly strained. "Come to me after, and I'll help you shed, like usual."

"Thanks," Lash said in a gruff tone. Then he followed Devlin to his bedroom.

When they were gone, I went to the kitchen, and grabbed a box of Oreos. If I couldn't drink, I was going to lose myself in some hydrogenated chocolate. I needed a mental escape of some kind because by the sounds of it, Lash wasn't just burying the body, he was doing something else to it. Whatever it was, I sure as hell didn't want to know.

* * * *

The law of being drunk didn't apply to everyone, however. The next night, I came down to see Lash finishing off a bottle of Laphroig on the veranda. Now he didn't act drunk at all; a human wouldn't have noticed anything out of the ordinary. But I smelled the scent of him was slightly altered, and it was obvious to me in how his hands moved just a little slower, and how he wobbled very slightly in his seat when he shifted his weight in the chair. Yet when Lars came in, Lash stood up fast, looking immediately like he was in full control. "What is it?" he hissed.

"I want to go into town," Lars pleaded. "I need some smokes, Lash."

"That all you need?" Lash hissed sarcastically. "I know you were into coke before, Lars. I see any of that shit here, you're dead meat. You know it's Devlin's life if we're discovered here."

"Just smokes. I'll pick up some for the other guys, too. And for you, if you want."

"My woman's got that taken care of," Lash hissed arrogantly. "But ask Kev, if he wants you to go for him this time into Rio. If he says yes, then you can go."

Lars gave him a grateful smile, and hurried off. I surmised that he went, as I didn't see him for several days. Kev was there, instead, watching from Lars's usual position on the roof with the high-powered rifle.

* * * *

A day after Lars left, Nick came to me, and asked me point blank if I'd consider taking a potion, to be a bear for him and Vince.

I looked at him in surprise. "How? I'm not a werebear."

"But you are were, Serena. You could handle us making love that way."

Nick was very persuasive when he wanted to be, or when he wanted something from me. But I admitted I liked him best of my lovers, and I usually gave in when he asked me for something, whether it was a new sexual position or just a back rub.

"How?"

"Devlin said he could have a potion for you here by tonight, if you agreed. It's not cheap, half a month's pay from each of us to cover it. But it's getting to the point we can't deal with not getting any in bear form."

Negotiation time. "What will you do for me?" I said, folding my arms across my chest.

Nick gave me an odd look, then he sat down on my bed. "Are you asking me to take you as my mate?" he asked in an unsettled tone.

I flushed redder than I ever had in my life. Finally, I got out, "Mate?"

"If you are with me and Vince as bears and in human form, and I give you something after, and you take it, you'll be my mate," Nick explained, sounding very nervous. "That's were law. It's what the mated bears who live here did with the women they call their own." He swallowed again hard. "With bears, more than one partner is allowed in a mating. Males usually outnumber females three to one as a rule, so it's males that usually share one female. So even doing what you do, it would be allowed."

I still couldn't get any words out, sudden feelings I'd never felt before now flooding me. *What would it be like to be someone's mate? Nick's mate?*

"But I'm not ready to be mated," Nick added carefully. "I like you a lot, Serena, but if that's what you're asking, I can't do it."

Make light of this, before he does think that's what you meant. I cleared my throat. "That's not what I'm asking. I was just teasing, really. But what you're asking is a lot. I wanted to know if there would be any extra perks." I softened my words with a smile.

"Please?" Nick said, taking my hand. "I'm going crazy, Baby, not being able to."

Pleading won't be enough by itself. But you can come to that conclusion on your own, Nick. I tuned him out for a while, thinking. Did I want to do this? *Not really.* But what would it be like to finally know what it would be like to be animal? Sex did bring out my animal side, as I sometimes changed partly during orgasm, though that had never amounted to more than temporary claws and a little fur that rapidly melted away as soon as I relaxed. This way I'd finally find out. Plus I didn't have to pay any of the cost, which must be extravagant. "How? And I mean, how will you get the potion? From who?"

"Devlin's got a magic man," Nick said eagerly. "A sorcerer, back in the states. He'll make it, and get it here tonight."

"And what, I'll take it, and turn into a bear? For how long? Will I remember anything?"

Nick considered. "For three hours, tops," he said slowly. "That's the limit, I believe. But as for what you'll remember, I'd think it would be everything. Bear brains are big, so memory wouldn't be compromised at all when changing form. But I'll ask to make sure."

Hearing that, I decided that here was something I wanted that was worth being bear. "Okay then. But on one condition."

Nick looked at me warily, and waited.

"I'll expect the same from you at some point in the future. And from Vince, too."

"To be fox for you?" Nick said, looking at me strangely. "Or coyote?"

"Either," I said with a shrug. "But I want my animal side sated too, if the time ever comes when I am able to change form."

"It would be odd. But it's still a predator, I guess. So sure."

"I will too," Vince said from the doorway, beaming at me. Then he turned to Nick. "Let's get to Devlin, before he hangs up with Titus!"

Nick kissed me, and left, almost running out the door. With a last smile, Vince followed him.

The next evening, I took the potion Vince offered me, swallowing it in a single gulp. And absolutely nothing happened.

I gave them a look after a few minutes had gone by. "Am I supposed to do something?"

Nick shot a questioning look to Vince.

"Turn, both of you," a cool voice called loudly.

Kev strode toward us, bare-assed naked. Before the other men had time to say a word, he grabbed hold of me, and bore me to the ground. I squirmed, trying to get away from him, and then felt his skin began to ripple. I went still as his body changed, getting bigger. Hair was brushing my bare arms and my ankles. I screamed, but instead of my scream, I let out a guttural roar.

My body was changing, too. I sprouted fur and claws, my body suddenly huge, so tall and wide! I rolled to my feet, swiping at the huge male next to me. *Because he is huge, and the scent of him is heavy in my nose. He's not proven himself. I'll not let him have me until he does. Or the other two bears, either, who are snarling at him.*

Nick gave a guttural roar, and charged, Vince right behind him. Kev fought hard with them, roaring over and over. Soon, the sand was wet with blood. Nick backed off first, whimpering a little with a large gash on his side. Vince followed suit, limping on three legs. But my eyes were all for my warrior, who was coming fast to me.

I crouched down for him, readying myself, and then I felt him roaring, thrusting hard into me like a jackhammer. He let out a roar as he came, and then withdrew. But in another moment, I felt him enter me again, just as roughly, and again, within seconds he finished. I swiped at him that time with my claws, my harsh bellow telling him he wasn't pleasing me. Kev chuffed in response, asking me to be patient with him. He mounted me again. This time, he lasted long enough so my roaring joined his, as we screamed out our pleasure into the night. The next time, a few seconds after, he lasted longer.

Forty-five minutes later, Kev tried to enter me again, and couldn't. He gave it one more attempt, and then walked away from me, lying in the shade of a palm tree some yards away.

My two other paramours were already coming towards me. Vince took Kev's place, growling, and snarling at Nick, who roared furiously back at him, yet backed away. Vince lasted one stroke in me, and came. Annoyed, I swiped at him, connecting this time with my claws. I drew blood from his nose, and he yelped. But he didn't strike me back, just grabbed hold of me again, pushing inside me even as I squirmed under him.

Soon, he was pleasuring me, and we were roaring together, losing ourselves in the rut until he was exhausted. Twenty minutes later, he joined Kev under the tree.

Nick came to me then, and I swiped at him, telling him there would be none of what had gone on before, to enter me at all without pleasing me. He chuffed at me, then rubbed his head against my side, weaving back and forth. The action strangely mellowed me, and I crouched for him obediently. When he mounted me, I got a pleasant surprise: he lasted long enough his first time to bring me. Even though we continued on after, he didn't grow soft, or withdraw. And every time he brought me, until finally he grew soft, and dismounted.

I turned to him questioningly. In my bear mind, I was completely sexually sated. But I also felt the need to run, to dig, and to eat. When he chuffed at me and ran away, I followed him.

He ran to a nearby sealed barrel, and knocked it over. Meat spilled out, and we both began eating greedily, bolting down the large chunks of raw meat. When I'd eaten my fill, he finished what I left. Then I noticed that Vince and Kev were also eating from a similar barrel under the tree.

Nick nipped me with his teeth, and I roared in mock annoyance. He ran into the surf with me in hot pursuit. We wrestled, the waves crashing over us, and Kev and Nick joined us.

The next hour was almost more fun than the sex. We played together in the surf, and rolled in the sand. I dunked all of them in waves, and they rose up, eyes closed, water dripping from their drooping ears to shake hard, spraying salt water everywhere.

Finally utterly exhausted, I walked up and sprawled on the sand and dozed. My body began to change back. My fur and claws receded, and my form grew smaller, and soon, I was human again.

The men saw me changing back, and changed back, too. As soon as they were human, Vince went right to Kev, and punched him in the face. "This was our idea!" Vince said angrily, and Nick echoed that he was right. "What right did you have to crash?"

"I was and am the strongest," Kev said arrogantly, wiping the blood off his mouth. "I'm alpha bear here, Vince. You're beta. And Nick, you aren't even ranked."

"Fuck you!" Nick roared. "You had no right. We aren't wolves, that there is any kind of pack hierarchy rules for mating!"

"I went in on that potion," Kev said, shrugging on his clothes, which lay draped on a nearby bush. "You think your salaries covered it? You needed mine to pay for the transportation of it here, which cost the same as to make it. It only keeps for a few days, so it needs to be teleported via demon. You're just lucky that I kept the other bears away from the beach tonight, Nick. Or there'd have been none of her left for you."

Nick swore at him, but he didn't move to hit him. Kev looked at us, eyes glittering, and then strode off.

Vince came to me, and hugged me. "Are you okay?" he asked hesitantly. "Please believe me, we didn't intend to hurt you, or to have you feel forced into taking on all three of us in one night."

"I'm okay," I said, giving him a smile as he let go of me. "I had a lot of fun. It felt really good, to be animal." I felt unshed tears gather in my eyes. "I never had any idea…"

Nick came over and hugged me. "We'll help you try to be fox," he whispered in a tender voice. "Males can usually bring females into their animal form and back, the way Kev did to trigger your bear transformation. We'll start trying tomorrow."

I was touched, and some of my tears spilled over, even as I smiled happily. "Thank you."

Vince grabbed me up in his arms, laughing, and carried me up to the house, Nick following with their weapons and our clothes.

Chapter Six

I walked inside that night feeling wonderful. The night was quiet, and I was very tired. After we'd dressed, Vince and Nick had left me to go to their posts, and I was feeling how exhausted I was. *I need to get to bed before I fall down.*

"Fuck me," a soft hissing voice said. I stopped dead in my tracks. It had come from above me, near my room.

"Not in my bedroom," a deeper hissing voice replied. "I told you that, Esperanza. Wait for me near the stairs. I'll only be a minute."

"Fuck me now, Lash, or I'm leaving!" she hissed back. "And I want to be in a real bed for a change!"

"I pay you, and I say where we fuck, and when!" he hissed angrily. "Wait for me there!"

"Bastard!" she spat at him. "You think you're so good of a lay that I need to put up with your shit? You aren't! There's a python I know who...."

There was the harsh sound of flesh striking flesh, and a woman's cry of pain.

"Wait for me near the stairs," Lash hissed in a low threatening tone. "And God help you if you aren't there when I get there, Esperanza."

I am not going up there, no way. I stayed quiet and motionless, right where I was.

A woman came slowly down the hallway, holding the right side of her face. She continued down to the bottom of the stairs. She was very pretty, with long dark hair, full lips, and a lush body.

Why would she ever bed Lash? She might be weresnake, but I knew she wasn't his species. And he'd just hit her. *What an asshole.*

Lash came walking fast down the upstairs hallway toward her, his gaze locked on her. From my hidden alcove, I felt a shiver of fear. Lash went down the stairs, grabbed Esperanza by the back of her neck, and gave her a shove. "Get to the couch," he hissed. "And drop your skirt, before I drop it for you."

I stayed still, riveted.

Esperanza backed away from him, showing him her own snake fangs in a warning hiss. Lash bared his fangs back at her, then grabbed hold of her, throwing her to the couch. He unzipped his pants. She got up, and tried to run, but he grabbed her again, pushing her face down on the couch.

"Hold still, you bitch!" he hissed. Esperanza tried to bite him in response. He slapped her hard, knocking her to the couch on her belly. She tried to crawl away from him over the back of the couch, but he grabbed her hips, tearing her underwear down. With a quick motion, he pulled her hips back against him hard. Esperanza let out a cry, going still. He pulled down her low cut tank top, baring her large breasts, and he grabbed hold of them in his hands, squeezing roughly. Lash let out a loud hiss of satisfaction, and then he was hammering himself into her, trapping her body against the couch as he thrust fiercely into her, and she was struggling, but she seemed to be moaning, too. He gripped her hard, his one hand moving up from her breast to wind in her hair, the other still fondling her breasts.

"Yes, lover, just like that!" Esperanza hissed. "Yes, stroke me! Fuck me! Harder!" *Her struggles are and were really her writhing in pleasure in his grip. This isn't force; it's more role-playing. Ugh. Maybe this is where Kev gets his ideas.*

Lash continued to pound himself into her, hissing fast and furiously, his eyes almost closed. Esperanza alternated demanding he fuck her harder with loud hissing noises of pleasure, her eyes tightly shut and her mouth slack with desire. In a few minutes, it was over. Lash jerked, as he came inside her, and Esperanza let out a soft cry of release, collapsing over the couch under him.

They'd been so quiet, compared to my lovers and me. *Maybe it's a snake thing?*

Lash stood up, and zipped his pants, looking down at her with an angry expression. "There had better not be any fucking python," he hissed in a dangerous tone. "I told you I'd pay you for every night, but I was going to be your only lover. That was our arrangement."

"There isn't," she hissed softly, turning to him almost lovingly. "There's only you."

"You're going to get tested tomorrow," Lash interrupted. "Before I fuck you again, you're going to show me you're safe to fuck."

"I'll do it," she said quickly, her fangs disappearing, her eyes soft and placating. "I'll bring you proof tomorrow."

"You had better, or you won't be having any more of me," he hissed at her. "When I fuck you, I want to feel your flesh against mine. I'm not going to wear a rubber."

"You don't have to, I told you," she pleaded, coming to him on her hands and knees on the couch. He helped her stand, and she reached up, sliding her hands around his neck. "I don't want you to, anyway. I'm on the pill."

"Go off it!" Lash hissed angrily. "I can't get you with child, I told you. So there's no reason for you to be on it, unless you're fucking someone else besides me."

"I will, tonight. I swear, there's only you. I like to feel you, too, Lash. So much…"

"I know you do," he said, hissing in an almost fond manner, and then he kissed her roughly. She wrapped her arms around him, kissing him back passionately.

He let her go after a moment, though she didn't take her arms from around him. "You care for me, don't you?" she said softly. "I like you a lot, Lash. I love being with you, feeling you loving me."

She must be crazy. Well, she's his lover, so she has to be just from that decision.

"You're nice," he said gently, looking down at her. "That's all I want in a woman, Esperanza. Just to have someone to be with, to coil with, and not have to share her with another snake."

"You have that, in me. But I'd like it, if we could be more," she offered, kissing his neck gently. "I could be your woman, Lash. There doesn't need to be money between us."

Lash took her arms off him gently, and pushed her away. "There is too much danger here for that. I'm not that kind of man, Sweetfang. You knew that when I first made arrangements with you. Things are better staying as they are."

He walked her to the door, and opened it for her.

"Okay," she said with a sultry smile. "I'll see you tomorrow then. I'll bring you the proof."

"Be safe going to your home," Lash hissed gently, and shut the door behind her.

I made a quick dash for the stairs. The movement caught Lash's attention. I blushed red as he gave me a knowing look. "You watched us."

I flushed deeper. "I'm sorry! I didn't mean to."

"You thought I was raping her, didn't you?" he said angrily, as I backed away from him.

"I didn't...I don't judge," I offered lamely.

"She likes me being rough with her, even sometimes to hurt her," Lash hissed softly. "I don't understand it myself, but she needs it, to get enjoyment out of sex. I do it, though some of what she asks me to do to her appalls me."

"I saw that," I uttered, hoping I wasn't making a bigger hole for myself. I hadn't expected him to be thoughtful enough to care what his partner needed, since he was paying her. *But my guys cared about my happiness. Why shouldn't he be the same?*

"I'd rather be gentler," Lash went on, looking at me with his cold eyes. "I like sharing soft caresses with a woman, to make love to one. I miss it badly. But I can't do that with her. And she is the only were in this place who will let me touch her."

I flushed dark crimson at his words, the reason for his explanation clear. *He wants me to reconsider, to let him come to me.*

I looked at his snake eyes and fangs, and knew I couldn't do it. I couldn't even imagine kissing him. *What if he wants some kind of fantasy, like Kev?* Bile rose in my throat, and I swallowed hard.

"I see your revulsion in your eyes," he hissed flatly. "Forget I said anything." He stalked past me, and up the stairs. His bedroom door closed with a slam, and I almost fell to my knees in relief. Somehow, I got to my bedroom, shut and locked the door, then collapsed on the bed.

While I felt badly for Lash's situation, what could I do? There was nothing he could do that would make me not fear him. And there was no way I wanted him inside me. *Not ever.*

* * * *

That next week, after four nights of attempting transformations with Nick and Vince, I finally changed form. I became coyote first, not a fox. It felt so good to finally run, to finally be what I'd always known on some subconscious level I was. Two nights later, I managed finally to take fox form. It was very different, though I wasn't that much smaller. I seemed way too short, and my legs too tiny to support me. Yet Vince and Nick encouraged me with their friendly chuffs. With their help, I adjusted to my new forms rapidly.

Of course, the inevitable happened. No sooner had I become animal than I wanted sex. I spent a good part of my first night in each form whining pitifully, rolling on my back, and scooting along on all fours with my tail raised in hopeless anticipation. Nick and Vince stroked my fur, and told me again and again they were sorry, but they couldn't do what I needed.

Vince came to me the night after I turned coyote, and told me he would put up the money to get a potion for himself to become coyote, as I hadn't earned enough yet from working with Devlin to pay what the potion would cost. After I became fox, Nick came to me and said the same thing the next day, in terms of that form. Devlin himself visited me the night after, and told me he was pleased with my "adventuresome spirit" and he would put up some of the money himself, as I'd been a "good sport" about Kev "joining us."

I got a little chill, thinking I'd been wise to accept Kev's extra money, and to do what he requested of me. Holding in my nervousness, I thanked Devlin and accepted his help, glad I'd maneuvered the tricky situation successfully.

Chapter Seven

I was reading in bed on the afternoon of Halloween. Vince and Nick were in the closest small tourist town, getting me some candy along with supplies for the estate: bullets, some meat, some new clothes for themselves, some bottled water, and some kind of discs for Devlin's laptop. There was a knock at the door.

I got up with surprise, and went to answer it. I had no one scheduled for that day until nine, when Vince got back.

Maybe it's Jazz. He'd come to me apologetically a few times now for sex. His mate, Valerie, sometimes said nasty things to me, and he apologized for that, too. According to him, though Valerie liked sex, she would permit it only one way. And like most men, he liked it another way sometimes, a way she wasn't willing to do for him. I'd asked Devlin about it the first time Jazz had approached me, not wanting to cause trouble. He replied that Jazz had come to him asking and requested that I comply. "Val will deal with it," he said, rolling his eyes. "If she'd just blow him once in a while, he'd never look at another woman. But it's her choice to say no. Just as it's his choice to look elsewhere for satisfaction."

I'd flushed and nodded. And the few times Jazz had come to me since then, I'd taken care of him.

To my surprise, Lars was the guard standing at my door, not Jazz. He looked anxious, almost rattled. "Serena, could you do me?" he said, sounding almost desperate. "I need it bad."

I hadn't seen him since he'd left for Rio weeks ago. I'd thought he'd decided I wasn't worth Dev's price, or something. But Devlin hadn't said he'd stopped paying. Maybe he'd been delayed in Rio? I opened my mouth to say "yes," and then got a good look in his eyes. They were glassy and bloodshot. *He's on something.* "No, I'm sorry," I said, closing the door. "Come back tomorrow. I have someone coming at six."

"They can fucking wait!" he roared, growing fangs. "I told you I need it, bitch! Now get undressed!"

"No!" I grabbed the door, and tried to slam it. He grabbed it too, and pushed back.

"Stop!" I screamed. "Help!"

I pushed back hard as he tried to push his way into the room, wishing Vince or Nick were here. Lars was stronger than I was, and with a crack, he pushed the door fully open, knocking me to the floor, and burying the doorknob in the bedroom wall.

"You whore! You're going to do what I say, and I'll call you anything I want to!" he said, starting towards me. "When I get through with you..."

A sharp crack sounded. Lars roared, and turned, a fresh stripe down his back bleeding through the hole in his shirt, just in time to get a bullet through the heart. He fell to his knees, and then Lash put another bullet between his eyes. Lars' body fell to the floor, twitching.

Lash came to me, and helped me to my feet. I was still so scared I hugged him. "Are you all right?" he hissed gently.

"Yes," I said, stepping away from him, and trying to compose myself. "He just went crazy."

Lash flicked out his tongue, and a good foot of it came out of his mouth, vibrating. I shivered slightly, as he repeatedly scented the air. "Meth," he pronounced disdainfully. "And probably coke, too." He paused, flicking his tongue out again. "And fresh VD, probably bear type, but I can't tell for sure." He looked over at me. "Good he didn't get to you, or you'd have caught it."

Another shiver went through me, this one more a convulsion. Then I let out a scream. Lars was stirring, already healing. Both bullets had fallen out of him, and his eyelids fluttered, then flicked open.

Lash rolled his eyes, gave a long-suffering sigh, and deftly reached down with both hands, using the doorjamb for a brace. With a dull crack, he broke Lars's neck. Lars stopped moving, though he kept breathing.

"Stay in your room," Lash hissed, picking up Lars's body in his arms with effort. "You may hear screaming, but ignore it. It won't last long."

I knew he expected me to be relieved, and I was. He'd saved me. Yet I was horrified, too, because I knew he'd kill Lars in some horrible torturous way as soon as possible. Covering my revulsion, I nodded, and closed my door with a click.

Vince was subdued when he came to me that night. But so was I, considering what had happened. "I'm sorry that happened to you," he said finally, as we lay sated together sometime around eleven. "I'd have kicked his ass, if I'd been here."

"Was he whipped to death?" I asked, afraid of the answer but compelled to know.

"No. Lash beheaded him, and stuck his head on a post as a warning. The body we buried."

I hugged him close to me, trying not to think how awful this was. But Lars would have hurt me. It was right to defend myself, and what had happened was deserved, just grisly.

"Shh," Vince said affectionately. "That potion will come in a few days, Baby. And we'll take care of your needs then, just like you took care of ours."

I hugged him and didn't explain my true feelings. Vince often misunderstood me, as did Nick. I knew he was trying to be kind the only way he knew how to be.

* * * *

My close call did drive home a point to me; I'd been blessed with how well my life was going now. It was truly past time that I gave thanks to the being who'd helped me so much. That next morning, I had Nick take me into town, where we went to my church. We were in time for afternoon mass. As always, there were more than a few of the local seniors in the pews. Several nodded to me and smiled, pleased to see me there with a male friend. I prayed a good deal, and thanked God, giving a fair tithing portion of what I'd earned so far in the collection plate. Nick looked incredulous at my offering, yet he was also generous, though not so much as me.

After, I went to the confessional, and made my confession. The priest was appalled at my new choice of work, but he forgave me, though he assigned a massive penance. I agreed to it, but I also decided that I'd leave what I did for money now out of any future confessions.

I wasn't hurting anyone. Animals did what I was doing in nature all the time, they were just paid with food and shelter and protection, which was the same as I was receiving. I was and had always been part animal. No human had the right to judge me, to say that what I was doing was a sin, or evil, or not according to God's plan for me. I'd felt the desire for sex as soon as I became animal; I had got that from God himself, it was hardwired into me, and it wasn't wrong. I was not going to sit in a booth in the dark, and let some man who'd never experienced it himself tell me that it was.

* * * *

In early November, both of the transformative potions came. Vince and Nick took them, as they had agreed to. Afterwards, I thought I'd never felt so good, so sated, as when I lay with my respective lovers in my own animal form, my head resting on his shoulder, his muzzle against mine.

In late November, Devlin called me to him, and asked me for my blood. But this time we did not have sex, or even kiss. His only touch was his light embrace as he fed from me, and then the brief press of his lips as he healed me.

I wasn't unhappy about giving him my blood. His bite was pleasurable, and I appreciated everything he had done for me. I didn't even expect to get any extra money out of it. Yet I found an extra two hundred dollars in my paycheck that week. I went to him immediately, and asked him about it. "Is this for the blood I gave you?"

"Yes, of course," he answered.

"You don't have to pay me for the little you took," I said.

"You are my employee," Devlin said patiently, his honey-colored eyes almost slitted. "I am not one who abuses that relationship, Serena. Besides, I appreciate your blood, both its taste, and that you give it to me willingly. You also recover faster than a mortal, and I can take more from you. Esperanza also 'donates' her blood to me once a month, and I give her four or five hundred, as that is her price."

Five hundred? *Maybe I should be offended.*

"But I take enough to make her pass out," he finished coolly, that addendum making me feel much better. "I take much less from you, the same amount I take from my guards when it's an absolute necessity. Not enough to make you weak, but enough to keep me strong for a week or so. That is the same amount I give them each time I'm forced to feed from them."

I wanted to ask him if he paid the families of the women he drained, but held back, reminding myself I had no proof of that at all.

Devlin sighed. "I miss hunting, and drinking from mortal women. It's hard, trying not to be noticed. I have spent my life being noticed, and my time since becoming vampire making it the point of my existence. It's hard trying to blend into the shadows now, and not to my liking."

This being in hiding was because of Perseus, the vampire whose territory he was in. And because of his tryst with that married woman. *You could have stayed in the limelight and your own territory, if you'd have kept it in your pants.* "I'm sorry," I said, feeling it was the only safe response.

"She did not respond to the card!" Devlin said bitterly, his eyes angry and accusing. "And I have e-mailed her poetry as well for a week now and she does not respond to those either!"

What should I say? "I'm sorry."

"That is all you have to say?" he hissed, baring his teeth. "You who gave me hope and made me believe that she might care for me?"

It had been a long day, and I was annoyed. *He's blaming me? When did I ask to be his love life counselor?* "Do you love her?" I asked bluntly.

"Yes, of course!" he hissed back at me. "But—"

"Then don't give up," I counseled calmly. "You seduce all these women, and they all tell you that you are so wonderful. Then one day, one woman doesn't tell you she'd just love to give up her life to be with you, and you get annoyed! Did you ever stop to think that maybe she's going through her own problems?"

Devlin looked shocked. I thought him abhorrent in how much he thought about himself, and not about this woman he professed to love. He thought of her in terms of how she related to him, not in any other way. That didn't sound like love to me, even if I'd never been in love myself.

"So what should I do?" His tone was respectful now, hushed. "Tell me."

"She liked what you did to her in that hotel room, yes?"

"Yes, of course."

Could his tone be any more confident? "So what did you do to her?"

"Everything she asked for and more besides." Now his tone was lustful, obviously remembering some sex scene with her.

Whatever had occurred was probably more involved than our night together, with so much emotion on Devlin's end. *I will never be that important to him. That's probably a good thing.* Nick had told me enough about Devlin to get my hackles at attention, coupled with what I'd seen of his mood swings. "Send her some of that poetry you seem to always be reading."

"I did that already," he answered, exasperated. "I wrote her some, even!"

"Write more! Send her flowers! Call her!"

"I can't call her, save at Danial's!" Devlin said angrily. "The same with flowers! I do not want her husband finding out about her and me! I shouldn't even be trying to contact her. I am supposed to be in hiding."

I thought briefly that he was a jackass, but held that thought inside. "Do what pleased her most when she was with you then, as discreetly as you can manage."

"Fine!" Devlin said, with a dismissive wave of his hand. "Leave me."

In early December, Devlin came to me, excited that his love had responded to him. "She said I should stop writing her poetry, that I was making it hard for her to let go of us! You were right!"

In the weeks after that, the sullen look returned to Devlin's face, and he spoke no more to me about his love. I also avoided the subject, heeding my animal side's warning to leave well enough alone.

Chapter Eight

It was nearly Christmas. Eager to see if there would be any type of holiday festivities, I asked about the coming weeks in terms of any change to my normal schedules. But none of my lovers mentioned any changes at all in their allotted times with me. From the absence of any decorations and my needing to ask for December 25th off instead of being offered the day, I deduced that Devlin and his men didn't celebrate Christmas.

The night before Christmas Eve, I came in from the surf to witness Lash drinking heavily in front of the TV, watching *The Bodyguard*. I was surprised he had chosen that over all the hundreds of DVDs in the nearby rack. What was more strange to me was Lash seemed to be getting emotional over it, something I hadn't known was possible.

Even though I was naturally curious, I intended to ignore him at first. Whatever past love he was mourning wasn't my concern or my business. Yet I went back, because like it or not, it was the Christian thing to do, and tomorrow being Christmas, I knew God might have done this on purpose to see if I'd take the bait, so to speak. I also felt I owed him a favor on some level; Lash had saved me from Lars, even if I'd been mortified about what he'd done afterwards as a punishment. "What is it?" I asked. "Do you want to talk about it?"

I expected Lash to tell me to leave him alone, or to tell me to fuck off, like I heard him tell the guards some variation of that almost every day. Instead, he answered me. "Do you think she loved him? That if he would have stayed with her, she might have loved him?"

"No," I replied honestly. "You should watch *The Best Little Whorehouse in Texas*. That's better use of that song, anyway." Nick had shown me that movie, said it was one of his favorites. He was a big Dolly Parton fan. He insisted his attraction to the star was her musical

182

talent, but I knew it was just her breasts. *Men.*

"You're probably right," Lash hissed sadly, with more emotion in his tone than I had ever heard. "It was stupid to think anything else."

"Did you leave someone behind?" I said, sitting down beside him. "A woman you cared for?"

"Just a friend," Lash hissed quietly. "Someone who was trying to be friends with me, anyways. But there might have been more, if I hadn't left."

"Why haven't you called her?" I said reproachfully. "I'll bet you haven't,"

"She loves another man, not me. I don't want to fuck that up for her."

This sounded familiar. "That hasn't stopped Devlin."

"I'm not Devlin," Lash interrupted, his tone an odd mixture of pleasure and sadness. "I don't love her, like he loves Sar. I care more that she's happy than that I get her for myself." He paused. "Besides, she's human. It wouldn't have worked anyway, it never does. I should fucking well know better, old as I am."

I held my tongue, a barrage of questions threatening to spill out. *He's putting her happiness ahead of his own. This sounds far more like love to me than Devlin's feelings for Sar. And what human had wanted Lash? What are these women seeing in him that I'm not? Is it because of my animal side, that I can never look at him and see anything but a snake?*

"You can't be sure," I said slowly. "Everyone's different. Some women can accept things other women wouldn't."

"No. It's better this way," Lash said with finality, getting up and turning off the movie. "And that's that."

"Call her," I said firmly. "She might be thinking of you. Maybe she can fly down here and visit."

Lash turned, and gave me a cold look. "Don't be giving me advice, like you give Dev. You're getting his hopes up for nothing, Serena. And I'm going to be pissed at you, if nothing comes of this, after all of your instructions to him about how to win her." He paused. "And he will be, too."

He gave me a final look of warning, then strode out of the room.

* * * *

On Christmas Eve I lit a candle at midnight, and told God I was thankful for all he had given me. It wasn't much by way of an offering, but I thought He would like it. I'd gone to church earlier again with Nick, and given my tithe and my thanks there, also. I truly was grateful. *That is what matters, right?*

I wasn't expecting any presents, but to my surprise, I got two gifts. Nick got me a dozen pink roses, and Vince got me a box of expensive chocolate, both of them saying a little sheepishly that their families had always celebrated Christmas. I took them, feeling happy and grateful enough, so I agreed to be in bear form for them again in a week, which made both men very happy.

* * * *

The night after Christmas, a hurricane moved close to the coast. The waves were huge, and the wind bent the palm trees almost double, snapping more than a few. I was uneasy, but got my flashlight ready in case. Lash had cautioned me that morning that we might need to evacuate, if it got bad enough. He also warned me that if an alarm sounded to make my way downstairs to the basement, where a shelter was equipped to help us ride out the storm.

But I needn't have worried. Vince came to me at dusk holding a duffel bag of supplies, telling me while he believed we were safe that he would sleep with me that night just in case the worst happened and we had to evacuate. I fell asleep with him holding me, feeling peaceful.

I woke up to hear the howling of the wind, and some thunder booming loud enough to shake the room. Vince slept on, snoring. I listened to the storm for five minutes, then decided I needed something soothing to restore my rattled nerves. I got out of bed, carefully moving Vince over, knowing better than to wake him. *He'll think sex is the perfect way to soothe me.*

I went downstairs in my robe, and made myself some hot chocolate. I was just taking it out of the microwave when a crash of thunder startled me. I took a sudden step backwards and bumped into the counter, letting out a cry of surprise. "Shit," I said under my breath, breathing a sigh of relief.

I took a sip from my steaming mug. *Ah, just right.*

A bolt of lightning illuminated the kitchen, and Lash in the doorway, watching me. I let out another cry, clutching the counter with my free hand.

"Sorry for startling you," he hissed, not sounding like he meant it at all.

"It's okay," I said, giving him a smile. "I couldn't sleep with the storm outside."

"I heard it, too," Lash hissed. "Want to share some cow?" he added a little awkwardly. "I wanted a little something before going back to bed myself."

Should I decline his request? He would be offended if I did. And I was hungry. "Sure. That would be nice."

Lash went to the refrigerator and removed a hunk of steak from the bottom drawer marked "Lash" in large block letters. He grabbed one of the kitchen knives, and divided it in half, handing me half on a plate, and taking the other half for himself. We went into the dining room and began to eat, using only our hands.

It was delicious, more so than the meat we usually had which was expensive steak. "This is wonderful. What is it that it's so much better than what we usually eat?"

"Organic," he said, licking his fingers. "No drugs. It gives the meat a sweeter taste."

"So you order this specially?"

"Yes. I like to have it for a treat a few times a week."

"So no chocolate for you?" I teased.

"No," he said, flicking his eyes to me then away. "No chocolate for me."

Our meat was soon finished. I gathered up the plates, and took them into the kitchen to wash. I turned on the faucet, rinsing them, as Lash came up behind me, putting his arms on either side of me and gripping the counter. I went still.

"Did you like the meat?" he hissed in my ear.

My body broke out in a cold sweat. "Yes," I said, swallowing hard. "Thank you for sharing it with me."

"I want to share something else with you," he hissed lustfully.

185

I trembled, wanting to scream and knowing if I did, a fight would ensue, a fight that Vince was sure not to win. "No, please."

Lash's hands went over mine, and held them down to the counter with force, so I couldn't move. He trapped my body between the sink and himself, his erection against my rear, hard and ready. "Just hold still," he hissed in my ear. "I want to feel your body against mine."

Snake! My animal side was petrified, frozen. I gathered my human courage. "No. Stop it, Lash."

"Be quiet," he hissed gently. "I won't hurt you." He pressed his body tight to my back, and taking hold of my wrists, he wrapped my arms around me without letting go. He rubbed his face in my hair, and then pressed it to the back of my neck, groaning. Then he began to slide my arms and his down toward my hips. I struggled, but he was stronger than I was, and I got nowhere, and still his hands slid lower. Finally, they were at my hips. He pushed his pelvis against mine, pulling back with his arms to force my body tight against his. "Tell me I can," he hissed to me, his voice full of need. "Please, I'll give you any price you want. Just let me inside. I want to be warm. Please, Serena."

I almost did it. My human side said to submit, that once I'd sated him I'd be free. With the sheer need in his voice, he wouldn't last long. Yet my nose was full of his snake scent, my animal half in rising panic, telling me I had to run or be killed, that he was death. I forced my growing anxiety down, trying to keep control. "No," I managed. "I'm sorry, but no."

"You know I don't need to ask you," he hissed angrily. "I'm asking to be nice. But if you aren't nice to me, I'll just do what I did to Esperanza." His voice dropped lower. "Only this time, it won't be role-playing."

My terror and panic mounting, I forced myself not to scream. No one would hear me anyway. The shutters were rattling loudly, the sound of breaking and falling palm trees barely audible over the howl of the wind. "Stop, or Devlin will—"

"Dev will do nothing," he hissed confidently in my ear. "Save request I pay you for your time. And I'll do that gladly, ten times over."

I began to shift form, thinking to escape him that way. Lash saw the fur sprouting on my arms and tightened his grip. "You turn, and I'll turn,

186

too, little coyote," he hissed darkly. "You want it that way?"

In his coils. I'll be in his snake coils! My dread shot up. "No! Stop!"

"Tell me 'yes'," he hissed menacingly. "Tell me 'yes' now, Serena." His voice dropped lower. "Or I'll just stop pretending you have a choice."

My thin veneer of control cracked in half, my fear bursting through in a long, loud wail of terror. "No!" I screamed, sobbing. "No! Let me go! I don't want you! Leave me alone!" I cried hard, waiting for Lash to pull up my nightgown, to take me as he'd threatened to, knowing I had no power to stop him.

Instead, he swore loudly and abruptly let me go, leaving the kitchen.

Swiping at my falling tears, I ran to my room as fast as I could, locked the door, and had a good long cry snuggled into Vince's sleeping arms. That night I promised myself never, ever to be alone with Lash again.

Chapter Nine

On December twenty-sixth, hell broke loose. I woke up to a pounding on my door. I got up, slipped on my robe, and ran to the door. Nick was there, his mood wild and happy. "Serena, we're going home!" he said with glee. "Pack your bags! We're leaving tonight."

"What?" I uttered, stunned.

"He said pack your shit!" Lash hissed loudly, stalking by. "The plane leaves in four hours. If you aren't on it, you'll be left behind."

Nick rolled his eyes, but didn't say anything until Lash was on his way downstairs. Then he pushed me inside the room, and shut the door. "Devlin's frantic. Something is very wrong at home. He talked to his brother last night, and he's been on the phone ever since, arranging the plane, and talking to Titus."

"Who's Titus?" I asked curiously.

"He's one of Devlin's men, the magic man who made those potions we've been using. He's been watching Hayden, Devlin's estate in the US, for the past few months. You'll like him, Serena."

I looked around at my bed, and everything I'd come to think of as mine. "Do we have to leave all this behind?"

"Hayden's beautiful," Nick assured me, slipping his arms around my shoulders. "It's true, this place is nice, but it's really too fancy for me, and the rest of the guys. It's not home."

"It's become home to me," I said sadly. "I was happy here, Nick."

"You'll be happy there, too," Nick said, brushing my cheek with his lips. "Vince and I'll be there with you, along with Kev, and the rest of the bears. We'll have good times."

I knew I didn't want to leave. I'd lived here my whole life. *But what choice do I have, really? What's left for me here, if I stay behind? Going back to the diner to work? Scraping by on macaroni and cheese?* I

188

couldn't do it, not after how I'd lived so well, these past few months. "I'd better get packing," I said, gently pulling away from his embrace. "I have a lot more to bring with me than I did months ago."

"I have to pack too," Nick said, letting me go. "But Vince and I'll help you like before. Just pile boxes near the door, and we'll take them out. There is a semi already here in the driveway, ready to take our stuff to the airport. Anything can be taken except furniture."

I began to pack as Nick left, shutting the door behind him. There was a lot to take. I'd spent a week's pay each month just on new clothing, another on books and music; all the things I hadn't been able to afford before. But I'd saved the rest, all of it that I hadn't given in tithe anyway. *There's a lot, but I haven't been too sinful.*

The hours passed quickly, Vince and Nick carrying my boxes downstairs as fast as I packed them. Other bears were also going back and forth hurriedly, carrying boxes and calling out questions, Lash and Devlin's voices sometimes heard giving curt answers.

"We're leaving for the airport, to guard the truck," Vince said, taking the last box from me. "We'll see you soon!"

"Thanks," I called after him, then shut the door. I took a moment and looked over the mostly empty room, saying good-bye to the place where I'd finally come to know happiness. *But Nick's right. I can be happy somewhere else.*

Suddenly, Lash banged on the door. "Serena! Serena?"

I opened it nervously. "Yes?"

He glared at me. "Are you ready? We're moving out."

"All ready," I replied quickly, and stepped out into the hallway with my purse with a sigh.

He shut my door, herding me downstairs. "Devlin is finishing up," Lash hissed, his eyes flicking everywhere in succession, taking stock that everything was packed. "I'm going to bring the Hummer around front. Come outside with him, and we'll leave. Everyone else is already waiting there for us except Brock and Justin, who will be guarding us on the way."

"Okay," I nodded, sitting down on the couch as he left by the front door.

In a moment, Devlin came bounding down the stairs, looking wired and stressed. "Serena, come on!" he said, irritated. "We have to hurry!"

"Lash is bringing the Hummer," I assured him, swiftly getting to my feet. "He said it would be a few minutes"

"Damn it!" he swore, upset.

I've never seen him so frantic. "What is it? Does Perseus know you're here?"

Devlin gave me a shocked look, then a quick smile, his hand on the door to open it. "No, he doesn't know." He opened the door.

Esperanza staggered in, falling against him. "He does!" She went to her knees holding her side, blood dripping from a huge gaping wound. "Get out!" she gasped, looking up at him with pain-filled eyes. "He's on his way, with men!" She swayed, then collapsed.

An explosion rocked the house. Devlin bent and gathered Esperanza up, then started for the front door. I ran behind him, wishing I'd taken up some of the guys' offers to get me a gun and give me shooting lessons. We emerged to the Hummer burning on the driveway, Justin's body on the pavement beside it, charred and shredded.

"Devlin Dalcon," a hissing voice called menacingly. "What a surprise to see you." A man came toward us with a gun pointed at Devlin.

"Victor," Devlin said, his words dripping malice. "Still working for Perseus?"

"He's on his way," Victor said, grinning to show his snake fangs. "He's very upset you've been here all this time, and never invited him over. He said you owe him, Dalcon, and he means to get paid in full."

Victor screamed as his chest was suddenly shredded as if from within. He convulsed hard, dropping the gun, and falling on his face at Devlin's feet.

"Get to the truck!" Lash hissed, running toward us from the road, his gun still smoking. "Hurry!" A red truck was behind him parked halfway up the yard, idling.

"Grab the gun!" Devlin shouted to me, as he began to run. I reached down and grabbed it up from the ground, sprinting hard after him. We got to the truck and got in. Lash closed the door behind me, and then he ducked as a bullet whined off the truck's reinforced armor. Devlin pushed me down as more bullets hit the truck, the impact rocking it on the tires but not penetrating it.

I peered out. Lash was fighting hand to hand with a huge red-skinned man. They were slashing at each other, their knives moving so fast they blurred.

"Take her!" Devlin said, handing me Esperanza. "Give me the gun! I have to help him! That's a demon!"

I took her limp form carefully, handing him the gun I'd taken from Victor as I tried to put pressure on Esperanza's wound. He fired out the window, the bullet striking Lash's assailant in his side. The huge demon jerked, but didn't go down.

Lash launched himself at the demon, stabbing him in the heart with all his momentum behind the deadly blow. With a snarl, the demon sliced again at Lash, opening up a huge gash on the side of his face in a spray of blood. Lash snarled, but he didn't let go of his knife, working it deeper into the demon's chest, shoving with all his might. His momentum forced the demon backward, its body banging into the driver's side door with a thud. Devlin shot the demon again and again. The supernatural being jerked, huge wounds opening in its' back, but the monster didn't let go of Lash. It squeezed with all its' strength, trying to crush him in its arms. Lash fought hard, his flailing denting the truck and cracks spider-webbing the driver's window. But he couldn't get loose.

"Serena, give me your cross!" Devlin shouted with an outstretched hand. I jerked it from my neck, throwing it to him. He snatched it out of the air, and punched through the cracked glass with his other, shattering the window. With a quick movement, he grabbed the demon's head and tossed the cross down its throat. The monster screamed, acrid black smoke boiling out of its mouth. It let Lash go, clutching at its neck.

Devlin shoved Lash into the backseat, the snakeman staggering but alert. The demon went to its knees, its torso on fire, screaming. A stench of sulfur and brimstone filled the air, along with the charred smell of burning meat. Devlin pushed Lash into the passenger seat, and he got behind the wheel, peeling out at top speed. Lash alternately hissed and groaned in pain, holding his injured face.

Devlin ripped off his shirt with difficulty as he drove, handing it to Lash. "Why isn't it healing?" he said frantically.

"I don't know," Lash answered, obviously scared. "The bastard must have had werepoison on his blades. He knew I'd be here guarding you."

"Keep pressure on it!" Devlin ordered. "We're almost there!"

We drove into the airport at eighty miles an hour, barely missing passengers leaving the terminal. Devlin drove to the farthest hanger, where a private plane waited. Nick ran up to the car with some of the other bears, guns drawn. Devlin stopped the car, and hopped out. "Everybody get on the plane!" he shouted. "Perseus will be here in ten minutes or less. We've got to get in the air!" Devlin grabbed hold of Lash, and helped him into the plane. He was still bleeding badly, and hissing in pain.

Nick hugged me so hard all the breath went out of me. "We couldn't get any answer on the cell," he said worriedly.

I pushed at him, worried more demons would come. "We have to leave. Can you help me with Esperanza?"

"She's dead," Vince said softly, holding Esperanza's limp body. "Should we bring her?"

"Bring her!" Devlin said, calling out to us from the plane's doorway. "She gave her life to try to warn us. Get the last bags from the car and get into the plane!"

We hurried fast to the portable stairs, climbing aboard the plane and taking our seats. Nervous, I clutched Vince's hand as we began our trip down the runway, the engine noise going from a thin whine to a steady roar. As the land disappeared beneath us, I glimpsed a line of car headlights racing to the entrance of the airport. I shivered in relief, knowing we had just escaped in time.

Chapter Ten

The journey was a long one to the United States. I slept most of the way. Most of the men slept, played with their various electronic devices, or talked. No one was drinking, though everyone obviously wanted to. The tension level was high, the unspoken question of what awaited us at our destination a very frightening possibility. *We escaped one enemy, but will another be waiting for us when we arrive? Perseus must have friends. And Dev was in hiding where we were. I wonder if we're not heading from the pan to the fire.*

Devlin spent much of his time beside Lash, by themselves in the front of the plane in first class. The bleeding from Lash's facial wound had stopped, but the gash remained raw with no signs of even clotting. After an hour with no indication of it closing, Devlin sewed up the gash with a first aid kit he'd found in the bathroom. Lash cursed him intermittently, whenever Devlin sank the needle into him.

"Damn it hurts!" Lash hissed. "That bastard better be frying in hell."

"He's there burning, and you're alive," Devlin assured, as he tied the last knot. "You're going to be pretty nasty-looking for a while, 'till it heals, but I think most women will see it as an improvement."

"Fuck you!" Lash hissed, grimacing. "I'm in pain and you're being a prick! Best friends are supposed to be supportive."

Devlin laughed, then he gave Lash a hug. "There. Feel better?"

I watched in silence, shocked. I hadn't known they were anything more than employer and employee. *Yet, Lash is the only one I've ever heard call Devlin "Dev."*

"Rest," Devlin said affectionately. "We'll be back in The States in another ten hours."

"Esperanza is dead, isn't she?" Lash asked. "I thought I saw Vince carrying her."

"Yes," Devlin said softly. "She came to warn us, but someone shot her with an explosive bullet. It shredded a lung and most of her heart. She died on the way to the airport."

"I told her she could come with us," Lash hissed sorrowfully. "I was going to help her start a new life in the US, maybe help her find a job. I didn't want a life with her, but I couldn't leave her behind."

"I'm sorry," Devlin consoled. "She only warned us because of you, Lash. She cared for you a lot."

"I know she did," he hissed softly. "And it led her to her death. Big surprise."

"It wasn't your fault," Devlin said firmly. "As it is, we're very lucky we were already leaving. If I hadn't learned Sar was dying—"

Sar is dying? No wonder Devlin was so worried.

"Sarelle's dying?" Lash interrupted, looking at Devlin in disbelief. "Of what?"

"Danial said she's colder," Devlin explained, deeply upset. "She hasn't had any blood from him, and he hasn't been with her, so she can't be turning! I think she might need regular doses of the virus to live now, but I won't know until I see her, or taste her…" He trailed off.

"You know Theo's not going to let you just be with her," Lash hissed meaningfully. "I don't know why she didn't tell him about you and she, Dev, but you're stupid if you think that's not going to come out."

"He might be leaving her, Lash," Devlin broke in, with barely restrained excitement. "He left today for Europe, to go see Tasha. The Russian girl, the one you found him with after he went missing."

"That fucking stupid cat!" Lash hissed spitefully. "He leaves his mate alone, when she's sick, to go to that girl? After all Sar did to find him? Could he be more of an asshole?"

I didn't understand any of this, except that Devlin thought he now had a clear path to Sarelle, and that she needed him. *Very romantic, especially if he saves her like he hopes to. But Lash is right, it's a dangerous game.*

"I need to get to her in time, Lash," Devlin said, desperate. "I'm asking Titus to meet us at the airport. He'll teleport me home, and I'll leave immediately for her house."

"Dev, it'll be day by then!" Lash hissed, his eyes wide. "I'm too hurt to go with you. You're being crazy. Don't go getting yourself killed for a broad who—"

"Nick will go with me," Devlin assured. "I've called Brian. He's got things in motion so I can get close enough to see her, to tell if she does need me."

"She fought you the last time you had her," Lash said harshly. "What makes you think this time will be any different?"

"If she needs me like I think she does, she won't fight me at all," Devlin assured him. "She'll want me badly, like she wanted Danial for months now. Like I've wanted her for months." His voice dropped lower, becoming husky. "And I told you, that last time with her, she seduced me, Lash, and after, when we talked…" He trailed off.

"And?" Lash prompted.

Dev gave a sigh. "I think deep down she always wanted me, from what she said. Things may be very different when she sees me again."

"Theo'll want to kill you, no matter what happens," Lash said. "And then I'll have to kill him, Dev, to keep you safe. She won't forgive you for killing her mate, no matter what he's done."

"If I'm right, Lash, I'll need you to do something else for me, besides keeping Theo out of my hair," Devlin said, appearing not to hear Lash. "But I'm not going to think about that until I see Sar. If I'm wrong, and she doesn't need me, then I'm going to let her go. We'll move operations to another state, and that'll be the end of it."

"Like hell!" Lash hissed, rolling his eyes. "You can't let her go, or you would have already! You're in love with her! You've talked of nothing else but her for months! For years! Her and her damned summer blood!"

"Fuck you!" Devlin growled angrily. "You've never been in love, Lash! I've got a chance to be with her again, maybe to claim her for my own! How can I not take it? How can I not try at least?"

"I'm sorry," Lash hissed less stridently. "You're right, I've never been in love, I don't understand. I want you to be happy, Dev. I'm just hurting bad."

"Lie there and rest," Devlin said forcefully, making Lash sit back in the seat and recline. "I'll get you some more painkillers. Vince has some." Devlin seemed to notice me for the first time. "Serena, go ask Vince for some of his pain pills."

I nodded, and went back to the rest of the men.

Vince was talking to Kev. "I told you, I heard him say we're going back for her."

"Vince," I interrupted. "Devlin asked me to ask you for some of your pain pills for Lash."

Vince fished out a few, and handed them to me.

"Serena, is it true Dev's going home for Sarelle?" Kev growled. "That he's going to try to take her for his own?"

I hesitated, then nodded.

He cursed. Vince cursed too. I left them telling each other loudly that they weren't going to guard her, this woman who'd killed their friends. Nick was trying to shush them, without looking like he was being too enthusiastic about their new duties.

I brought the pills back to Devlin, and he handed them to Lash with some water. Lash swallowed them, and groaned a little.

"I'll buy you a new cross, when we get settled in," Devlin said, giving me a smile. He patted me on the shoulder. "You don't have to worry Serena. The worst is over."

"Okay," I said, giving him a smile back, even as I knew he was lying. *He has some master plan, and it's going to endanger us all. All for love. It would be so romantic, if it wasn't my future on the line along with his love.*

* * * *

When the plane landed, Devlin got off first, with Nick following to guard him. Afterwards, I didn't see either of them for several days.

Lash might have been badly injured, but it didn't impede him getting everyone organized and off the plane. We left in a convoy for Devlin's home, a place Vince said was called Hayden. A few hours later, we arrived.

Hayden was a beautiful house, yet it looked as though a war had been fought there. According to Vince, one had been. "Titus, Devlin's sorcerer was fighting with his witch woman Leri," he explained in a whisper. "He's a good guy, Titus, especially in a fight. But Leri's good too, she's healed me up more than once."

I looked around, appalled at the destruction. There were huge holes in the walls and ceilings, many furnishings were broken or blackened as if by fire, and almost all the decorations were missing. "What did they fight about?"

"Leri got pregnant years ago. Titus kind of made it happen, from what I heard, and she didn't want it, or know what he'd done. So she hid the pregnancy, and left the baby out west, after it was born." He paused. "But it found its way home. Titus finally found out this past fall that he has a son named Terian. When he found out, he hit the roof." He paused again. "Letting them stay here to watch things was a mistake, if you ask me. A full assault by the vampire hunters would have caused less damage."

I nodded. *This sounds like a soap opera.*

"I don't want you to worry, because he's a demon, and she's a witch," Vince continued, hugging me close. "I know how religious you are. But Titus won't hurt you, though he sometimes 'feels bad,' which is the best I can put it. Leri keeps to herself mostly. She's not staying here right now anyway, though I think she's still Devlin's employee."

This was too confusing for me. "Okay."

"Let's get you settled in," Vince said, grabbing a few boxes of mine and heading upstairs. "Devlin said you're in the room next to Lash's."

Oh no. "Are you sure?" I said plaintively, as I followed him upstairs.

"Dev's room is in there," he pointed to a heavy oak door. "Lash's room is next to his. So yours is here." He set down the boxes, and opened the door.

The room wasn't the opulent palace my old one had been. But it was still lavishly decorated, with a king-size bed, two large maple dressers, and a large walk-in closet. Strangely, it was also cozy, the way my room in South America hadn't been. The bathroom was lush, too, with a built-in Jacuzzi tub attached to a large shower built for at least two. *Have other women like me been stabled here in the many years Devlin's lived here? Was this built specifically for the house's...female...?* I stumbled mentally, not wanting to use the word "whore." *But what other word is there? "Salaried lover"?*

"Can you unpack yourself, if I get the boxes up here?" Vince said, concerned. "I know you must be rattled after all that's happened. I'd love to stay and be in your arms." He kissed me chastely. "But I need to report for guard duty in an hour."

"Sure," I said, managing a smile. "When will Nick be back?"

Vince scowled. "Not for days." Then he left, before I could ask what he meant.

* * * *

I was reading in bed that night when I felt a very bad feeling, as if something oppressive was drawing near, like a physical warning of some evil event to come. There was a knock at my door.

I got up to answer it, sure it must be Vince. But it wasn't. A huge man stood there with red skin and very short dull black horns just noticeable above his close cropped black hair. *This has to be Titus, the demon.* The heat coming off him was intense. His hair was even waving just a little in the heat waves coming off him. "Good evening," he said pleasantly. "I'm Titus. I'll be rooming next door to you."

Argh! Lash on one side, and a demon on the other? "Good to meet you," I forced out.

He reached for my hand, and I recoiled. Titus stopped, taking his hand back. "You have nothing to fear from me," he assured in a rumbling bass voice that sounded amused. "I am here just to introduce myself. Devlin's told me of your beliefs." He winced a little. "And I am not the kind of male that would come calling for your services after knowing how you feel, even were I not already spoken for."

"Thanks," I said quickly, then blushed. "Most everyone I've met has been respectful."

"Most?" Titus rumbled, then his red eyes flashed briefly. "You must be referring to Lash."

"Yes."

"Settling in?" a sarcastic hissing voice said. "Ah, I see you've lost no time in introducing yourself, Titus. But then I heard you're single now." Lash came sauntering up the hall, his face still looking raw under the stitch marks. "Makes sense you want to get in line."

"Why couldn't you have been blown up in Rio?" Titus rumbled, sarcasm and obvious real dislike in each harsh word. "I heard you lost Brock and Justin, not to mention Lars."

"Cannon fodder," Lash hissed coldly. "You know how it is." He grabbed hold of me suddenly, making me give a startled cry. "But we found Serena here." Lash rubbed his cheek on mine. I winced, feeling the rough edges of his fresh stitches raking my skin. "And that might be worth all the bullshit. She fucks for pay. The bears love her, though I've yet to sample her myself."

Titus gave Lash a sudden shove. He wasn't expecting it, and fell to one knee, as I grabbed hold of my door, breaking my own fall. "Leave her alone, Snake," he growled. "You aren't going to force her to accept you, not while I'm around. And it's obvious you already tried to, from the scent of fear on her."

"Then maybe it's time you went back to Hell," Lash said with a grin, taking out his gun.

Titus laughed. "As if your gun would work to do the job! Did you lose your brains in Rio, along with your face?"

"These bullets were blessed," Lash hissed. "I brushed them with holy water."

"That will burn off, when you fire them at me," Titus said resolutely, unmoving.

"Want to take the chance?" Lash offered, baring his fangs, his scarred face twisting. "*I* do."

"You shoot me, and no matter what happens, I won't heal you," Titus said, not moving. "And your face isn't healing, like it should. Want to know why?"

"Poison," Lash hissed, his finger tightening on the trigger. "Another of your kind had it on his blade. But he's in hell now, you can say 'hi' when you get there."

"It's not poison," Titus said mysteriously. "I would smell it, and I don't."

Lash looked at him for a long moment, then lowered his weapon. "Then why?"

"Come with me," Titus said, pushing past him, and heading downstairs. "And I'll do my best to find out." He turned back, focusing on Lash. "We need you, if Devlin does what I'm guessing he's going to. He's supposed to call in an hour or so. We need to be ready when he does."

Lash holstered his gun, and followed Titus, without a backward look.

* * * *

I was still unpacking that night when Vince came to say he was leaving. "We have to go tonight on a mission."

I was surprised to see he had on some type of armor, dull black in color, and a ton of ammunition and guns strapped to him. "Are those grenades?" I asked. "What's going on?"

He hugged me tight. "I may not come back, Serena," he whispered gruffly. "Everyone's saying this is a suicide mission." He pulled back from me to gaze into my eyes. "But Lash and Titus are going," he said, confident. "With them along, we'll make it, at least some of us." He gathered himself. "They would send us by ourselves and go in separately, if there wasn't any hope of getting out alive, if we were just supposed to be a distraction."

He cupped my face in his hands. "I'll come back to you, if I can. If I don't, I want you to know I left you my money."

I'd always thought of Vince with affection, and nothing more intense than that. Yet his sudden admission of feelings made my chest tight. "Vince, I don't want your money."

"I don't have anyone, no family, except for Nick and you, and the other bears," he said gruffly. "I always liked it that way. But I stand here, knowing I have to go, and that this might be it for me, and I can't say that I didn't want there to be more to my life than what it is now." He gave a derisive snort. "Listen to me, being a candy ass, like this is my first mission! Jesus!" He cast me a quick look. "Sorry."

"It's okay," I assured, feeling overwhelmed. "I'll pray for you. Be safe."

"Tell me that you want me to come back," he asked hesitantly. "Please?"

I hugged him tight. "Of course I want you to come back," I said, swallowing hard. "Please be careful."

"Vince!" Kev shouted from downstairs. "Let's go!"

Vince gave me a rough last kiss, and then he was out the door, his footsteps moving fast down the stairs.

Chapter Eleven

I didn't sleep much that night, waking often to look at the clock and then toss and turn until the next ten minutes had passed and I did it all over again. In the morning, there was still no word. Jazz was the only werebear left guarding the main house, his jealous wife Valerie with him, dogging his steps as he waited. Nick was still with Devlin, guarding him wherever he was. Some other werebears I'd never met before manned the gatehouse, with orders to stay there until either Devlin or Lash returned. Everyone else was gone, doing their part for Devlin's still-secret master plan. A snowstorm was raging outside, burying the land in drifts of white.

I'd always longed to see snow, wondering what it felt like, hoping someday to find out, and go skiing, or build a snowman, or other winter activities. But the actuality of a real Northeastern American winter was bitter cold that chilled my tropical blood, and drove me back to my room as soon as I'd eaten my breakfast.

The day passed slowly, then the night. I fell asleep with my book on my face, not having comprehended the last page for hours. I was awoken at five a.m. by a bloodcurdling scream. *Valerie.* I dashed to my feet, and ran downstairs, pushing through the kitchen door.

Kev was prone on the kitchen floor, covered in blood and many cuts, his torso riddled with bullet wounds. His right arm had been severed, and was just a stump, though I saw Titus was trying to reattach the twitching limb. Kev breathed raggedly as the demon worked, a piece of worked polished steel in his mouth, growling in pain.

Vince was worse. He lay unmoving, also covered in blood and bullet wounds. His middle was slashed open in four huge deep gashes, his innards exposed. A woman knelt beside him, working frantically.

I went quickly to her, and knelt beside her. "What can I do?"

201

"Clean off his intestines, and his other organs. Push them inside, and sew up the wound. I'll heal it, as you sew it closed, but I need all my concentration to keep him breathing! He's losing too much blood!"

"How do I—?"

She tossed some heavy thread to me, a needle stuck in it. "Bring the edges together with the thread. I can't heal a wound that big!"

I hurried to obey, threading the needle with shaking hands. My skin crawled with the first poke of the metal into Vince's body, but once I was sewing, my tension eased. As I brought the edges of his skin together, the woman healed him, leaving unbroken flesh in our wake. After his torso was closed, she turned to me, fixing me with her calm brown eyes. "Clean him up as best you can," she ordered. "I've got to take over for Titus, before he makes a mess of Kev's arm and cripples him for good."

She turned from me, rushing to Kev. Titus bounded to his feet and raced out of the room to the basement. A faint bellowing sounded, a furious voice that seemed to go through the walls. I didn't understand the language. *Was that German?*

"Serena!" the woman shouted to me. "Get working, or he'll die!"

I grabbed a dishcloth and ran some hot water into the dishpan, grabbed the first aid kit from beneath the kitchen sink, then turned my attention back to Vince. I slowly cleaned him off, sewing up all the larger wounds and bandaging the others. They were not healing as they should. *None of them. Werepoison? Or some other dark magic?*

Soon, I had all Vince's visible wounds taken care of. Surmising he might have others, I removed the rest of his clothes, and found a few more wounds. When I had those cleaned and bandaged, I turned to the woman. She was still working on Kev. His arm was now reattached, and his larger wounds were healed. Within a few moments, she was finished. She turned to me, and gave me a smile. "I'm Leri. Thanks for helping."

"What do we do now?"

"I'll teleport them to their beds. With a little rest, and a lot of meat, they'll be good as new." She got to her feet. "But you won't have anyone visiting you for at least a few days."

I felt a chill. "Where are the others who went with them?"

"Dead," Lash hissed, striding into the room. "Ebediah didn't come easily. He's trying to tear his cell apart right now. We'll need to reinforce the bars with magic, a holding spell of some kind."

"Devlin's an idiot!" Leri exclaimed loudly. "Ebediah's the only vampire Ruler who himself knows magic. He'd have been much smarter to go after Zane!"

"Zane's the weakest of the Rulers, even weaker than Danial," Lash hissed, looking at her coldly. "Devlin's got to be strong. To do that, he needs to drain someone strong. And Ebediah was the only one so confident he would not be attacked that an attack with so few men would have worked."

Leri just looked at him, then away, her blatant opinion that an 80% loss and 100% injury rate didn't constitute a successful attack. I noticed belatedly that Lash seemed fine, though he was covered in blood spatters, and his whip was caked with it, like his boots. His knife and its sheathe was oddly missing.

"Titus asked you to come below, when you're done," Lash added. "He needs your help with Sola. He can't keep blocking them both."

Leri whipped her head back, incredulous. "You brought her back alive too? She's the one that taught him magic!"

Lash nodded. "Devlin's orders. And he's still your boss, Leri."

"That's fucking great," Leri said sarcastically. "Tell Titus I'll be down in a minute." She got up, and motioned with her hands to two prone guards. Kev's and Vince's bodies rose in the air a few feet, and she strode off, the bodies floating behind her like attentive dogs.

Lash turned to me. "Go back to bed," he hissed tiredly. "The worst is over." Then he turned, and headed going downstairs. The bellowing was even louder now. *Is that Ebediah?*

I did as he asked, though I didn't sleep for some time, wondering where all this was leading, and what it would mean for me.

* * * *

The next morning, I attended a mass funeral at dawn in the estate graveyard located behind the house. The other bears that had gone on the mission had been killed, as Lash had said, including my former lovers Matt, Van, Harald, and Gerry. But the saddest thing to me was that four other bears had died, ones I hadn't known or spent time with, because those had been mated bears who had stayed behind at Hayden, and never came to South America at all. Their widows were crying loudly as a local priest gave a simple blessing. One widow was hysterical, screaming that her mate couldn't be gone, he was coming back, he'd promised her he would, and so he couldn't be dead. Jazz finally slapped her, and she quieted, but the tension remained high. I excused myself as soon as possible, heading toward the house.

When I got back, Nick was in the kitchen. He hugged me so hard I couldn't breathe, and I hugged him back just as hard, relieved he was back. "I heard what happened," he said. "I'm sorry we didn't get back until now."

"Nick!" Devlin shouted from the basement, impatient. "Get down here!"

Nick gave me an anxious look and left.

I'm tired of being passive, of never knowing what's going to happen next. My eyes narrowed and I followed Nick down the stairs. He went through what looked like some kind of workshop, and then through the door at its far end. I went to the door and listened. It wasn't hard to hear, with my fox-coyote hearing.

"How dare you, Dalcon?" It was the same old voice from last night, calmer now and speaking English, albeit with a very odd inflection.

"You know me, Ebediah," Devlin said in rolling tones. "I dare most anything."

"Where is Sola?" Ebediah roared. "What have you done with my Oathed One?"

"She is dead," Lash hissed nastily. "Devlin drained her this morning."

There was utter silence. I held my breath.

"You broke our most sacred law, to do such a thing," Ebediah said in hushed tones. "Laws you yourself wrote! Have you no respect for love?"

Lash laughed raucously, but someone stifled him, as he stopped abruptly. Again, silence.

"You'll drain me, too. I see your men there, and your demon," Ebediah said, sounding already lost. "Without her, I've no desire to go on anyway."

"I do have respect for love," Devlin said in slow measured tones. "You have had centuries with yours, Ebediah, while I have mourned my broken heart. I must do right by my own love. And everything else must give way before it, including yours."

"So be it. I give you this gift then, along with my blood." Ebediah paused. "I curse you, Devlin Dalcon, that whatever you most desired, whatever you really hoped to gain from doing this, you will not attain it. I promise you it will slip through your fingers like grains of sand."

"Shut your mouth!" Devlin growled. "Leri, silence him."

"May your darkest fears find you on the cusp of your happiest moment with your love." Ebediah went on in sepulcher tones. "And may all that you most feared come to pass, shredding that happiness like straw in the wind."

"Beware, Devlin. What he says is true," Leri cautioned. "He has the power to make his words reality!"

"Then silence him with a spell, before he says anymore!" Devlin snarled. "Hold him fast!"

There was a clang of steel, and the movement of hurrying feet.

"And may your love share in your suffering!" Ebediah shouted, struggling. "May she suffer the same fate when all she cherishes dies in flame!"

Ebediah cut off with a scream, the sounds of loud sucking and struggling punctuated with more intermittent screams as he was drained.

I crept back upstairs to my room, and huddled in a chair, a blanket around my shoulders, turning up my iPod as high as I could, so I didn't hear the screams.

Chapter Twelve

It was a clear spring day. Sarelle or Sar, as she liked me to call her had come to paint some of the recently finished repaired walls of Hayden. She'd done that a lot lately, since she'd begun to be a regular guest here at Hayden.

Devlin's plan of draining a powerful vampire to reclaim his seat of power as one of the world's Vampire Rulers had worked. He'd become the Master of Canada, taking Ebediah's spot. Sar had accepted him, as he'd hoped. In fact, they were now promised to one another under vampire law called officially the Oath. Sar was already pregnant with his child, a cross between a vampire and a human called a dhamphir. Sar's husband had left her, then come back again, though the details of that I wasn't sure of. There seemed to be some odd love/sex triangle with Devlin, his brother Danial, and now Theo, Sar's wayfaring husband, taking place that had all four of them on edge most of the time. As with other intrigues, I'd planned to keep to myself and avoid her. But Devlin had come to me himself right after New Years' Eve, when all this had first happened, and asked me to spend time with her when she visited.

I'd stared at him, incredulous. "But isn't she here to spend time with you?"

He'd looked uncomfortable, but didn't say anything.

"I cannot help you if you won't tell me the truth," I said, using the direct yet calm tone I usually used for his new hires. "What is it you want me to do?"

"I want you to be her friend," he admitted finally.

"Why?" I stammered.

"Because I think it would be good for both of you," he cajoled with a sudden winning smile. "You must miss a woman's company, Serena, after all these months with only men that have for the most part one thing on their mind."

I'd grown a little daring in the last month with all that had happened, no longer too shy to speak my mind. "You never worried about my lack of female friends before, Devlin."

He scowled at me. "Very well. She has friends at Danial's home. I want her to have one here, and Valerie is not very nice to any females, no matter what species. I want you to make her feel that she has a friend here to confide in."

I folded my hands across my chest. "You want me to spy on her?"

He shook his head, then shrugged. "Women tell things to other women that they would never tell a man. I want you to tell me if she voices unhappiness to you."

All women alive do that, and likely daily. I certainly did it frequently enough with Nick, whose mind never seemed to be on me, where I thought it belonged. "And?"

"And I'll do my best to correct it, so she is happy," Devlin finished. "There has not been a mistress at Hayden in some time, Serena. I am out of practice at being a husband, so to speak. The hardest years of a relationship are the first ones. I want my relationship with Sar to work very much. I'm asking for your help." He paused. "I will of course double your salary, for indulging me in this."

I gave an inward sigh at his love for her, feeling a sharp pang that likely no one would do such a thing to ensure my happiness. *Perhaps a man needs to be four hundred years old to be a full adult.* "Agreed. Will you introduce us? Or am I supposed to chance on her some morning on my own?"

"I will tell her that you are interested in learning some of her skills, like sewing and baking," Devlin said. "I'm sure that Nick or Vince might enjoy a pie or cookies occasionally. And I know that your own attempts to make bread did not turn out very well."

Vince, Dev's right, you need to learn to keep your mouth shut. "I already know sewing. But yes, I'd like to learn baking, if she's good at it."

"Very good, or so it's said," Devlin affirmed. "Good. I will arrange a time with her, and let you know. Thank you, little dove." He kissed the back of my hand, then left.

I sat down, thinking on his proposed plan, and realized that the idea of having a female friend was something I wanted very much. I had settled into my role here, and I still enjoyed my work. But there were only so many movies I could watch and so many books I could read. This country was new to me, and I longed to explore more of it, but I didn't want to go by myself. I wanted someone to go with me, to show me the sights and ensure that it was fun, not scary. It would be fun to have someone to take walks with, and talk to about all the things that I couldn't talk to Vince or Nick about. And lately, that seemed like most things.

Vince had been a little distant since his mission for Devlin. It was hard for me to remember his loving words before he left, or imagine him uttering similar endearments to me again. I had chalked up his parting words that night to his worry about dying. Because he'd survived, he likely regretted saying them at all. But he was still friendly to me, and sometimes we would watch a DVD together, or just talk after sex.

Nick was even more distant, to the point I thought something had happened to our friendship. Now his caresses were purely lust, and as soon as the sex was over, he found some excuse to leave. I minded on one level, but on another, it was a relief. Of the bearmen I'd initially met, only Kev, Vince, Nick, and Jazz were still alive. I worried about that, worried that one of them would die next. I had of course made acquaintances with a new set of guards who had taken the place of those dead. But my relations with those men were very unemotional to me. I thought of them as strangers I was intimate with, not like the group I'd been part of in Rio. Because the truth was, that a majority of them would probably die in a short time, and others would come to replace them. It wasn't healthy to get attached if I was only going to have to say goodbye right after I said hello.

I was a lot more cautious now than I had been six months ago. I was even cautious of Sar, not knowing if Devlin had told her my function at Hayden, or how she would take the news, if he hadn't. I hadn't expected to like her, knowing her part in my various lovers' deaths, and how Vince and Kev felt about her. Even though it had been Devlin's decision to go after Ebediah, they both blamed her for the dead guards, as well as for the deaths of their other friends years ago when Devlin had stormed her house in an effort to capture her. And so had the remaining werebear widows. Most of them were gone now. As was custom, Devlin had given them their widow's severance "blood money" as it was called in guard slang, the day after the funerals were held, and they had left for their new lives elsewhere.

But life went on. And I grew to like Sar, and the time we spent together.

She and I would be baking today, provided she had the time and energy after her painting was done. There had been no attacks on Hayden so far. Even Perseus had only come that once for an official visit, and none of our people had died, which I had to admit was Sar's work, as it had been her intercession and the announcement of her dhamphir in the making which had driven that vampire asshole away. Even Lash seemed to be mellow lately, spending a good deal of his time reading. Last week it had been the Bible. *Just when I think he's past all redemption...*

There was a knock at the door. Knowing I had no appointments, I opened it quizzically to find Lash. *Think of the snake, and he appears.* "Yes?"

"Come downstairs, please," he hissed, his tone more gentle than I'd ever heard it. "I need to speak to you."

Uneasy, I followed him downstairs. We both sat at the dining room table. Lash looked at me and away, then spoke in that same gentle tone. "Vince and Kev tried to hurt Sar. I stopped them in time, Serena."

"What?" I couldn't believe what I was hearing. "There must be some mistake. They're guards, her guards."

"Serena, don't play the fool," Lash hissed, his tone harder. "You know how Kev was with you, what he asked for. You know who he was fantasizing about. I thought what you were doing for him was good, alleviating his rage. Now I'm wondering if it wasn't just making it worse."

I flushed, dropping my eyes. "I believe he could do it. But not Vince."

"Vince is a surprise to me too," Lash hissed tiredly. "I know he was...well, he felt something for you. It's your name on his blood money."

I couldn't think straight, ugly horror seeping into my mind. *This can't be happening.* Another inner voice of my animal side said it not only was happening, I should have seen it. *Yes, his rough style of intimacy has been the same. But he hasn't smiled in a long time, or laughed either. He's been distracted, withdrawn.* "What's going to happen to him?"

"It was Sar he attacked," Lash said with finality. "Devlin's got to make an example."

"Are you sure it was him," I repeated again, my fear rising. "This had to be Kev's idea. Maybe there was a misunderstanding of some kind?"

"There's no misunderstanding," Lash interrupted. "They meant to rape her. I'm sure Vince was talked into it, that Kev's been working on him since our attack on Ebediah's estate."

I stood and faced him down, my own anger turning my arms furry and my eyes yellow. "So? I'm not advocating rape's a good thing, Lash. But didn't Devlin take Sar against her will himself? How is it that he metes out death for a crime he committed himself?"

"You're colder than I thought," Lash hissed softly, studying me. "I thought you were her friend."

"I care about Vince," I said just as coldly. "I can't forgive what he's done. Sar is a victim, and she deserves justice. But its' not the Christian thing to do, punishing Vince with death when you know it wasn't his fault." My anger ratcheted up a notch. "And where was all this judgment when I was being bear for Nick and Vince, and Kev took advantage of me? You did nothing to him for that, Lash! Devlin did nothing, either, except thank me for my fucking understanding!"

"I didn't know you swore, either," Lash said sarcastically. "It's a surprise we don't get along better, Serena." He paused. "The truth is, if it were up to Devlin, he would likely let both of them off with a beating and a castration, both of which they'd heal from in good time, but not before they changed their attitude. But it's not up to him, Serena. Sar and Devlin are not alone in their Oath: Theo and Danial are equal parties. And they are both calling for the death of the two werebears. And his favorites or not, if Dev doesn't serve up Kev and Vince, he will likely lose Sar and his unborn child for good."

This is all Sar's fault. Hers and Devlin's. But that didn't matter now, did it? Devlin was master here. "Is he dead?"

"No, but he will be in a few hours," Lash said gently. "Do you want me to take you to see him, to say goodbye? He's out cold, but—"

"No," I said, wiping at my filling eyes. "I don't want to see him, knowing he did this. I want to remember him how he was, how we were together. There's nothing to say." I grabbed a tissue, and wiped off my face, then crumpled it in my hand. "Even though it's unfair he's going to die, Vince had to know what would happen. And he did it anyway, knowing it was wrong."

"Sar wants to see you," Lash said abruptly, standing. "Take her condolences, then excuse yourself."

He left. A moment later, Sar came into the kitchen. She hugged me, and told me she was sorry. And I told her it was okay, even though it wasn't. Then she left, and I made my way upstairs, closing my bedroom door. As I went to lock my door for a good cry, Lash's voice again came through my door. "I asked you to wait for me," he hissed, his tone still gentle. "Open this door."

I'd seen him break doors down before when he wasn't let in, so I opened it. He sauntered in, closing it behind him. I felt suddenly unnerved having him alone in my bedroom. He took my hand, and led me to my couch, where we both sat down.

"Do you want the money?" he hissed gently. "Devlin asked me to take care of that, while he speaks to Sar."

"No," I said, wiping away more tears. "Give it to the church I go to, please. They have an abused women center they support. Send it there."

Lash nodded. "I'll take care of it." He looked at me, and then quickly away, remaining silent.

"Just say it," I said, exhausted. "Please."

"I was the one who went to get Devlin's Oathing ring made. You know the one he wears, that's similar to the ring Danial gave Sarelle? The one with the many colors?"

I nodded.

"Vince had this made for you," Lash hissed softly, handing me a box. "He ordered it months ago. I picked it up and gave it to him at least a month back. I don't know why he didn't give it to you yet. But I noticed you weren't wearing it, so I checked. It was there in his locker, way in the back."

"You already looked through his locker?" I blurted, holding the box unsteadily.

"Guards get killed often in Devlin's employ," Lash said. "Most of them have no one to leave their things to and no will if they aren't mated. Usually the others divide them up." He paused. "He wouldn't have cared if someone took any of his other shit. But he'd have wanted you to have this. And it would have pissed me off to see one of the bearwives wearing it, when I know who it was supposed to go to."

Against my better judgment, I opened the box. Inside was a beautiful ring, set with an emerald. It was a very delicate and feminine design, the stone not large. Yet it sparkled very brightly.

Lash got up, and went to leave. "I will let you know about funeral arrangements."

"Why did he get this for me?" I said in confusion, looking up at Lash.

"You know why," he hissed gently as he left, shutting the door after him.

* * * *

Nick came to me that night. For a long time, we just held one another and cried. He managed to say finally that he didn't blame Sar, Devlin, or anybody but Kev, that he'd known of Kev's plan, and had refused to participate. But he cursed himself as he cried for not doing more to stop them. And I cursed him too that night, for not finding a way to save Vince, even from himself.

Chapter Thirteen

It would be winter soon, I thought wearily. I'd lived here a year at Hayden now, and seen a hell of a lot in only twelve months. *Too much, actually.*

I got up, and went to my window. The sun was shining brightly, though it would be setting shortly. I took out my emerald ring and put it on, enjoying the reassuring sparkle. I often wore it to bed, when no one was coming to visit and it was time to actually sleep. That way, Devlin and Sar's dhamphir daughter V, was the only one who saw it. She wasn't talking yet, so there were no explanations needed.

Even though the spring had turned to summer, and now back to winter, not much had changed for me except we'd lost a few more guards. Well, truthfully, more than a few.

Sar had given birth in late summer. Venus, V for short, lived here with Devlin full time. Even with all his talk, Devlin had been in the end like most men, and his little head had gotten the rest of him in trouble when Sar had found him with an old flame in bed coupling. Devlin and Sar were currently back together unofficially after a few huge fights and separations, but I wasn't sure how long that would last.

Another old enemy of Devlin's had come out of the woodwork, by the name of Ulysses. He'd captured both Sar and Devlin one night, putting the latter through horrific torture to the point I was sure that Ebediah's curse had come true, as Leri had warned it would. I also worried for Sarelle, who against my reservations was my closest girlfriend now. *Ebediah hadn't only put a curse of suffering on Devlin, he'd cursed her, too.* She'd lost her infant son with Theo to crib death, precipitating that couple's permanent breakup. That "cougar thug," as I thought of Theo, was already engaged to someone else. And her house had burned, Sar escaping only because of Lash's apparently lucky visit

213

to check some suspicious activity Sar had reported. I hoped that was enough suffering to satisfy the apparent curse, saying daily prayers that things would get better. Ulysses had attacked several times now, enacting vengeance for his dead sister. While I understood his motivations, my nerves were shot, as were the nerves of most everyone else at Hayden.

I turned off the light and got in bed. Nick would wake me up, when he got back from his resupply trip into town.

* * * *

I woke up, and stretched, glancing at the clock. *God, oversleeping shouldn't be a bad thing, it always feels so good.*

I sat bolt upright, looking again at my clock. *It's almost six now, and Nick isn't here.*

I hurried downstairs, and checked the kitchen. *No Nick.*

Pushing open the door to the attached garage, I noticed that the Hummer H2 at the far side was missing. With a scream, I ran down the stairs to Titus's shop, and found he wasn't there, either. I ran for the kitchen phone, and called his house. A sleepy sounding Leri answered. "Hello?"

"Get here!" I screamed. "Nick is missing! He never came home last night!"

Leri yelled for Titus. Dropping the phone, I ran upstairs, and began pounding on Devlin's door. I knew he was there, and so was Sar. *She'll be concerned, even if he isn't. She knows I'm in love with Nick.*

Devlin and Sar came downstairs with me. Titus arrived via teleportation in the kitchen, located Nick magically via his tracking spell, and a few minutes later, he arrived holding a bloody form. But it wasn't the Nick I knew. Because this man had been skinned. He was just muscle, bone, and red rawness dripping blood in a steady pat-pat-pat onto the bright yellow tiles.

Sar fled the kitchen and ran to the bathroom, dragging her girl child with her. The bathroom door shut with a click.

"He'll die soon," Devlin said forlornly, looking down at Nick's twitching body. "Damn it, I'm losing men left and right."

"Isn't there anything we can do?" I screamed. "We have to save him!"

214

"We have no skin to heal together," Leri said, appearing suddenly from the living room. "There's nothing to cover him."

"Maybe we do," Titus rumbled, eying me. He fixed his gaze on me. "If you help us."

"Tell me what to do!" I shouted.

"We need a skin, a wereanimal's skin, to drape him with," Titus rumbled. "Something to sew closed, that his body hopefully won't reject."

Danial excused himself to look after Sar, to keep V out of the kitchen.

"Are you willing, Serena?" Devlin said seriously, taking my hand in his cool one. "You'll lose one of your animal forms, and the pain's going to be bad, even with a spell. You're under no obligation to do this."

"I can help with the pain," Leri said quickly. "But he's right, essentially you're going to be losing part of your soul. And it's a part that won't heal. Nick's dying in part because the bear half of him has been ripped away. Losing your animal side if you're were is not like losing an arm, or a kidney. It can't grow back."

"We do this now, or it's too late," Titus rumbled loudly. "He has another ten minutes, at best."

"Do it," I said, letting my robe drop. I shifted form to coyote, laying down on the floor and stretching out, steeling myself for what was to come.

The next ten minutes were the worst of my life. Devlin pulled my skin off slowly with a skinning knife of Titus's. Even with Leri stopping the bleeding, and helping the physical pain, she was right, it was pure agony. There was the feeling of my soul being cloven, of part of myself being separated from the rest. I screamed over and over, struggling and flinching even as I tried to keep still. Finally, when my coyote skin was fully off, Leri and Titus began to work on Nick. Devlin grabbed hold of me. "Change to fox!" he whispered urgently. "Please, Serena!"

It's the first time he's ever said please to me. I began to shift, my orange-red fox fur covering my bare muscles. The change completed, I lay panting on my side as fox, my soul still feeling shattered.

My sacrifice hadn't been in vain. Titus and Leri had somehow made the skin larger, and it was adhering to Nick's body, as his bloody form shrunk to fill the skin. Soon he was lying in the coyote form, somewhat larger than I'd been as a coyote. He was panting hard, but no longer hurt.

"They must both rest," Leri whispered to Devlin. "And be left with raw meat, blood, and water, as much as they'll eat, when they wake." She paused. "I can't believe that worked."

"I'm not a novice, witch wife," Titus said irritably.

"You're a hero," Leri said tenderly, kissing him. She clearly meant it as a light kiss, but he grabbed hold of her, sitting her on his lap, and hugging her tightly. "And a genius," she added, with a sultry smile.

"I couldn't bear it, if I lost you," he rumbled.

"You aren't going to," she said tenderly. Then she kissed him again, as I lost consciousness.

* * * *

When I awoke, Nick was near me, also awake and still in coyote form. He caught my gaze and shifted back. So did I. As soon as we had arms, we grabbed each other tight, holding fast.

"What did he do to me?" Nick whispered in fear. "What did Titus do to me? I can't feel my bear self, Serena. But I feel something else. It's like when I was fox for you, but different."

I squeezed him reassuringly. "You were skinned. I gave you my coyote form, so you wouldn't die."

"Why?" he choked out. "Why did you save me?"

"I love you," I said, enough longing and feeling in the words to rend my heart.

There was so much I hoped he would tell me, so much I wanted him to say. Instead, he looked at me in silence. "When?" he got out finally.

"For a while," I stammered, thinking back.

"Since Vince died?" Nick asked.

I didn't reply

"I know he was going to ask you to be mated to him, even though some of us laughed at him for it. I've seen the ring that you wear, the emerald ring he got for you." Nick wouldn't meet my eyes. "But my answer is still the same, Serena. I'm not ready to be mated."

I felt floored. *I'd have done it anyway,* I told myself, squeezing the tears back. *It doesn't matter that he doesn't love me.*

Then I registered what he'd said. "You laughed at him, for caring about me? For not just thinking of me as…as what, a good fuck?"

"I'm sorry," Nick said in the same solemn tone. "I should've gone after Sar with Kev. Then Vince would've been here with you, and you'd still have both your forms."

"Just leave," I said bitterly, pushing him away. "Leave, Nick, and don't ever come back."

Nick gave me an anguished look, but he grabbed a blanket from my bed, and left.

I cried for a long, long time. *I told you if love was going to hurt, I didn't want it, God. This isn't a blessing, to feel this strongly for someone and not have them feel the same in return.*

That night, everyone stayed away. Everyone that is, except for my newest lover, Sar's adult dhamphir son, T. I heard his knock, and murmured, "Go away."

The door opened. *Stupid, I didn't lock it after Nick left.* T stood there, looking confused. Then he saw I was upset. "Are you okay?" he whispered, coming over and holding me. "You're crying."

He's here for his session. Nice as he is, I just can't make myself do it. "No," I said, dissolving into tears again. "I'm not okay. I feel like I'm dying!"

"Shh," he said calmly, holding me. "I'm here, Serena. Let it out if you need to."

I blinked at him. "You're telling me to cry?"

"Mom says to always let it out," he said calmly. "She's right, keeping it inside hurts. Let it go, so you can feel better."

So I cried for another hour, lamenting my choice in men, my profession, and the day I'd met Devlin Dalcon. In time, the tears stopped and became sniffling, then sometime after I fell asleep.

I awoke in T's arms, in bed. "Are you feeling better?" he said, brushing my cheek with his hand. "I can bring you breakfast, if you want some."

"You can cook?" I said in shock.

T laughed. "Breakfast, sure. My sister Elle taught me. She said not to expect a woman to be around all the time to cook for me. And she was right, there usually hasn't been one, unless Mom's home. Though Elle or Cia sometimes feels in a mood to take pity on me."

His voice was matter of fact, and not angry or resentful. I managed a smile for him. "Sure, that would be nice."

I expected him to bring me some burnt toast, and maybe, if I was lucky, some water and undercooked eggs. But he came back in thirty minutes with eggs over-easy, toast, bacon, sausage, pancakes, and also a bagel, along with some water, and a vaseful of black and yellow daisies.

He handed me the tray, and took the daisies, putting them on the end table.

"Thanks," I said gratefully. "They're beautiful."

"Mom likes roses best," T said, shrugging. "But you look like more of a daisy kind of girl. Sorry they're not in a prettier arrangement."

"I've always liked daisies," I said, digging into the food with gusto. "Especially those black and yellow ones." I didn't have the heart to tell him that he was the only one besides Nick who'd ever gotten me flowers.

"They're called Black-Eyed Susans," T offered. "Elle said so, anyway. I had Terian teleport down south just now, to grab me some for you."

How can T be so thoughtful of me and Nick be such an asshole? "You didn't have to."

"I wanted to," T said, reclining beside me. "We're intimate, Serena. I think you deserve to be treated well."

There was something of Devlin in the way he said it, and in the manner of how he was reclining so casually on my bed. But there was a difference in that there was real feeling behind T's words, that he meant them and that he cared about how I felt emotionally, not just as a satisfied lover to whom he was teaching sexual tricks.

I finished my food in a few moments. I'd been hungrier than I thought. I put the plate aside, and turned to him. "Are you visiting Hayden to see your uncle?" I asked. I'd been going to say see Lash, then remembered with embarrassment that Lash was in jail. My coworker had gotten framed by Ulysses, and was doing his month or so of remaining time in the county lockup. Sar had just accepted Devlin's explanation, when he'd told her of Lash's confinement. Yet I'd scented there was some lie behind why Lash remained in jail, when I knew that Devlin could have found many ways to facilitate his escape. *He's staying there for a reason.*

"To see you," T said with a boyish grin, snapping me back from memory to the present. He turned solemn. "I want to know why you were crying though first, please."

With halting words, I related what had happened, all of it, between Nick and myself, adding in what Vince was planning to ask me, and even how I'd met them, just over a year ago. When I finished, T held me to him gently. "Please don't be sad. Vince loved you a lot to want to make you the promise it sounds like he was going to make to you. And you saved Nick's life, which was very brave, even if he was an asshole who didn't deserve the sacrifice you made."

"I know," I whispered. "I just feel stupid."

"Love makes us all stupid, at least that's what Devlin told me once. He said he'd only been in love twice, but both times it happened, he'd done stupid things."

I didn't reply. *Devlin had been very stupid about a lot of things.* The thought of him admitting that, however, was surreal.

T gave me a kiss on the cheek and got up. "I'll come back tomorrow, if that's okay," he said gently as he started to leave.

"We can now, if you want," I said, mustering up a smile.

"Is that what you want?" T said, shooting me a concerned look. "I can wait."

I'd been pretending that so many of my lovers were Nick for months now. The first few times with T, I'd done that. And I wanted to be with him now, to think of him, and not Nick. I walked to him, and kissed him passionately. He kissed me back with abandon, wrapping me tight in his embrace.

Chapter Fourteen

Over the next few months, a sort of healing took place. T came to me a few times a week, and I began to look forward to our times together, the way I hadn't looked forward to anything before loving Nick. It wasn't love, but it was comforting and good to find some solace in his arms.

Devlin came to me within a week of my break with Nick, and asked me to consider taking Nick back to my bed. He offered me double my usual rates as retribution for Nick's insult to me, and thanked me again for saving his life. I agreed, permitting Nick to visit me again but only in animal form. His coyote could mate with my fox, enough for both of us to get by. With Vince gone, there was no one willing to pay the money for a potion to do that for me. And while I could easily afford it now, I didn't want to solicit a new animal lover from my client list. I still enjoyed sex, but I'd had enough of emotional ties. I was not making any new ones if I could avoid it.

The uneasy truce between Nick and I lasted until December, when I found out from Titus the real reason Nick had gone to town the night he'd lost his skin.

The demon was in his workshop in Hayden's cellar, working on an animal pelt. I looked closer, realizing it was a bear skin. "Is that his?"

I'd meant Nick's, but Titus's mind was elsewhere, and he thought I meant someone else. "No," he rumbled. "That was sent to his widow. This is Klara's pelt. Hers was the only skin recovered that wasn't claimed by next of kin for burial."

I felt a cold feeling. "Who was Klara?"

Titus gave me an odd look, and then his face darkened, until its normal flushed hue was a dark burgundy wine color. It hit me suddenly that he was blushing; the odd darkening was because the color of his blood was black. "She's the female werebear who lived in town," he rumbled. "Some of the men went to her to be bear for them, sometimes human, too."

Shock washed through me. Then utter rage. I turned without a word, and went to my room. Once there, I called Nick on his cell, and asked him to come to me, pleading it was an emergency. When he got there a minute later, I slugged him with everything I had, knocking him to the floor. "You bastard!"

Nick looked up at me from the floor, pissed. "What's gotten into you?"

"Tell me I didn't save you with part of my soul when the reason you were caught and skinned was because you were visiting another woman for sex! Tell me that isn't true."

Nick got to his feet. "Serena, we aren't mated!" His tone was strident. "This is why I don't want to be mated, to have a woman telling me I can't be with anyone I want to be!"

"Should I get checked for diseases?" I said sarcastically.

"She got checked as you do, and the same rules were in effect for her, though she had no one watching out for her, like Devlin watches out for you." Nick's tone was now neutral. "I wasn't the only one who saw her."

Don't make this seem like its normal, like it's nothing! "I was bear for you!"

"Serena, that was six months ago."

"Yes, it was! When were you last fox for me? Almost a year ago! If I were like most other werewoman are, I'd have gone insane by now!"

"I can't afford the potion's price on my own," Nick whispered. "I've never been good with money. And there isn't anyone that I feel I can approach to help. These new guys aren't as close with me as Vince and Kev were."

I looked at him, standing there looking so removed from me, his lame words still echoing in my ears, his eyes not meeting mine. *God, he's such an utter jerk.* "Get out! Get out and don't come back!"

Nick left, and I wept again as if I'd hadn't cried in years.

That night, T came to me, again finding me crying. As he had before, he held me, and asked me what was wrong. As before, I told him, leaving nothing out. "Are you free tomorrow?" he asked.

I nodded.

"Come to me," T said. "Around midnight. I'll send Rip for you, okay?"

I nodded. He kissed my forehead gently, then excused himself.

As he'd said, Rip came for me a little before midnight, and teleported me to T's home. The handsome dhamphir met me in his large great room, where we shared a glass of wine and some light double-entendres. Together, we walked out into the forest, admiring the night.

T suddenly turned to me in mid-sentence, and bore me to the ground. At once, we were changing forms. In mere moments, I was looking at him in surprise from all fours through my fox eyes, because he was fox, also. He was a different type of fox than I was; a dark color, almost grey, but I didn't care. I lay down almost desperately, mewling at him to hurry, hoping he wouldn't be too gentle. Then he was on me, taking me, barking out sharply that I was his, and no other fox's. And I lost myself in pleasure and relief, to finally feel whole once more.

Three hours later, he began to change back, and I changed with him. When we were human, I dressed, and so did he, and together, we walked back to his home. There, I led T to his bedroom, telling him gently that Devlin had shown me some secrets of his, and if he'd permit me to, I'd like to share all I knew of them with him, by way of thanks for what he'd done for me. He replied with a smile that he'd learned from Devlin, too, and that he'd reciprocate, if I felt that way.

We passed that entire night together.

After, things between us were a little more... serious, I guess is the word. T had me come to him every week, though he still came to me at Hayden, as well as to visit his mother, and other family, and he was fox for me every time I visited him. And after being together as animals, I spent the rest of the night with him as human, loving him that way until my strength left me.

When he invited me to spend Christmas with him though, I was a little apprehensive. "What will your mother say?"

"She'll ask me if I'm happy, and if this is what I want," he said reassuringly. "And it is."

But she knows what I do for my living. So does your father. So does everyone we know. "You won't be embarrassed of me?"

"My mother is not embarrassed to be with Lash, though she isn't snake," he replied evenly. "It's well known they are lovers now, and that they care for each other."

"But she's not a…" *Why don't you just say whore? It's what you are.*

"She is also Oathed to my father, and Devlin," T said in a calm but concise tone that brooked no argument. "Please, do not concern yourself. No one will make you feel ill at ease."

I agreed, hoping for the best. After attending church in the early evening, I had Terian, Titus's son, teleport me to T's home.

Christmas at T's house was beautiful. Theo and his new werecougar female, Jenny, had brought in an enormous tree, with the help of Elle, T, and me. We decorated it together while singing some carols, though I admitted none of us could sing very well, except T. And when we were done, Theo crowned the tree with a large star.

After, we sat around, talking about Christmases past. By that, I mean mostly listening to Jenny tell of her Christmases past. I didn't have very many happy ones to share, and no one, not even T or Elle, was going to bring up Sarelle, who'd orchestrated all the past Christmases that they had shared as a family. But it was cozy, being part of a group. Before long, Theo and Jenny excused themselves to bed, and soon after Elle did as well, saying with pleasure and a good deal of relish that she was spending the night with the foxes, as Demi was telling Brian at their holiday gathering that night that she was pregnant, and she didn't want to miss the announcement. T asked to pass on congratulations for him, and also to make sure Demi went with Brian to see Dr. Camlyn next week, to make sure everything was as it should be. Elle left with a nod, to say she'd pass that on.

For a while, T and I sat on the couch, beside the tree, watching it sparkle. And then he handed me a small box, saying "Merry Christmas" in his sexy voice.

I opened it, and found some beautiful earrings, shaped like tiny chunks of gold. I put them on, and thanked him.

"My father gave similar ones to my mother, many years ago when they were dating," T said a little absently. "I hope you like them."

I assured him I did, and then told him in a hesitant voice that I had something for him as well. He looked at me expectantly.

"You have everything you need," I said getting the words out with effort. "I don't have much to offer you that you can't buy for yourself, T. But I have myself, and I can offer you that."

T looked at me, and something like nervousness flitted through his eyes, but he just kept looking at me.

"I know Devlin took care of the money for me, until the New Year," I said delicately, feeling embarrassed yet determined to see this through. "But I'm telling you now, come to me whenever you like, T, for as long as you like." I blushed, thinking this was a shameful way to celebrate my Lord's birth. But it was true, I didn't have anything else he needed. And a lover he could trust was something T did need. *And I want that lover to be me.*

T took my hand and kissed it. "That's thoughtful of you, Serena, but it's not necessary."

"It is for me," I said more forcefully, trying to be strong. "I want to give you a gift that means something, T."

"All right then," T said, nodding. "When you come to me here at my house, that's just you and I. But when I come to you at Hayden, that's on the books, so to speak. Agreed?"

"Agreed," I said, biting my lip. *Does he not want us to have a relationship? Am I reading his signals wrong, the way I did Nick?*

"Come with me," T said, taking my hand. "I'll make us a fire, and we'll sleep in front of it for a while. I know you like that."

I gave him a smile, and followed him into his bedroom. For a while we slept, our bodies warmed by the heat of the flames. But when we awoke, T groaned a little in annoyance.

I looked over at him curiously. "What is it?"

"I'm hungry," he said, embarrassed. "And with the holidays, I forgot to arrange for donors."

It dawned on me what he was referring to, and I gave him a smile. "Take some of mine, then."

T gave me a look of shock. "Did you...had you wanted me to bite you, Serena?"

Now I was the one blushing. "Um, really, I've kind of wondered why you didn't. I thought all vampires wanted blood when they had sex."

T looked away. "Devlin said it would make the sex better," he whispered. "But my father said not to feed on...not to mix the two." He gave me a worried look. "I'm the first dhamphir, Serena, I have no idea what to expect for so many things!" He cursed, sounding much like Sar did when she was upset. "I almost wish I was full vampire sometimes, it would make things easier. I'd know just what I could and couldn't do."

I sat closer to him, and took his hand. "Make love with me, and drink from me," I offered easily. "I'm not a human; I'll heal the blood loss easily. Even if I pass out from it, I'll just sleep for a while and awaken."

T gave me a funny look. "You sure? It's okay, if you don't want to."

"Do you not like wereblood? I've heard your father doesn't."

"I don't know," T said, again looking away uneasily. "I've had only human blood, and some of Brian's, when he first found me after I escaped from Ulysses's men."

"Come try it," I said, getting to my feet. "It's okay either way, T, but I'd like to do this for you, if you'll let me."

T got to his feet, and came with me to the bed. We were already in robes, so we lay down.

T hesitantly kissed me, and then moved down my neck. I expected him to do as Devlin had, to kiss me for a few minutes, and then bite down completely. But he immediately moved his teeth across my neck in a deft motion, making a small but deep cut. Then I felt his mouth fastening on me, sucking gently. His arms tightened around me, and I held him close. Unlike Devlin, he made no sounds of pleasure, and a few minutes later, he healed my cut with some of his blood. For some reason, it took him longer to heal me than Devlin had. *Probably because he's only part vampire.*

When T drew back from me, he looked much less tired, and his complexion was almost ruddy. But he didn't look especially happy. "Thank you."

Hadn't he liked the taste? "You're welcome."

T held me close, rubbing my shoulder as we lay there, saying nothing. I wanted badly to ask him if he'd liked my blood. But because he didn't say anything, I guessed that he hadn't.

Desperate to do something he would enjoy, I initiated sex with him. He responded immediately to my caresses, as he always did. The intimacy was good for both of us. But afterward, I could feel something was different between us, even though T was as gentle and loving as he'd always been with me.

* * * *

The next morning, I got a surprise. Cia was in the kitchen, making breakfast. And so were the other female foxes.

On a previous visit a few years ago, Cia and another fox, Janice, had verbally attacked me, and Sar had to come to my defense. Since then, I'd avoided the werefoxes whenever T wasn't with me, nervous of a repeat incident. This morning, when I went out hesitantly to make T some breakfast, they welcomed me. "Hi Serena," Janice said, as she mixed up what looked like a batch of scones. "Come to help?"

"Sure," I said, taking a bowl and spoon another woman offered me. I began mixing, and Cia began telling me some joke that Aran had got from Theo. Just like that, I was accepted.

Breakfast was a wonderful affair. The table was crowded, and Brian was doting on the pregnant Demi, getting her everything as soon as she made to move to get it herself. When breakfast had been served, Jenny and Theo appeared, smelling of sex. They said hello to everyone, then sat down and began eating with gusto. I wanted to say both times that the couples reminded me of how Devlin and Lash had been with Sar in the mornings where she had been making breakfast, but held my tongue, knowing to bring up Sar here wouldn't be a good idea. Yet I did feel a pang for her, alone at Hayden with her lovers. These were her former friends, and it seemed wrong she wasn't welcome here with them, just because of the men she loved now.

* * * *

Later that afternoon, when T did his emails, I readied my things to leave. And Janice stopped me. "You know, you don't have to go back there," she said quietly. "You could stay here with us, Serena."

I looked over at her quizzically. "I live there. My job and all my things are there."

"You aren't coyote anymore, you're all fox. That means you're one of us. You belong with your own kind."

I felt the pull of her words, even as my animal side assured me that she was right. "But what about my job?" I gave her a forced smile. "Don't tell me you want me plying my trade here, Janice."

"T would hire you, I'm betting." Janice said meaningfully, avoiding my second comment. "Jenny doesn't mind housework, but she hates computers, and she does the filing only under duress. You could take over that job."

Sar's old job. But when she'd had it, she'd been Oathed to Danial…well, actually, she hadn't been, not at first. They'd been lovers, and trying for a baby, she'd said. *A baby. What would it be like to be here, to belong here, and not have only T, but a ready-made family of my own kind, too?*

"Serena?"

I snapped back into the conversation out of my fantasy, before I lost myself in it. "Thank you, but I don't want to push things with T, not until…" *Until what? He tells me he loves me? That he wants to marry me? Is that what I want? And will it ever come to that, after how last night seemed?*

"Until?"

"Until I think it's what we both really want," I said firmly. "Right now, he seems happy with how things are. And so am I."

"Nice earrings," Janice said, giving me a pointed grin. "Another woman wore similar ones years ago, and said kind of the same thing about T's father. She was Oathed to him a few months later, and was pregnant with his baby a year and a half after that."

I flushed, abruptly told her goodbye, and walked out to a waiting Rip.

When I got home, I found I had someone waiting for me, leaning against my door. And it was the last person I expected to see. "What are you doing here, Nick?"

I was irritated to see that he was just as appetizing as he'd been the last time I'd seen him. But then, I'd always liked him in blue.

"Serena, I wanted to come to you, to say I was sorry," he said contritely. "I never meant to hurt you." He raked his hands through his hair. "I never thought you cared for me, any more than you care for any of the others. I don't have any standing here at Hayden, not any more than I ever had. I'm saying I know I'm never going to be someone Lash or Devlin asked to do anything important, or someone they asked for advice." He paused, and looked at the wall, as if words were written there.

"And?" I prompted.

"I knew you liked Vince," he said finally. "I thought maybe when his contract was up with Devlin, he might leave and take you with him."

"Nick, what's your point?" I cut him off sharply. "You saying all of this, it doesn't matter now."

"It does matter! I need—"

"I don't care what you need," I interrupted flatly. "I have needs, too. And they come first." I felt an amazing sense of fulfillment when I said those words. With belated pride, I realized for the first time, I myself believed them.

"I'm saying I'll meet your needs," Nick said, swallowing hard. "I will be animal for you, if you—"

"You don't need to," I interrupted again in a lilting tone. "T has been taking care of my needs, Nick. All of them."

Nick growled low and mean. "I heard that. Some of the bears are complaining, saying he's taking up all your time."

"I have time for anyone who needs me," I countered. "But I never said I wouldn't have a boyfriend of my own."

"I need you," Nick said earnestly. "And the truth is…the truth is, I do love you, Serena."

I'd been feeling so sure, so strong, and the moment he said the words, I felt all my new armor evaporating, leaving me pink and defenseless as a newborn cub. "Don't tell me lies."

"I love the quiet way of you," Nick said in a rough sexy tone, coming close to me. "I love that you're gentle, that you make me breakfast, and fix my clothes." He paused, and his next words were full of emotion, enough to almost physically see. "I love I was your first, that until me, a man hadn't touched you, hadn't even kissed you. I love that most of all." He came close to me. "Have you ever loved anyone but me?"

"No," I whispered, before I was able to lie. I—"

Nick cut me off with a passionate kiss. I kissed him back, melting into him, my longing for him a raging force that felt like it would swallow me whole.

We made love that day until we were covered in sweat, and our voices were rough from our cries of passion. And when he held me close, and asked me to let him come to me again, I agreed.

Sar, Lash, Dev, and Titus saw Nick and I later the next morning, as we were finishing breakfast. I heard Titus make some comment as he took my hand, guiding me from the kitchen, but took no note of it. My eyes were all for Nick, as he pulled me into the forest.

Chapter Fifteen

New Years was a great affair. Devlin threw a large party, in part I think to celebrate his triumph over Ulysses, and the return of his brother Danial to the waking world. After their long drawn out guerilla war that had lasted all fall, Devin had finally bested Ulysses in a challenge fight via a better double-cross involving a fight on holy ground. Sar had used her teleportation skills—which Ulysses was unaware of—to bring him to Hayden, where Devlin and Danial had drained him almost to the point of death. Shortly thereafter, Lash and Sar had burned the newly turned vampire to death, ending his reign of terror over us.

Nick was manning the gatehouse that night, and didn't attend the party. But T was there, and he spent most of the night in my company, when he wasn't with his mother, or his sisters. Everything went well, until it was seven minutes to midnight, and the shift change happened.

Lash often did that, change shifts at odd times, so that would-be attackers had no pattern to follow. He also favored a change early in the evening, so that those watching at night were fresher. But Lash's good planning tactics worked together to ensure that Nick came looking for me the moment he clocked out, wanting to share a New Year's kiss like we had last year. He caught me coming out of the ladies room, and grabbed me from behind. I let out a shriek of surprise, making him laugh. "You're so spooked," he said in my ear. "I know what you need to relax you."

I pushed him away gently. "Not now. I'm due back soon, I'm helping Sar keep an eye on V."

"Come on, Serena."

"Why don't you go with him?" a familiar cool voice said in an unfamiliar dark tone. "He can't seem to wait."

I turned, and so did Nick. T walked up to us, his steps so graceful he

230

was almost gliding. "I'll help Mom," T said in a noncommittal tone. "And the party will be over soon anyway."

Nick looked at me, then back at T. He was clearly jealous by his scent, but it was also clear he had no idea what to say, because T didn't seem angry or jealous himself.

I smiled politely at T. "Thanks, but I should go back."

"Don't bother." T turned to Nick. "And you should treat her better, jerk." He walked off, both of us too shocked to say anything.

"Well, he's Sar's son," a melodious voice intoned. Devlin came up to us, smiling, though his eyes were tinged red. "You had to expect he was going to say something."

He stopped before us. "I'd hoped to not have to interfere," he said, obviously irritated. "But I've heard enough complaints about you that I have to address this tonight, even in the midst of celebration."

I felt my face flush red. "I'm sorry, Devlin—"

"Not you," Devlin said, his tone more irritated. He turned to Nick. "You." His eyes were completely red now. "Lash has told me you've not been at your post, or you've been late to it three times this past week. What's the problem?"

"I was with Serena," Nick said immediately. "I hadn't been with her or anyone for more than a month, and I lost track of time."

"That's an adequate excuse for one time," Devlin growled. "But not for more than once. You've never before had trouble leaving her after sex. Do you have anything else to say in your defense?"

"No." Nick swallowed. "Except I know I deserve punishment, and I swear it won't happen again."

"You're damn right it won't," Lash hissed from behind Devlin. "Or you'll be fired, Nick. And being as you know the complete lay of Hayden's inside, you know when I say 'fired' I mean 'dead'."

Lash stepped closer. "Come downstairs with me now," he said, baring his fangs. "And I'll give you your punishment. And you're to be at the gatehouse at eight a.m. tomorrow, unless you want that again twice after that shift ends."

Nick cast a glance at me, and then followed Lash down the basement stairs.

I thought about asking Devlin for mercy for him. *Don't bother. He won't be swayed.* Even Sar herself usually didn't get anywhere with him.

"Rejoin the party," Devlin ordered. "Lash has plans for later tonight, so Nick's beating won't be long. But he won't be seeing you for a few days, probably."

I hesitated a second, and then Devlin cut me off, glaring down at me. Yet his voice when he spoke was more resigned than angry. "It's been a year and a half since you joined my employ. But the work you do seems to have lost its excitement for you."

"May we walk for a few minutes where we won't be overheard, to discuss my future?" I asked, moving back toward the door.

"Of course." Devlin fell in step beside me.

"I'm not unhappy," I said, when we were out of hearing of Devlin's guests. "But no, it's not something I want to do the rest of my life, Devlin."

"You have no special feelings for T, or for Nick? You don't love them?"

It hit me then, that my feelings had changed, the shock of it bringing me to a sudden stop. "No," I said. "I like them both very much. I like spending time with them, being intimate with them, more so than the others who see me. But I don't love Nick anymore. T... I might come to love him, if he decides he wants something serious, but right now he's acting distant. I'm not sure why."

Devlin looked surprised, but then he beamed. "Good," he purred. "I was worried you did love Nick. I like our arrangement very much, Serena." He took my hand, and kissed it. "I'd let you be mate to one of the bears, if you wanted, or T, if he asked for you. But from what I know of you, and them, it wouldn't be a good match if you stayed working for me." He paused, and then laughed out loud, his rich tone making me shiver. "But then again, what do I know? Probably no one who knew me or Sar years ago thought we'd end up Oathed to each other, or be happy living together at Hayden." He took my hand. "Come on, little dove," he said, moving away. "I can hear the New Year counting down."

I followed him, feeling happy and a little excited about what this New Year would bring.

We arrived back at the party, with only seconds to spare. "Go to him," Devlin whispered, indicating T. My handsome dhamphir was standing alone near the doorway, as if he planned to make a hasty exit as soon as the clock struck midnight, and everyone's attention was on their date. "I should not be saying this, as it's not in my best interest. But I'm a romantic at heart."

I shook my head. "I told you he's angry with me."

"He's not, he's jealous," Devlin said conspiratorially. "But he does care for you, Serena." He embraced me from behind, leaning in close. "He's much like his father, covering hurt with cold words. Don't let him push you away."

"He doesn't like my blood," I confided. "I gave it to him one night, and he didn't seem to enjoy it."

"Wereblood isn't a born appreciation for a vampire, it's an acquired taste," Devlin interrupted with a chuckle. "T is only a few years old in experience, though he looks an adult. Remember that he's not as mature as he looks, though Danial instilled a good deal of responsibility into his son in the short time he was a child." He paused, then gave me a push in T's direction. "Go and try for the gold, Serena. T deserves happiness and so do you." He walked past T with a smile, hurrying to Sar's side as the clock struck midnight.

I went to T, clasping his hand in mine. He turned to me, a scowl on his face. "Aren't you busy?" he said coolly.

"Only if you're available for a kiss," I said lovingly, slipping my arms around his neck.

T held his cool expression for another moment, then his face softened, as he hugged me, then planted a kiss on my forehead. "Happy New Year."

I took his face in my hands, then kissed him for all I was worth, as sensuously as I dared. When we parted, we were both breathing hard. *Devlin's right. I deserve to be happy.* "I want to be with you," I said, throwing caution to the wind. "If you don't want my blood as part of the deal, it's okay. But I really like being with you, T."

T let out a sigh of relief, then hugged me hard. "I want to be with you too, Serena. The blood issue…if it doesn't bother you, it doesn't bother me."

I kissed his cheek. "Good. Do you want to leave?"

"Not yet," T said with a dazzling smile, taking my hand. "We have some dancing to do, my sweet fox."

"I like the sound of that," I giggled, following him to the dance floor.

"You know I've never heard you giggle before," T said with a happy smile. "I hope you'll resolve to do more giggling in the New Year."

"I promise," I teased. "If you're around to provoke me by calling me your sweet fox."

He brought me in for a kiss. "I will be," he murmured lovingly. "I promise you, my sweet fox."

THE END

About the Author

Tara Fox Hall's writing credits include nonfiction, horror, suspense, action-adventure, erotica, and contemporary and historical paranormal romance. She is the author of the paranormal action-adventure *Lash* series and the vampire romantic suspense *Promise Me* series. Tara divides her free time unequally between writing novels and short stories, chainsawing firewood, caring for stray animals, sewing cat and dog beds for donation to animal shelters, and target practice.

www.tarafoxhall.com

Other works by the author with Melange Books, LLC

Return To Me
Surrender to Me
The Origin of Fear in Spellbound 2011 Anthology
Night Music in Midnight Thirsts II Anthology
Partners in Midnight Thirsts II Anthology
Kink in Wicked Christmas Wishes Anthology
The Oath in Wicked Christmas Wishes Anthology
Bedtime Shadows Anthology
Make Me Behave Anthology
Latham's Landing, An Anthology
The Oath
Her Frozen Heart, in Frozen Anthology
Night Music, a Novella
One Perfect Moment, in Propose to Me, A Romance Anthology

The Promise Me Series

Promise Me, Book 1
Broken Promise, Book 2
Taken in the Night, Book 3
Taken for his Own, Book 4
Promise Me Anthology, Book 4.5
Immortal Confessions, Book 5
Her Secret, Book 6
Point of No Return, Book 7
Lost Paradise, Book 8
Dark Solace, Book 9
Eye of the Storm, Book 10
Tempest of Vengeance, Book 11
Sundown-Serena, Book 12

Coming Soon

Hope's Return—Promise Me Series, Book 13

www.ingramcontent.com/pod-product-compliance
Lightning Source LLC
Chambersburg PA
CBHW050514260626
47157CB00004B/1321